SNOW AT SUNSET

SEASON OF WITCHES

AMY PROKOPIS

Amy Prokopis

For those who are the black sheep in their family.
Nothing is more beautiful than being yourself.

Chapter 1

THIS BOOK IS BEAUTIFULLY WRITTEN, but none of the characters have any passion or depth worth caring about.

IT WAS the review that ruined my whole career. At least, I thought it had. I still wasn't sure. I wasn't even sure you could call making a couple hundred dollars a month a career; a couple hundred dollars being a good month at that. All of Yale University would laugh at me if they knew. Thank God I wrote under a pen name. It really would have been the end of my career if I hadn't.

It had to be a form of self-torture that I kept a browser on my phone open to that stupid book review at all times since I noticed it last month. My fingers navigated there practically on their own now, pulling up that stupid screen whenever I found a little down time. Here I was, preparing for what was supposed to be a girls' night out to celebrate the end of the fall semester, and I was sitting on the toilet staring at the damn review for my book. Pants down and all.

There wasn't anything more humiliating.

"Marlee!"

I locked my phone screen and sat it on the counter beside me. "Almost done!"

I flushed and turned for the mirror. We weren't going far, just a few floors up actually, so Callie made me swap out my comfy joggers and leather jacket for my short black dress. I had been in a perfectly good mood until just an hour ago when she reminded me that our podcast episode had gone live. I'd told our listeners I was going to publish a book so different than my last, one that was trendy, and I'd only said it because our topic for the episode was about writing to market and Callie's constant pushing to "write something that's just for fun" had finally gotten to me. Of course, it was the worst moment for me to give in to the peer pressure.

On the fucking internet!

I had no idea what that book was going to be about, but I'd already carved out the time in my school schedule for the next release. So, the next great novel by M. A. Jennings would be published in May and all I knew was that it would be totally different than my newly-released book about a young writer trying to break through all the sexist noise in political journalism with a romantic sub-plot. I slipped into my dress, preparing to walk back my statement until I checked my phone to see that I'd gained a hundred new followers on my social media. The comments on our newest podcast episode were all speculation about my new book. It was Callie's idea to check my pre-orders for the untitled next book, which was intended to be book two in my political journalist series. I had twelve pre-orders, twelve more pre-orders than I'd had when I released my last book. It wasn't Callie-level of success, but it was significant enough to ruin my mood and make me sequester myself in our tiny bathroom.

Callie J. Cody became internet famous seemingly overnight. My roommate had been class valedictorian in a tiny town in Oklahoma, which I did not take as seriously as I should've. Her SAT was a point higher than mine. She was on a full-ride scholarship as a pre-med student and her very first book blew up online and was funding all her personal expenses. So, my sudden influx of followers and the pre-orders on my next book were absolutely a matter of my connection to her and the fact that I said I was writing something trendy, which was exactly what her books were. Trendy. Writing to market. Romantic. Spicy as hell.

So, yeah. Fuck me. I was screwed.

"Marlee, the guys from the apartment downstairs are taking shots!"

Callie had beef with the guys who lived below us. Well, more like they had beef with her. They would bang on the floor of our apartment whenever she would practice her cheerleading dances. Callie J. Cody was a class valedictorian, scholarship recipient, pre-med student, bestselling romance author, and a Yale cheerleader. She was my best friend and I loved her, but damn.

"I'm coming!" I dried my hands and stepped into the main room of our apartment only to have my wallet and a pair of Callie's heels shoved into my hands. She was already pulling her ID from her wallet and stuffing it into the pocket of her skirt before I could ask any questions.

"Take your ID just in case," she said as she adjusted the strap on her left heel. "And let's go before those boys drink anymore. It's *not* worth me bringing up last weekend."

Last weekend being the first time that they made enough noise that we could hear it in our apartment. Callie had been looking for an opportunity for payback just as much as she wanted a reason to talk to the cute blond boy who lived in that downstairs apartment.

"Sounds like the perfect meet-cute inspiration for your next book," I said, the words sounding more bitter than like the joke I'd intended.

She stuck out her tongue at me as she opened the front door, that twinkle in her eye telling me that romance was exactly what she was hoping to get out of our post-finals celebration tonight. I tucked my ID in the pocket of my leather jacket, ignoring her groan as I pulled it on over my low-cut dress. It didn't matter that I was a winter witch. I knew it was ironic, but I hated the cold weather. It reminded me of home, where I was an outcast no matter how good I was in school or how much I tried to relate to people. I didn't fit in and I didn't care anymore. When I was warm, I didn't feel like a part of the winter witch coven back home and it made it easier to pretend like I belonged somewhere else.

"Hurry up! I'd like to at least learn what cute boy from apartment 27's name is tonight," Callie groaned, waiting until I'd slipped into the heels to tug me into the hallway. I started for the elevator while she locked our apartment door, ignoring her gasp as I pressed the button on the wall.

"I'm not promising that I'll talk to anyone," I told her.

"Says the girl with her ass out!" Callie laughed.

I swore my heart stopped for a moment as I tugged the hem of my skirt free from my underwear, smoothing it in place and checking my reflection in the doors of the elevator to make sure I was covered. The doors slid apart and my entire body was displayed in the mirrored wall, face bright red as Callie laughed behind me.

"I hate my life," I grumbled and moved into the elevator, already regretting my decision to press the button for the eleventh floor.

"You could've worn a cuter pair of underwear, at least," Callie said as the doors slid shut. "What if you actually do meet someone you're interested in?"

It didn't matter that the elevator was on its way up, it felt like the decent to hell.

"Maybe I'm asexual."

"You'd know if you were asexual."

Damn her and all those romance movies we watched for being right.

I sucked in a deep breath, not getting a chance to express what was really bothering me before the elevator doors slid apart to reveal the thick crowd of people in the hallway.

"Let's get you a drink," Callie said, gripping my wrist before launching us into the crowd.

"If all they have is cheap beer, I'm leaving!"

I wasn't sure she heard me as I was towed through the sea of people. She must've known where she was heading, because she passed the first few open doors in favor of the third on the right. The lights were low, with only a couple of lamps providing light around the room. A short strand of blue Christmas lights were stretched above the tiny kitchen where all the half-empty bottles of liquor sat.

"I have to be at the airport tomorrow," I told her as she pulled two Solo cups from the stack on the counter.

"Your flight is at one. You'll make it," she said and began pouring a helping of vodka into one of the cups. I didn't argue, just pressed my plastic cup to hers a moment later and downed the shot. She took the cup from me and I turned away to take in the crowd as she made rum and Cokes for both of us.

Our apartment building was close enough to campus that it was mostly filled with students and staff. It took a lot for the cops to be called to a college party in this building, but if they were going to make an appearance it would be on a night like this. I recognized several faces in the crowd from my morning mailbox check or my walk to campus along with a lot more who I didn't recognize. It was almost eleven and it seemed like there was a clear split between those who were drunk and those who were eager to be.

Part of me was reluctant and the other part was glad to take the cup from Callie. I downed half of it in one go as she cheered and when I looked up, the three boys who lived in the apartment below ours were on the opposite side of the counter. Callie leaned across it to talk to the blond guy, leaving me to decide which of the two I would entertain while she was busy flirting.

"I'm guessing it's not you who makes all the noise," the boy with dark hair said, sliding his empty cup my way like I was the party bartender. I didn't hesitate before sweeping his cup into the trashcan at the end of the countertop.

"I'm studying pre-law at Yale. How about you?" I asked, feeling a little better as the guy's smile faded. His friend beside him only laughed harder, pushing him aside so he could stand in front of me.

"I'm Tate. I'm a business major at Yale and I'm not at all interested in sleeping with you."

Tate was blond, had the same blue eyes as the guy who was talking to Callie now, and I could tell from the way he talked and the hopeful look he gave me that his lack of attraction to me had nothing to do with the way I looked or my personality. Thank God.

"Would you like a drink?" I asked and pulled a Solo cup from the stack.

Tate pushed away his friend when he tried to whisper in his ear, leaning across the counter to point out which bottle of rum he'd like, and then left me to mix his drink. It didn't take long for Callie and her blond boy to move into the dancing crowd, the dark-haired guy following shortly after.

"Is he your brother?" I asked Tate. I'd made his drink and he told me he wasn't interested in me. It didn't take me long to figure out that the trio had only made their way to this apartment for him, so he could make a move on the redheaded guy keeping track of what song was playing and how much liquor was left. It wasn't until the redhead had stopped by the bar a second time to check on supplies that I felt brave enough to ask my new friend about his plans for the night. "I mean, the blond guy talking to my friend now."

Tate looked down the bar where Callie was, leaning against the blond boy who had his arms wrapped around her waist as she swayed to the pop song. If you didn't know better, you'd think they were boyfriend and girlfriend and not two people who had just met within the last hour.

"Yeah. He's my brother. They got in a fight in the elevator a few weeks ago and he's been talking about her since," Tate said.

It had actually been more like a month ago, but I knew what he meant. Callie had been annoyed by the boys all semester, but she'd only talked about the blond boy for the past month. I assumed something had happened, but hadn't told me what.

"She's my best friend and my roommate," I told him.

"I know," Tate said, raising his voice over the crowd as they cheered on the start of a new song. "Want to dance?"

I should've said no.

It wasn't like I had to get up early, but I should've said no.

If I had known that the next day would be worse than today, worse than building up my next book to be some trendy romance story, then I would've stayed home in my comfy joggers.

No, the eleventh-floor party was just the beginning.

Chapter 2

WHEN I OPENED MY EYES, I didn't get a chance to come to terms with where I was. I fell against the toilet, smashing my head into the side of the bowl before I could catch myself. I massaged my temple as I stood up, looking at myself in the mirror to make sure nothing was seriously amiss.

I was still dressed in my black dress, mascara a little streaked under my eyes, but otherwise totally fine. A panicked glance at my phone told me that it was a little after eight in the morning, well within the time frame needed to finish preparing for my journey home. I took a deep breath. We must've been out of soap since the plastic bottle was missing, even though I was sure I'd bought a new bottle just a week ago. I checked under the sink where we usually stashed cleaning supplies only to find a plunger and a box of cat litter.

We didn't have a cat.

This wasn't my apartment.

I made sure my ID and phone were still in my pocket before I opened the bathroom door, walking into the main room of the apartment and racing for the door. I carefully shut it before going to the elevator, realizing I was still on the eleventh floor as I waited on the doors to open. My heart was racing throughout the entire trip, not slowing until I unlocked my apartment door and opened it only to see Callie behind the kitchen counter with an index finger pressed to her lips, urging me to be quiet.

I followed her gaze to the couch where the blond guy she'd spent the previous night talking to was sleeping, one leg resting against the floor and the other draped over one lone throw pillow. I rounded the couch to join her in the small kitchen where she was trying to rip open a package of frozen waffles without making much noise.

"It's not what it looks like," she whispered. "I like him, but we're just friends and it would never work out. He did tell me that he'll stop complaining about the noise though, so that's good."

I skirted past her for the cabinet that I knew contained a bottle of painkillers, swallowing a couple of pills before reaching for the box of cereal. I didn't bother to reach for a bowl and just shoved my hand in the box instead.

"I'm going to finish packing," I told her and went for my bedroom, popping a handful of cereal into my mouth.

"I'll go wake up our neighbor," Callie said and started for the man on the couch. "And not in the way I thought I would."

I left her to deal with her new friend and closed my bedroom door behind me, glad I'd mostly packed the night before so I could crawl into my bed now and sleep for a while longer.

MADISON THREW her arms around me outside the Denver airport, squealing like she hadn't seen me in years and not just since I'd been home at Thanksgiving. Her fiancé stood a few feet back, watching her with a smile on his face like she could do no wrong. Jared McAdams, although not a warlock, perfect for her. But sometimes I wished he wasn't so easygoing and would challenge her a little more. I mean, he'd agreed to all the rose gold for their wedding décor and having the wedding and reception at the lodge in Crescent Peak, witches and all. The man was so wound

9

around her finger that it was amazing the Christmas trees on his family farm weren't adorn with pink bows. The whole town knew that the uptick in sales from the mercantile in the barn was thanks to Madison's clothing business.

"Margot got here yesterday," Madison said when she pulled away from our hug. "Everyone's already in Crescent Peak, so we're heading there."

Jared loaded my suitcase into the back of Madison's pink Jeep before leaning toward me to say, "I'm sorry in advance."

"What?" I asked. He was already opening the passenger-side door, leaving the back door of the car open for me like the old-fashioned gentleman he was. Pop music poured from the Jeep and my question was answered as I climbed into the backseat. Sitting in the seat next to me was a three-inch binder with pieces of lace, pink fabrics, and tabs sticking from the pages. I withheld my annoyance at the wedding overkill until I realized it wasn't Madison's wedding binder.

I tried to lift the book for emphasis, but it was so heavy that I just let it thud against the seat as we pulled into the airport traffic. "Tell me you didn't make a giant binder like this for every bridesmaid."

"The wedding party is small, so it's not like it took long," Madison said. She didn't notice the humor on Jared's face. While I was horrified, he seemed to think her obsession with all the tiny details was just another one of her cute quirks.

"So, what are Mom and Dad in charge of?" I asked as I peeked at the first page of the binder. It was a lengthy table of contents. She had thought of everything.

The Jeep had gone quiet enough that I looked up, noticing that the humor was gone from Jared's face and Madison was pretending to check all the mirrors even though we were stopped at a red light. Things hadn't been great with my parents for years, but the divorce was becoming contentious. Splitting their assets had become a task and Mom was pissed that my dad started a remodeling project on the cabin without letting her know. She wanted to sell it as soon as she could and now, they had to wait.

She wanted Dad to handle the whole project, but Margot told me just a week ago that Mom had some strong opinions about the construction crew and their fights now were about who to hire to finish the project.

"There's a man from the lodge who's helping coordinate the details," Jared said, turning a little in his seat to look at me. "He'll be there for the day of the wedding and the rehearsal dinner."

This already sounded like a whole drama-filled production. Gross.

"Margot is in charge of Mom and Dad," Madison said as we merged onto the highway.

Of course, she was. Mommy Margot to the rescue.

"Well, I am exhausted and I plan on taking a nap when we get there, so no one bother me," I said and slumped a little in my seat, still deciding if I wanted to try sleeping in the car.

"Well, Margot and Dax are staying with the Krunes and Mom is at the lodge," Madison said.

"We're staying at the farm house with my family," Jared added.

"So, it's just Dad and me at the cabin," I said, relaxing a little more knowing he'd be too busy with work to bug me.

"You, Dad, and the construction crew," Madison said in her sing-song tone.

"Perfect," I said reaching into my backpack at my feet for my book. The car went quiet aside from the pop music and they left me alone to read until we pulled into Crescent Peak.

It was unchanged from last winter. There were lights strung around the square and Christmas wreaths and painted windows that added to the festive cheer of the tiny town. It must have snowed recently, because a light dusting still covered the lesser-traveled roads and the sidewalks. Madison turned onto that steep road that led up to our cabin, adjusting a little as the Jeep slid as she reached the corner.

"Did you notice anything different?" she asked, the upward inflection of her voice telling me that I was in for it because I had not noticed anything different.

"Different how?" I asked and tucked my book into my backpack.

She groaned. "The Crescent City sign."

"What about it?" I asked.

"It said *Welcome Sinclair/ McAdams Wedding Party*," she said as we approached the driveway. Unlike the other cabins, our driveway had been cleared of snow. Dad must've really been trying to keep up the curb appeal, because we didn't normally bother with shoveling snow.

"Does this binder have a full list of events?" I asked, hoping it did so I wouldn't have to worry about the constant texts and phone calls. It was wishful thinking, I knew, because it seemed unlikely that I'd go the entirety of Christmas Break without some kind of wedding drama. I was happy for them. I was. I loved my sister and I loved Jared, but I really just wanted to be told when to show up somewhere so I could prepare ahead for all the social interactions. This was my break from school too and I wanted to spend it writing.

I could feel a headache building at the thought of my own recent drama.

"It has a full itinerary of events starting with the welcome party tonight," Madison told me and put the Jeep in park.

"Welcome party?" I asked, pulling my backpack into my lap. "Isn't there already a bachelorette party *and* a rehearsal dinner? What's a welcome party for?"

Jared let out a laugh and got out of the car.

"The welcome party is open-invite. Anyone can come. It's to celebrate the wedding week," Madison said and mumbled something under her breath before climbing out of the front seat. Part of me wanted to ask her what she said, because I was sure it was something rude. The argument wasn't worth it though. I wanted to get out of my traveling clothes and into my fluffy pajama pants, take off my bra, and dissociate in my oversized sweatshirt while I still had the chance.

My door opened and I turned to see Jared standing there with my suitcase at his side.

"Thanks," I said and stepped out of the Jeep.

"I got it," he said as I adjusted my backpack straps over my shoulders. I ignored him and took the handle of the suitcase anyway. With the snow gone, it made rolling it across the concrete easy.

"I told you I'd be nice, but was that not bitchy?" Madison asked from behind.

"It's been a long day for her. She probably needs the rest."

Great. I was either the bitchy little sister or the cranky toddler throwing a temper tantrum.

"Dad's here," I called back at them as I passed Dad's SUV in the open garage. I didn't wait for them before opening the door and walking straight into the kitchen. It was clean other than the tile samples sitting on the countertop and a wall across the room that had paint swatches in three different shades of white across it.

"I'm going to my room," I said.

"Hold on!" Dad yelled from somewhere in the house. He appeared a moment later from the den with a laptop in his hands. "You're late. I thought I'd miss you."

Miss me?

"Hey, Dad," Madison said as she entered behind me. Our dad's face lit up and he crossed the kitchen to pull her into his arms. He took Jared's hand next, already mid-conversation about football before I could say a word. I started toward the living room, getting just a few steps before Dad stopped me again.

"Hold on, Marlee! I haven't seen you since Thanksgiving," he said, leaving Madison and Jared next to the kitchen island to join me in the living room.

"Hi, Dad," I said and let go of my suitcase to give him a hug. "I'm just tired. It's been a long day and I stayed up late. It was a whole thing. I'm going to need a nap if I'm going to make it to this welcome party thing later. Can we talk in like an hour?"

"Well, I'll be gone in about fifteen," he said and looked back toward the kitchen counter where he had sat his laptop. I noticed the handle of a suitcase peeking over the top of the counter. I figured he wouldn't be here much, but I didn't expect him to leave Crescent City entirely.

"Where are you going?" I asked, noticing the hurt on Madison's face. A pit settled in my stomach.

Dad patted my shoulder. "I'm going to stay at the lodge. It'll make things easier that way."

"Dad, I told you we didn't book a room for you after you said you didn't need one. The whole lodge is booked. It was hard enough to get rooms for the bridal party six months ago," Madison said. Jared slipped his hand into hers and I saw her shoulders relax. The way he looked at us was enough to tell me that it wasn't the lodging situation that was the problem.

"I know that. I'm going to stay with Lori," he said.

Lori. I only knew one Lori.

"Lori Maxwell?" I asked, looking from him to Jared and Madison. Madison tipped her head back dramatically and groaned.

"Yes. I told you I met Mrs. Maxwell at a charity banquet in town a few months ago and we hit it off over drinks. I also told you we've been together since."

"I thought you said *Mr.* Maxwell, the finance guy. You said you needed someone to do the books for your business. I thought you said he'd been with you since then," I said, understanding now why Madison has seemed more irritable than usual and why Jared seemed to tip-toe around the whole situation on the drive up here. I thought there was enough drama around the wedding with just our parents' divorce, and now Dad was bringing a girlfriend into it.

"No, *Mrs.* Maxwell. Lori," Dad corrected. "I'm sorry. I thought you knew we were together. Maybe I should've been clearer about it."

I pressed a hand to my forehead. "I'm going to take a nap. I'll see you guys later."

I turned for the stairs and heard the door to the garage slam shut a second later, Dad halfway into his apology to Madison when it did.

"I'll talk to her," Jared said.

"Marlee," Dad called from behind.

"I'll see you at the party," I said, not bothering to look back as I dragged my suitcase upstairs. There was new flooring throughout the upstairs, light-colored hardwood that matched the newly painted walls. Everything was light, giving the place less of a cabin feel. I hated it. I'd liked the dark academia vibes from before. The old doorknob to my room had been changed out with a black handle. Hell, the whole door was new now that I was standing close enough to get a look.

I pulled my suitcase into the room before shutting the door. I kicked the whole thing over and unzipped the top, upsetting the neatly folded stack inside to tug my pajama pants free. They were fluffy with a pattern of little skeletons and perfect for lying around the house. I tossed them onto the bed along with my Yale sweatshirt and then stripped, eager to get out of my bra.

I tossed the black bra toward the corner where the hamper was, surprised when it landed among the stack of clothes. I'd barely tried aiming.

"That's probably the only thing that's gone well today," I grumbled as I tugged the pajama pants over my ass, realizing a second later that the hamper was already full. I crossed the room to investigate. Pushing my bra aside, I noticed a stack of dirt- and grease-smudged rags. No, not rags. There was a pair of jeans near the bottom and a couple of socks. The rags were actually shirts and it all smelled like that one time I tried going to the gym on campus.

I jumped when the bathroom door opened, a wave of heat and steam warming my face. Standing in front of me was all six-feet of a dark-haired man, drying his face with one of my towels while the rest of him was proudly on display. And he wasn't the only one undressed.

I covered my bare chest with my arms and I screamed.

Chapter 3

"Fuck!" The man lowered the towel from his face and wrapped it around his waist, not nearly as offended as I was.

"Who the fuck are you?" I screamed, looking for my sweatshirt.

"I live here," he said.

"*You* live here?" I said and inched toward my sweatshirt at the corner of the bed, not turning my back to keep my eyes on him. "No, *I* live here."

"Sure, but I bet you don't know what color the tile is in there," he said, inclining his head toward the steamy bathroom.

"Why—How long—Ugh!" I groaned in frustration, finally reaching my sweatshirt. I almost grabbed it before I remembered what my hands were covering.

"I'll turn around so you can get dressed," he said.

"Like I'd trust you not to look," I said and turned my back before taking the sweatshirt from the mattress.

"There's a mirror right—" he let out a sigh.

It was too late to do anything about it. I'd already lowered my arms. I could see his reflection in the full-length mirror on the back of the bedroom door. He'd turned his head away and lifted a hand to his eyes. I slipped the sweatshirt over my head and turned around again to face him.

The bedroom door flew open, startling us both this time. The guy nearly lost his towel, managing to hang on to the front of it so he could hike it back in place a second later.

"What's wrong?" Dad asked, looking from me to the intruder. His expression fell and he gave a nod. "Guess I should've been clearer about that, too."

"Yeah. We're all really good at communicating around here," I said and squeezed past him in the doorway. I stormed downstairs, going straight into the kitchen and opening the cabinet where we normally kept the dishes and finding it empty. I opened the next few. Empty. The silverware drawer contained a cardboard box of plastic cutlery. Mom must have taken all the dishware.

"Marlee," Dad said as he followed me. "I'm sorry. I thought Madison would've told you."

"Who's that?" I asked and turned around to face him.

He scratched the back of his head and I noticed just how gray his hair has gotten over the past year. "It's complicated."

"What's complicated about it?"

"That's Jace. He's living here for now. He needed a place to go."

"That doesn't tell me why you'd just take him in," I said, glancing toward the stairs in case he could hear us.

"It was a favor. Mom didn't like any of the contractors I chose, but I'd already started the project. Things were just half-done around here and then Nolan called me. I needed someone to handle the remodel. His son needed somewhere to go for a while. I told him he could live here, no expenses, if he'd take care of finishing the projects," Dad said.

The kitchen was quiet as I thought over what he said. My parents were at work so much that all their friends were connected to their jobs in some way, either as a coworker or a potential business deal. Nolan Blackthorne was a bit different. He'd been my dad's college roommate, friends before either of them developed their companies and got rich. I didn't know a ton about him except that he and my dad talked often and that Nolen lost his wife a couple years ago. I didn't know he had a son.

"Fine, but what was he doing in my room?" I asked just as Jace joined us. He'd dressed in a pair of sweatpants and a white T-shirt, his hair still damp from his shower.

"Your room has the only working shower right now besides the master," Jace said on his way to the fridge. He pulled out a bottle of water and unscrewed the cap. "The plumber comes tomorrow to work on the one in the room I'm staying in. I'll tile the third one tomorrow."

It was annoying, but I guess that's the way it was. I could stay in a number of other places, but I didn't want to third-wheel it with Madison and Jared. The Krunes' house was always full of people. The lodge was so packed that I'd have to bunk with Mom, and even though I could afford a room at the motel in town I didn't want to spend Christmas Break in a tiny room with the tourists making noise down the hall. I wanted to stay in the family cabin where I'd spent every winter, reading in the little bay window in my room, and figuring out what I was going to do about this new trendy romance book I was supposed to be writing.

Shit. I'd almost forgotten about that book.

"Fine," I said. They both just stared at me for a moment, the humor in Jace's expression annoying enough that I planned on setting some house rules the moment Dad left.

"Fine. Okay," Dad said and clapped his hands together. He let out a deep breath, awkwardly walking to where he'd left his luggage and laptop. "I will see you at the welcome party tonight."

The only sound in the room was of the wheels of his suitcase as he dragged it across the kitchen. Jace and I stood in silence, staring at each other, as the hum of my dad's SUV faded in the background.

"You better have that bathroom in your room ready the next time you need a shower," I told him, turning for the fridge.

"It'll be tiled, but it won't be ..." He let out a groan. "I guess I'll use the master bathroom."

The fridge was stocked with so much fresh produce and meat that I knew it had to be his. My dad liked to grill, but he'd never buy so many vegetables. The protein powder sitting on the counter must've been Jace's too. I scoffed when I saw that the bottom shelf of the fridge was stocked with beer, but the labels had me do a double-take. They were all craft beers from different breweries in Denver, like he'd gone on his own tour of the city before coming here. At least the guy had some taste.

"I didn't know Nolan Blackthorne had a son," I said and shut the fridge.

"He doesn't like to claim me," Jace said and moved around the end of the counter to stand in front of me. He leaned against the cabinet I wanted to check. "I know Peter Sinclair has three daughters. Which are you?"

"I'm that bitch you live with. That's all you need to know," I said and motioned for him to move. He let out a laugh and scooted just far enough so I could open the bottom cabinet. I let out a sigh of relief and pulled out the box. Dad hadn't planned to stay here during the holiday, but at least he'd stocked my favorite peanut butter granola bars. "If you stay out of my way and leave me alone, maybe I'll drop the bitch part."

Jace nodded his head, making a face like he was considering the words as he watched me tear open a granola bar. I handed him the box and turned for the stairs, glad that those fancy new door handles had locks.

"DAMN IT!"

I picked up the shampoo bottle and sat it on the counter next to my straightener with the rest of Jace's toiletries. The guy didn't have much hair, but he used both shampoo and conditioner instead of a two-in-one like I'd assumed. The bathroom wasn't that large, so once I got all my toiletries in the room there wasn't a lot of space in the shower. I thought the counter had been a better option since I planned to go and dump all his things in his room after anyway.

I finished straightening my hair and went into my bedroom to do a final check in the mirror on the back of the door. The itinerary in the wedding binder said the welcome party was a casual affair, which meant it was a little more dressed-up by Madison's standards. I wore a long black skirt and a red sweater. I wanted to pull on my combat boots, but I strapped on the only pair of heels I'd brought with me for the occasion.

I'd stalled as long as I could without being noticeably late, so I grabbed my purse from my dresser and shoved my hand inside for my keys before remembering that I hadn't driven here. My orange Jeep wasn't even in Crescent Peak. My whole family would already be at the party too, so it wasn't like I could just ask someone to pick me up on the way there. I didn't have any friends here either.

I went across the hall to Madison's room, the room where Jace was staying. The door was cracked open a bit. It was neat inside, almost like no one lived in it at all aside from the leather motorcycle jacket that was draped over the bedpost. I went downstairs next, hating that I would have to break the silent treatment to ask him to drop me off.

"Don't you need a coat?" Jace asked, standing up from the couch with his car keys in hand. He'd changed clothes again. He wore a pair of gray slacks and a black button-up, no tie or blazer. How he'd managed an invite to the welcome party was beyond me.

"Nope," I said and adjusted my purse on my shoulder on the way toward the front door. "Don't you?"

"Nope," he said as he followed, catching the door before I could close it on him.

It was snowing and Jace looked up at the sky like the fact had ruined his whole day. He lowered his head and strode past me toward the little Honda sitting in the driveway. I climbed into the passenger seat, moving the rental paperwork onto the dash only for him to toss them in the backseat a moment later.

"Doesn't seem like your vibe," I said and clicked my seatbelt in place.

He let out a deep breath and checked his appearance in the rearview mirror. He didn't seem to care about the cold or the snowflakes that clung to the tips of his hair, other than brush them away in annoyance.

"You wouldn't like my vibe," he said and started the car.

"You ride a motorcycle?" I asked as he backed into the street.

Jace looked ahead and put the car in drive, waiting until we'd gotten halfway down the street to speak. "Do I fit the stereotype?"

"You have a motorcycle jacket," I said, wondering if he planned on touching the controls on the car at all. It was silent. No music. Not even the heater was on.

"A little hypocritical of you to be mad at me for being in your room when you just walked into mine," he scoffed and turned onto the main road that headed outside of town.

"Anyone can see what's in your room when you leave the door open," I said. The windows had started to fog, so I turned on the defroster for him. "You're a summer warlock."

It was why he didn't bother with the heater. Summer and winter witches could regulate their temperature. Fall witches had control of weather in a totally different way than we did. I could control ice and snow. Jace could summon fire and heat. My roommate Callie could actually predict natural weather patterns and use her powers to summon or shift storms. It seemed like a stupid ability to me until she told me about how her small town in Oklahoma never got hit by tornados or bad storms. Spring witches could create new life and connect with nature. I'd never met a spring witch or a summer witch until now.

It was no surprise that I didn't like Jace Blackthorne. He was a summer warlock. I was a winter witch. Fire and ice. Put it together and you just get a wet mess—or maybe steam. I thought about that cloud of steam that wafted from the bathroom earlier and I couldn't deny the way my face heated now at the memory. He did manual labor for a living and had the body to prove it. He was covered in tattoos, though I hadn't been focused on them at the time. He was sexy as hell, not super tall but built like a truck, and the brief moment that I saw what he was working with told me he had to be good in bed.

If only he wasn't such an ass …

"I can handle the beach, but it couldn't handle me," he said, his tone thick with sarcasm that hinted at a long story.

"You mean your coven," I said. I was so sure of the fact that I didn't need to ask and the way his body tensed told me I was right. Dad told me that Jace was sent here by his father. He was an adult, so it wasn't like he had to agree to leave. There was something back home he needed to separate himself from. Drugs? Legal trouble? On the run?

"The coven set their rules," he said as we slowed to join the line of cars turning into the parking lot of the McAdams Mercantile. "I made my choice."

My phone buzzed in my lap. I thought about answering Callie's text, but got distracted when I saw just how many people were here. Jace didn't bother going for the front of the parking lot and pulled into one of the few spots left at the back. Judging from the line of cars waiting to turn off the highway, lots of them would have to park in the snow.

"God. I bet the whole coven is here," I groaned and took off my seatbelt.

"There's got to be some people here you're friends with," Jace said in disbelief.

I glared his way before getting out of the car. I adjusted my skirt and let out a deep breath.

Let's get this over with.

Chapter 4

THERE WERE SO MANY PEOPLE. The large barn of the mercantile was so full of people that I didn't even bother walking through the doors. I skirted around it for the back deck and the Christmas tree farm. The stringed lights were on, casting a magical glow over the trees as snow fluttered around them. The trees directly in front of the deck were wrapped in thick rose-gold ribbons. One of them had a pink neon sign hanging from the branches.

Madison and Jared McAdams

"WE SHOULD EXCHANGE NUMBERS FOR LATER," Jace said, appearing at my side a second after he'd spoken.

"No," I said. I glanced at him when he didn't respond. I could tell he wanted to, judging by the mischievous smirk on his face.

"Marlee!"

I turned just in time for Winnie Maxwell to throw her arms around me and whisper, "Good for you, girl." She sent me a coy smile before she looked at Jace.

"This is Madison's friend. Winnie Maxwell," I told him, not able to soften my annoyance.

"I didn't know Marlee had a boyfriend," Winnie said.

Jace chuckled and that mischievous grin only got wider. "We're not together. She's just that bitch I live with."

I couldn't believe it. If it hadn't been for the stab at me, I would've laughed at the shock that painted Winnie's face red.

"He's here as a favor to one of my dad's friends," I said and patted Jace's bicep twice. "My dad was nice enough to take in a stray."

Winnie looked at each of us in turn, clearly not knowing what to make of the situation.

"Don't worry. I don't bite," Jace said.

Winnie laughed a little too hard at the joke before promising to talk to me later before she hurried back into the crowd. I turned to face Jace.

"I'll find a different ride home. Don't wait up," I said.

He barked, actually barked at me, before vanishing into the crowd and finally leaving me alone. I scanned the crowd for a quiet place to park it for the night and caught Margot's eye instead. My older sister had gotten more muscular since I last saw her, probably hitting the weight room extra hard ahead of the spring soccer season. Dax Krune, a winter warlock, was shaped like an upside-down triangle, thick shoulders and long arms that he wrapped around my sister from behind. She said something to him and he looked up, smiling when he noticed me.

There went my master plan of keeping to myself.

I crossed the deck to meet them near the buffet. Dax pulled me into a side hug.

"You look mad," Margot said.

I groaned. "Just the stupid guy Dad let stay at the cabin. It's fine."

"Did no one tell you before? Madison was supposed to ask you about it when she picked you up from the airport! I told Dad to call you about it weeks ago!"

Dax let go of me to pat Margot's back. She had a high tolerance for stress, being a college athlete and the one person who seemed to manage our family, but she looked stressed already and a glance at Dax told me she'd been dealing with a lot. Madison said they had a wedding planner, but I bet Margot was somehow in charge of that person, too.

"Margot organized the welcome party and the caterers arrived late and the bartender is just getting set up," Dax said, glancing toward the bar set up near the doors of the mercantile. There were three men rushing to set out bottles and stemware.

"Mom's been on a phone call for the last twenty minutes," Margot said and pointed to our mother near the neon sign. She was dressed in a red cocktail dress with a pair of black pumps, her phone pressed to her ear and face scrunched up in frustration. Margot pointed toward the lounge area across the deck where several people were gathered. Dad sat at the end of the couch, talking with two men sitting on the edge of their armchairs across from him. "And Dad came hand-in-hand with his new girlfriend."

My stomach twisted. Sitting on the armrest next to him was Lori Maxwell. She looked so much like Winnie, like she should've been her older sister or cool aunt and not her mother. She wore a dress similar to my mom's but in a deep green. I scanned the crowd for Madison and Jared next, but couldn't find them. They were probably in the congested barn where most of the party-goers were.

"It's fine," I said, feeling the tension settle into my shoulders despite the words. "Mom and Dad are going to be Mom and Dad."

"I know that and you know that, but Madison can't just enjoy herself unless things go to plan or get resolved," Margot said. "We need to keep our parents away from her, if we can, unless she asks for them. Out of sight, out of mind." Mommy Margot was at it again, always taking on everyone else's problems as her own. I swear, if I lived like that, I would be a nervous wreck.

"How late does this thing go anyway?" I asked. Margot gave me a nervous look and I added, "Don't worry. I'm not trying to bail."

Yet. Maybe I would once it was close enough to the end of the party or if people drank enough not to notice me.

"Party is open-ended, but food and drinks stop at ten."

"Cool," I said and looked over the table. Chicken. Salmon. Several different kinds of vegetables. At the very end was a display of pink-and-white cupcakes.

"Eat a cupcake for me," Dax said and nudged my elbow with his. "I'm in the middle of training and can't have sweets."

"Me too. So, go back for seconds," Margot said, forcing a smile and patting my shoulder.

I moved to the end of the table to join the growing line for dinner. I tugged my phone from my purse and finally opened the text Callie sent earlier.

I told you that you'd be good at this! Let your freak flag fly! Finally!

I STARED at the message for a moment. I had no idea what she was referencing. The podcast episode where I said my next book would be different than anything I'd written before had come out over a week ago. We'd already talked about it. That wasn't anything new and I hadn't said anything about what that book was, just that it was trendy and very different than my last one. I typed out my response, just a bunch of question marks. Instead of replying, she called.

"What are you talking about?" I asked as soon as I raised the phone to my ear. She let out a gasp that I was sure the man in front of me could hear despite the hearing aid behind his ear. "Callie, what the hell?"

"Tell me you didn't!"

"Didn't what?" I asked, the man in front of me glancing over his shoulder as I raised my voice.

"Marlee, did you get drunk and announce your next book at that party?" Callie asked, sending my stomach plummeting and my heartrate skyrocketing. I felt empty for a moment before the panic hit me full force.

No. I didn't. Did I?

I ignored her questions and hung up my phone, my fingers finding the app and our podcast social media account seconds later. The most recent post was a video of me. I didn't recognize where I was. There was a canvas painting behind me of a bulldog and a small floating shelf next to it that held a little ceramic bulldog and a sign that said *Oh, shit!*

Oh, shit was right.

If I panned the camera a little to the right, you'd see that toilet I'd woken up next to a few hours later. I must have filmed this video in the bathroom of that apartment and then fallen asleep on the floor after.

"Fuck," I whispered, ignoring the grumbles of the man in front of me. I moved out of the line, knowing I'd regret it later judging by how long it was now. I hurried toward the barn, going to the far side where there were no guests. I leaned against the wall and hit play on the video.

I opened with our signature podcast intro, "Hello, readers, writers, and curious listeners. My name is M. A. Jenson, one of the cohosts of the *Romance Night Writers Podcast*. It's just me. I have an announcement and I can't believe it!"

Video-me laughed and the camera shook in my hand. God, I looked crazy. Until now, I'd been totally anonymous, not even appearing in videos or photos on our social media account. Sure, I used a pen name, but I'd been faceless until now. Video-me took a deep breath and adjusted my hair over one shoulder before looking straight into the camera and saying the words that sealed my fate, made my blood run cold, and probably forever ruined my career.

"My next book will be a spicy one, a contemporary romance that will have you blushing. I'm probably blushing right now just thinking about all the steamy moments," I said.

What steamy moments? You don't even have an outline!

The video version of me laughed before recovering enough to make the big announcement. "I don't have an official title yet, but you can pre-order it and you should! It's going to be angsty and sexy. If you loved anything Callie J. Cody has written, I promise you will love the next M. A. Jenson book."

The video blurred before stopping. I exited the app and went to find my book online, logging into my account to check orders to see that not only was I up to forty pre-orders but I'd also updated the book's description online.

A spicy contemporary romance coming soon!

Fuck my life.

There was nothing I could do now. There's no way I could just walk back the announcement, not that it would make sense to anyway. I'd linked myself to Callie's fanbase and I was sure the influx of pre-orders had to do with this single video. I could only imagine how this would grow if I stuck with it and actually started marketing the book.

I just had to write it first.

I opened my text messages and typed out the message to Callie.

I guess I'm writing smutty books now.

SHE SENT me several excited emojis in reply and then a GIF of a woman doing a happy dance. I shoved my phone into my purse and took a deep breath, raising my head toward the sky to let the snow collect on my cheeks.

This decision had just changed my entire career as an author. I hoped it would be worth it.

Chapter 5

CALLIE SET the next deadline for me, or at least tried to. The day after the welcome party I shut myself in my room and tried brainstorming for this new book with no luck. Then, I got online to record our next podcast episode. The entire episode was supposed to center around two best-selling romance books that were just announced to be adapted into movies, but Callie decided to go off script at the end and pitch an idea. It wasn't like we were live, but it felt like it in the moment and I went along with her idea.

So, now I had this new book to plan for and I had to record an audio segment teasing it to go out in next week's episode. Someone needed to take the shovel away from me so I would stop digging all these holes.

"You seem on edge," Margot said, pulling my attention away from the coffee shop window.

I blew at the steam that wafted into my face from my mug. "I'm not on edge. I'm just annoyed with all this wedding stuff."

"I know," Margot said under her breath. I raised my eyes to her, ready to point out how particular Madison was being about this wedding stuff when I noticed how tired my sister looked. She'd been in charge of making sure all the details happened, planning all the parties, and coordinating everything between everyone. We met up at the coffee shop to hang out, but it was also to go over the plans for the bachelorette trip that was just another day away.

I pushed my mug forward so I could lean my elbows on the table. "How can I help?"

Margot shrugged. "The bachelorette trip is already planned. The Airbnb is booked. Dinner is booked. You could be in charge of the decorations at the house. I'm driving Madison, so if you get there an hour early, that should be enough time to set up before she gets there. You can ask Winnie to come early and help."

I would not be asking Winnie to come early. A whole hour of just her gossiping was worse than putting up all those frilly pink decorations. If I was going to do it, I'd rather do it alone.

"Okay," I said.

"Are you sure there's nothing else bothering you?" she asked, giving me that concerned "mom" look she always did. Margot was the only person I ever considered sharing secrets with. We'd always been that way. I got slime stuck in my hair once when I was five and I was afraid that I'd get the slime taken away if my parents found out. It was Margot who cut it all out and then took the fall for cutting my hair after the fact. It was still our little secret that she'd been trying to save my butt and not just using me to play hairdresser. Still, finding out how I spent my free time at college would change the way everyone saw me, especially now that I was planning to write something full of sex.

"I'm just thinking about school stuff," I said and forced a shrug.

She sent me a knowing look and said, "The semester just ended and the next one doesn't start for weeks."

"And I'm taking some harder classes next semester. I want to plan ahead."

"Over the holiday?"

I groaned. I would not tell her. There were so many reasons not to beside the embarrassment of everyone finding out about this book.

"I'm going to check out the bookstore," I said, downing the last of my coffee.

"You sure you can handle decorating the Airbnb?" Margot asked as I stood.

I raised a finger gun to my head, ignoring the worried look that crossed her face as I pulled the imaginary trigger. "I got it. It'll be fine. I'll go early and set up."

"Okay …" Margot's mouth hung open like she had more to say. It made me pause, which was just long enough to usher a new problem into my life. "I need my backseat clear, so I'll bring all the bachelorette décor by the cabin tomorrow and we can move it from my Jeep to yours. Do you think you can pick it up by then?"

My Jeep.

We usually stopped by our family house in Heritage City before we came to Crescent Peak for Christmas Break. This was the first year that I came straight to the cabin. My Jeep was still parked in the garage in Heritage City. Great.

"Yeah. Tomorrow," I said and adjusted my backpack on my shoulder. I left the coffee shop for the cold sidewalk. Crescent Peak Books was just across the street, a tiny little shop with rooftop seating that only got used to watch the lodge's firework display on Independence Day.

I waited until a Subaru passed to cross the street, raising my phone to my ear as I went. It continued to ring when I moved inside the tiny shop, my dad's voice telling me to leave a voicemail with my name and phone number as a small, elderly woman came out from the back room. She smiled in recognition when she saw me.

"Marlee Sinclair, I was starting to worry," she teased as she crossed the room. She walked with more of a wobble than I remembered and there were more wrinkles around her eyes than just a year ago, but she smiled with that same youthful grace.

"I only got here yesterday, Mrs. Dorthy," I said, meeting her halfway across the store.

She shook her head. "You're too old now to call me that. Call me Dottie," she said and pulled me into a hug. She was short enough that I could almost rest my chin on the top of her head.

"Have you read Callie's new book?" I asked when we broke the hug.

She smiled and a flush rose to her cheeks. "Of course! I read it the week it released. Your roommate just keeps writing sexier and sexier books."

I slipped my backpack off my shoulder and sat it on the table full of bookmarks and jewelry so I could open it. Callie had started publishing this series after last winter, so I had two signed books ready to hand over to Dottie. She gasped when I held them out to her.

"These are for you," I told her. It was a little funny to see such a little old lady hugging the books to her chest—books with bare-chested men plastered across both covers. "I almost forgot. She signed some bookmarks for you to put out in the store."

"Oh, don't give them all to me. Keep some for yourself. Maybe drop them off at the bookstore in Heritage City or in Denver when you fly out again," she said as I pulled a stack of bookmarks from the side pocket of my backpack. Her words made me pause. Callie sent enough for her store specifically, so there weren't many to begin with. I sat the stack in Dottie's open hand, noticing the way her lips curved downward for a second before she recovered and smiled.

"Um, so, what's new around here?" I asked, gesturing to the store. I let my eyes wander, only now noticing that the jewelry table beside us wasn't as well-stocked as it normally was. There were so few items that she'd moved all the "bookstore favorite" books to the table instead of leaving them on the front shelf. Now that I was scanning the room, the shelf reserved for those books and other bestsellers was missing entirely. There were spaces along the remaining shelves, like she was waiting on a shipment of books to arrive or hadn't ordered more at all.

"Dottie—"

"Robert's health isn't doing too great," she said before I got the chance to ask. "I never needed the money. The store was my passion project. But now, my passions are a little closer to home."

She didn't have to be direct. She was closing the store.

"Crescent Peak's going to miss having a bookstore in town," I told her, patting her shoulder.

She smiled and started toward the counter to my right, setting the books behind it. "Well, it may still be around. I'm not for sure yet."

"What do you mean?"

"A man already bought the store as is. We have a meeting next week to finalize things," Dottie said, setting the signed bookmarks next to her kiosk.

The store wouldn't be the same without Dottie, but I felt a little better knowing there was hope of keeping a bookstore in Crescent Peak. I loved how quiet this tiny town was. It had always been the perfect background to unplug and get some reading or writing done. My family never understood why I was more reclusive here. While they obsessed about social gatherings and recharged in the company of others, I craved the silence of the snowy bay window in my room that overlooked the street. Dottie knew that, which is why despite the missing shelves in the room, the little couch I sat at most days was still there by the front window.

My phone started to buzz. When I saw that it was my dad, I excused myself to sit on that couch, remembering why escaping reality for the bookstore had been so important to me in the first place.

"Hey, Dad! I didn't mean to interrupt or anything," I said. He didn't speak right away, pausing until the laughter in the background died out.

"I just stepped away for a moment to return your call. I wanted to make sure everything was okay," he said as another round of laughter came from the background.

"I need to go get my Jeep from the house in Heritage City. Margot is busy planning for the bachelorette trip next week and I don't want to bother Madison with this since it's kind of for her anyway. Could you take me later?"

More like, I didn't want to listen to Margot's prodding to make sure I was all right and Madison and I rarely got along long enough to make it through a cross-town trip, let alone the drive down the mountain to Heritage City.

"Sure! Yeah! I can take care of that. We'll get it done, Marlee Bear."

My stomach twisted with nerves for a moment. I'd been canceled on by my dad enough times to make asking him for help feel like a gamble.

"Okay. Meet me at the house in an hour? Is that enough time?"

"Um, let me just ..." I heard him speaking to someone, the voices low enough that I couldn't make out a word. "Marlee?"

"I'm still here, Dad." I couldn't keep the annoyance from my tone.

"I need to make a quick call and then we'll get your Jeep, okay?" he asked.

I held my breath. I shouldn't be so quick to judge, but when you're usually right ...

"Sounds good. I'll see you at the cabin in an hour," I said, repeating the instructions in hope that he'd follow through. This is why I asked him today and not tomorrow morning. I had a few days to get my Jeep, but I figured it would take a few tries before I could get on his schedule.

I tucked my phone in my backpack and sat it on the couch next to me, pulling my laptop free next. The screen lit up when I opened it, bright like a beacon reminding me of the blank page I had yet to fill. I told myself that I didn't have to write the book just yet. I didn't even need a full outline; I wasn't much of a plotter anyway. All I needed was a pitch, something long enough to fill even just a minute, maybe two of a podcast episode.

When I looked up from the screen, I caught Dottie watching me. She looked just as somber as I felt, offering me a sad smile

before she went back to scrolling through the kiosk in front
of her.

Chapter 6

I WAS at the bookstore for over an hour, mostly staring at the blank document on my computer. I managed to write a short paragraph, but I didn't like the idea I'd come up with for this spicy new book. The whole mess I'd gotten myself into pissed me off again enough that I didn't stress about getting back to the cabin in time to meet my dad. When I did finally go back to the coffee shop to ask Margot for a ride, I was twenty minutes late and I didn't even care.

Jace's rental was the only car sitting in the driveway. I punched in the code for the garage door only to find the space empty. Dad had either forgotten or bailed on me. I dug my phone from the pocket of my backpack as I went inside, getting to the living room when he spoke.

"You could've told me you'd be late. I would've been finished tiling the bathroom by now," Jace said.

I looked up from my phone, ready to shoot a retort his way before I saw him in his thick leather jacket with his car keys in hand. My heart sank. Dad said he had to make a call before we got the Jeep. Annoyance churned in my stomach when I put the pieces together.

"I'm going to drop off my stuff first," I said and started for the stairs. I went to my room and tossed my backpack on my bed, remembering that the keys to my Jeep and my wallet were still inside a moment after. I fished them out and opened my phone, finally checking the lone text from Dad to confirm my suspicions.

Jace will drive you to get the Jeep.

I GRABBED my wallet and keys, took a deep breath, and exhaled with a groan as I made my way back to the stairs. Jace was just where I'd left him, sitting on the couch and turning his car keys between his fingers. He stood up when he saw me coming, leading the way to the front door. He waited on the porch while I locked the door. I brushed past him for the rental sitting in the driveway, the car beeping as the doors unlocked ahead of us.

It was warm when I got in the passenger side. He must've started the heater while he waited on me to drop off my things upstairs. I tossed my keys and wallet on the floorboard and clicked my seatbelt in place. Finally, Jace got in. I felt his eyes on me for a moment and I sank back in the seat in response, hoping my obvious bad mood would keep him from testing my patience any further.

"You thought your dad was driving you, didn't you?" he asked.

"I did ask him and not you," I grumbled.

We were silent as we started down the road. I leaned over to turn on the radio, tuning it until I found a rock station. I zoned out to the loud guitar and the singer's rough voice, the trees along the winding mountain road whooshing by. I couldn't keep my mind from wandering though, and I felt my chest tighten as I thought about this stupid book. I should've just told our podcast followers that I had a made the announcement without thinking it through. I still could take it back, but also not really. Would people ever trust what I said again? There was the issue that every day since the announcement, people had been preordering this unwritten sexy book and it was already set to make more on release day than my last book had all year. God, I was an idiot. I was on scholarship to an Ivy League school, valedictorian of my high school, and I was still a fucking idiot.

It wasn't like I was totally ill-equipped to write this book. I'd kissed a few boys before, but I didn't have the experience that Callie had. She might not be doing some of the wild things the characters in her books did, but at least she'd had sex a few times. But then again, I had never been to a warzone, but the main character of my last book had and I managed to write that just fine. That's what reading was, a way to be transported to places you've never been and experiences you've never had. It was the same for authors, so who's to say I couldn't do all the research and imaging for this book too?

I focused less on the plot and more on the people, imaging my characters together. Maybe my main character was a virgin too and we could figure out the whole sex thing together. No one could fault me for not knowing what I was writing about if my character hadn't experienced it either, right? So, I'd write about an inexperienced girl and an experienced man. I imagined her in lingerie, the way it must feel for the first time to be draped in lace in someone else's bedroom. I could picture the way she might look at herself in a mirror, pull her arms close to hide the scar at her hip from a past she'd never told anyone about. Standing there in his bedroom would mean more than just sex; it was a moment of revelation for her. It was a moment she'd reveal something deeper about herself for the first time, let someone important to her in on a secret.

Maybe she wanted to be rid of her past all together and she would strip off the lingerie, uncovering herself physically and figuratively. I imagined her slipping the lace from her shoulders and hips, letting the sheer garment gather around her ankles before she stepped out and strode toward the hazy bathroom. She walked into the hot room, the space so thick with steam that it obscured the dark-haired figure behind the glass shower doors. She'd open the shower door, and the man would turn to face her, steam billowing around him. Water would slide down his muscular arms and over his abs.

Just as I felt my face heat and my heart pick up pace at the thought of what would sit between that man's thick thighs, the image changed and *I* was the one standing in that bathroom. Only, it was my steamy bathroom in the cabin and Jace's dark eyes staring back at me from the doorway, just like the day we met.

I gasped.

"You okay?" Jace asked.

"Jesus!" I groaned, fighting to rid myself of the memory. I hated that it was etched into my brain no matter how good he was to look at, no matter how *much* of him there was to look at. Fuck.

"I'm fine," I said a little too forcefully.

Jace shook his head in disbelief, his jaw tensing as he mumbled, "Always so dramatic."

"Hold on. Me?" I asked, feeling like every nerve it my body was awake now. "You think I'm dramatic?"

"I sure as hell wasn't talking about myself." Jace laughed.

"You've never met my sister, clearly," I said and turned the heater down. I'd been so absorbed in my thoughts that I hadn't realized we'd passed through Heritage City and were on our way toward the gated entrance of the neighborhood.

"More dramatic than you, huh?" he said and rolled his window down.

"I'm not dramatic," I said firmly enough that I hoped he would drop the subject, and we could go back to sitting in silence. On second thought, maybe arguing was better. I didn't trust where my mind might take me right now.

"What's got you so keyed up? Did you not hear me?" he asked.

Shit. No, I hadn't heard him, but from the amused look on his face now and the way one hand was poised over the keypad just outside the window, he must've asked for the gate code once already.

"I'm not dramatic," I repeated before telling him the code.

He laughed as he typed it on the keypad, waiting until the window was fully rolled up to say, "I really hit a nerve."

I groaned. "I'm focused on my classes back at school and how my oldest sister, who's actually the dramatic one by the way, is so obsessed with making her wedding perfect that she's driving everyone crazy and stressing out our other sister. She's usually the level-headed one and she's practically in tears over keeping all the planning details straight and making sure our stupid parents keep their selfishness from ruining the whole thing. I'm not dramatic and I just have a lot going on, okay?"

The car was quiet as we passed the gates and took the next turn. I looked from the road when I heard him scoff. He was smiling.

"What?" I asked. It was a challenge as much as a question. He only smiled wider after glancing at me.

"You talk an awful lot of shit about your family for someone who grew up like this." he gestured at the house as we turned into the long driveway.

"It's not like I'm the sole heir of all of this, unlike you," I said, turning in my seat to face him. "Your father is every bit as rich as my family and you grew up sucking the same silver spoon I did. But I didn't walk out on my family like you did to go and mooch off someone else's."

His smile didn't fade like I'd hoped, but it did change. All genuineness of it slipped away and it was almost like a mask covering something much deeper.

"Money can buy a lot of things and solve a lot of problems, but it can't solve everything," he said as he stopped just in front of the garage. "You can dress up or down as much as you want, but you're still the same baby doll as the rest of them."

I flashed him both of my middle fingers before climbing out of the car and slamming the door. I dropped my phone and my wallet a second later, which only made me angrier. I scooped them up and put the passcode in the garage door, opening my phone to check my messages while I waited on the door to roll all the way up. My fingers found Instagram before I could stop myself, all those unread messages drawing me in before I remembered what they were about.

I backed out of the first message about my upcoming book and went to the search bar instead. I typed in Jace's name, but no account came up. I did the same on the rest of my social media only to get the same result. Pausing to get into my orange Jeep and turn on the radio for a background music, I opened a browser on my phone and searched his name. My heart thudded heavily in my chest at the headline. My skin cooled when I recognized the man in the mugshot.

Millionaire's Son Arrested in Connection with Mother's Murder

THERE'S NO WAY. Dad wouldn't invite a murderer to live with his own daughter. My dad did a lot of questionable things and wasn't always there when it came to decisions that included his family, but there's no way he'd do this. I backed out of the article and refined the search so that it was specifically about Jace's case. There were several pages of search results, the headlines featuring one of two mugshots I'd seen so far and a few featured photos of Jace in an Armani suit in a courtroom. The headlines refuted the murder accusation, but came with additional information that didn't make Jace look innocent in the slightest.

Jace Blackthorne, Son of Millionaire Nolan Blackthorne, Connected to Seaside Gang

Son of Millionaire Sells Drugs on the Street

. . .

Jace Blackthorne, Son of Millionaire Nolan Blackthorne, Appears in Court

Court Date Set for Millionaire Son Turned Gang Member

Jace Blackthorne, Millionaire Nolan Blackthorne's Son, Acquitted Due to Lack of Evidence

I WASN'T sure what to do with the information. The sun was setting and the garage was dark. My family was busy enough and I was tired of asking my parents for help only to be let down. So, I started the ignition, ready to face the gang member himself.

Chapter 7

I MUST'VE SAT in my Jeep in the garage for a long time; it was dark for most of the drive back to Crescent Peak. It snowed the whole way, lowering visibility enough that I had to drive slowly on top of it all. The driveway was clear despite the snow and when I parked next to Jace's car and got out, I could feel the graininess of the salt beneath my shoes. I unlocked the front door and I heard feet pounding at the stairs before I'd even fully stepped inside.

Jace paused halfway down the stairs, looking over me with concern before his shoulders sagged with a sigh. "You said you were coming straight here."

"I did."

"Okay, so you drove what, thirty miles an hour the whole way?"

I tossed my keys and wallet onto the nearest armchair and started toward the kitchen. "Just because we live together doesn't mean you're in charge of me."

"Your dad would kick my ass if something happened to you on my watch," Jace said.

I heard him follow me, his footsteps pausing once I reached

the kitchen. I went to the little wine and beer fridge on the far side of the room, the entire unit disguised to look like the rest of the wooden cabinets.

"My dad is so busy with his own drama that he'd probably never know," I groaned as I pulled out two chilled glasses.

"Then I'd kick my own ass for letting something happen to you," he said.

I turned to find him standing on the opposite side of the kitchen island from me. I sat both frosty glasses on the granite and slid one his way. He caught it with both hands. "So now you choose to be a gentleman, huh?"

"I'm not going to be a doormat and just take all your cheap shots and listen to that bratty mouth of yours run all day, baby doll. But, where I come from, we look out for each other no matter how much we'd like to duke it out in the back alley," he said, tapping the bottom of the glass against the counter.

I paused, glaring straight at him for a moment as I thought about what he'd said. Hell, all I could think about was where he came from and what he was doing there. I let out a sigh and turned for the fridge, pulling down two cans of beer from one of the Denver craft breweries. I slid one toward him just like I had the glass before I popped the tab on my own and started to pour it into the cold glass.

"Let's talk about why you're really here," I said and lowered the can to the granite.

He didn't react, not even a flinch as I hinted at the truth. "My dad told me to get out, sent me with enough money to figure out what to do next."

I let out a low hum. "Did he kick you out before or after you were acquitted?"

He froze with his hands on the tab of his beer. Now, we were getting somewhere. He opened the beer with a loud crack, and I waited while he filled his glass.

"What do you want to know?" he asked, voice even, like he'd expected this very thing to happen. Honestly, I should've looked him up sooner.

"Were you guilty? Were you selling drugs?" I asked and took a sip of my beer.

"There wasn't any evidence. There was barely a case."

"We're both witches though," I said and motioned between us with my glass. "Winter witch. Summer warlock. The evidence doesn't matter. Did you do it?"

"I'm going to need you to be more specific." He shrugged and drank.

I groaned. "Fine. Are you in a gang?"

He lowered his glass to the counter, turning it between both of his hands. A frown pulled at his lips. "I was."

"For how long?"

He exhaled and leaned his forearms on the granite. "I jumped in almost a year before my mom died."

"Jumped in? Like an initiation?" I asked. A pit formed in my stomach as I thought about what it meant to be accepted into a gang. He must've known where my head would go, because he lifted his eyes to mine and that look ... It was soft, sincere, and expressive in such a way that I just knew he'd never been violent.

"They jumped me on the street, covered my head, and tied me up. I thought they were going to kill me," he said, giving a laugh of disbelief. "They took me to this warehouse, uncovered my head, and then two guys took turns beating on me. They screamed, spat on me, and I choked on the barrel of a gun a few times. When they were done, they untied me and gave me my role. I'd already been dealing for a little while. They gave me my own team of guys, told me I didn't have to deal anymore as long as I kept track of them and brought in the cash."

My heart was racing. "You were in charge of a bunch of drug dealers?"

He nodded and took another drink from his beer. "I was."

"But you're not in that gang anymore?" I asked.

He nodded. "I paid them off to get out, agreed not to sell them out when I was arrested, and without witnesses there was no evidence against me."

"Pretty crazy there wasn't a single fingerprint or something considering how deep you were," I said, still recovering from the initial shock of learning he'd been in a gang.

Jace smiled and lifted a hand, snapping his fingers and conjuring a single flame on the tip of his thumb. "It's just like you said. Summer warlock. I think the son of a millionaire thing was what kept me out of prison though." He blew out the flame and lowered his hands to his glass.

"So, what exactly happened that got you arrested?" I asked slowly. Jace Blackthorne drove me crazy and as much as I'd like to slap the man, I felt horrible about what happened to his mom.

His smile faded and he lowered his eyes to his glass, turning it around and around between his hands. "One of my dealers was skimming product. I tried handling it myself, but someone he sold to complained to the right person. Someone above me got to him first, beat him up, and took all his money. He thought I called the shots, so he came for me and managed to get past the gates, into my family's house where he found my mom in the kitchen. My parents weren't doing great at the time and Dad was away on business. She'd been having a hard time sleeping, so she was up late making tea. He shot her. Killed her."

It didn't matter that I was a winter witch and could regulate my own temperature. I felt cold. "I'm sorry."

"When the police were looking for motive, they found my name in the guy's phone. It wasn't my phone number. Well, it was a burner phone I used, but the police didn't know that. They probably assumed, but they couldn't prove it. Again, summer warlock," Jace said and lifted a hand, not conjuring the flames this time. "They arrested me because the gang was known to be violent, and they thought they had more evidence. It turned out that they didn't and when it all went to trial all they had was my name in some guy's cellphone. Case was dropped. I went home. My dad told me the coven was threatening to shun our whole family if he didn't do something to keep from drawing attention to our magical corner of the beach. My dad chose the coven. We got into a fist fight, and he gave me a couple million dollars and told me to get the fuck out."

"I can't believe he just kicked you out like that, after losing your mom, and choosing the coven over his own son ..." My parents weren't very involved in our lives, but they wouldn't do that.

Jace laughed. "He came around one morning and told me I could either go to rehab or come live here with your dad."

Weird couple of options, but okay. "Rehab? Were you using *and* dealing?" I asked.

Jace shook his head. "Things are complicated. I don't think my dad can stand the sight of me right now, but I also think he wanted me somewhere he could keep tabs on me."

I took a long drink, letting the silence settle between us. Jace let out a deep sigh and leaned on his forearms.

"My turn," he said and nodded toward me.

"No," I said, not giving him even a second to ask his first question.

He raised his eyebrows, like he was challenging me to deny him again.

"You don't need to know anything about me," I said and straightened up, preparing to down the last half of my glass and head to my room.

"You made a good point about knowing what kind of person is living in your house," Jace said, rising to his full height. He was just a little taller than me. His shirt clung to his stomach from where he'd been leaning against the edge of the counter, revealing just a sliver of skin at his hips before he flattened the shirt. "I should probably make sure that the bitch I live with isn't a murderer."

"You don't need to know what I do," I said, leaning back against the fridge with the lip of my glass resting on my chin.

The corners of his mouth lifted in a smirk that made my face heat and stomach clench. "You don't want to explain why you have recording equipment in your room and a notebook on your desk with the words 'Spicy Ideas' across the top?"

Holy shit!

"I'm not doing—I'm not a sex worker!" I blurted, the words

flying from my lips so fast that they practically ran together. *Fuck*. How long had he been thinking about this? How long ago had I started that list? "Why are you looking at my things anyway?"

"You left it open on your desk and your room has the only working bathroom."

I scoffed. "Because you said the bathroom in your room would be done like a day ago."

"I'll get right on that, after you tell me all about these spicy ideas." He laughed, raising his brows again in that questioning way I was starting to hate. God, why was it so easy for him to get me all flustered like this? What excuse even was there for someone to have a book of spicy ideas? I was sure I'd paused too long to come up with anything believable. I couldn't believe I was evening considering telling him the truth. The words were out before I could rethink them.

"I have a podcast with my roommate, and we talk about books and we're doing a month of dark romance," I told him. It wasn't far from the truth.

"Dark romance?"

"Yes, like books with more smut than plot."

"I know what it is. I just find it hard to believe that the serious Ivy League girl who rolls her eyes at the mention of her sister's girly wedding is into romance novels, let alone has a whole podcast dedicated to them," he said.

At least he acted like he believed me.

"I'm not uptight like people think I am," I said. He scoffed and suddenly I found it difficult to stand still. Shit. Maybe I was uptight. At least, I was on the outside.

"You don't drink like a college girl either," Jace said, downing the last of his beer.

"You expected me to chug cheap beer, didn't you?"

He shrugged. "I didn't expect you to get a chilled glass and sip on craft beer."

"Partying is overrated and the only beer I drink are craft brews, especially dark beers," I said, pretending to study the remaining liquid in my glass while I was actually trying to calm the butterflies in my stomach.

"I'm a decent cook. What's your favorite meal?" Jace asked.

There was no way I was eating with him. That was too close to a date, which reminded me of the uncontrollable blushing and the fact that a few hours ago I couldn't brainstorm for my damn book without imagining him naked in my bedroom.

I shook my head. "That's all you need to know," I said and drank the last of my beer. "And I'm not playing house with you."

I sat the glass on the kitchen island and walked into the living room, practically racing upstairs once I was sure he couldn't see me.

Chapter 8

JACE MADE chicken and rice and left the last of the meal on a plate in the kitchen for me to find. I almost tossed it in the trash, but it was late and I was so hungry by that point and didn't feel like making my own dinner. It was amazing, much better than anything I would've made. I devoured the entire plate while standing in the middle of the kitchen, thinking about the somber details he'd revealed about his past. I was so exhausted that I rinsed my plate and left it in the sink to deal with later before heading to bed.

I had such a hard time going to sleep that I stayed up to work on my book and after loosening up with another glass of beer, I decided to ignore my inner critic, and I started to write. I wrote the entire scene I'd imagined in the car earlier, adding more details and extending the scene until it was the length of a whole chapter. I still wasn't sure what this book was going to be about, but I hoped getting the sexy images out of my head and making them my own would help to separate them from my embarrassing introduction to Jace Blackthorne.

I woke up the next morning to a loud crash outside. It had snowed enough overnight that I couldn't make out the cause of the noise past the snowdrift outside my window. I wrapped my fluffy robe around myself and ran downstairs, slipping into my snow boots before I threw the front door open to reveal the large PODS truck parked at the end of the driveway.

"Woah! Hey!" Jace yelled from behind the POD. At first, I thought he was yelling at the truck driver, but he walked past the truck and continued to the street where a brown delivery truck was parked. While he talked with the truck driver—more like negotiated with him, judging by the bills Jace pulled from his wallet—the PODS driver unloaded the giant shipping container on the lefthand side of the driveway. Jace turned from the delivery truck as it pulled away from the curb just in time to wave at the PODS truck driver as he turned into the street.

Jace noticed me standing on the sidewalk and paused before starting toward the POD container. The snow crunched under my boots as I followed, stopping just behind him as he worked to open the container. With a metallic squeal, the door slid upward to reveal stacks of boxes bearing Jace's name. He stood still for a moment, and I could almost feel the sadness radiating from him. My stomach churned with guilt for being so cold to him. I raised a hand, ready to place it on his shoulder, when he surged forward and lifted a box from the floor of the POD.

"Do you want me? I mean need—" I took a step aside when he turned to face me, the box nearly pressed between our chests. "Do you want some help?"

He lowered his eyes to look over me and I worried for a second that my robe had slipped to reveal more than I intended. "Maybe put some real clothes on first, baby doll."

"Did you forget? I'm a winter witch," I said and raised my hand the way he had last night, only instead of flames I conjured an ice cube. "I'm fine."

He snorted and cast me an onery look before he started for the front door. I picked up a medium-sized box from the floor of the container and followed after him. I carried the box upstairs and into Jace's bedroom where he was already unpacking the box he'd carried up here. He pulled a white button-up from the box, more expensive-looking dress clothes neatly folded in the box beneath it. He sat the dress shirt on Madison's pink comforter before glancing at me in the doorway.

"For someone just staying here until he gets back on his feet, you sure are moving right on in," I said and shifted the box to my hip.

Jace didn't look amused, but also didn't have a well-timed retort prepared like normal. He clearly didn't care for the banter as he left the stack of shirts on the bed to join me in the doorway.

"I'm not in the mood," he said and took the box from me. Now that it was in his hands, I could see the black Sharpie along the side that labeled the box. *Harvard.* I moved farther into the room, watching as he sat the box on a chair in the corner. I didn't ask for permission. The top of the box wasn't sealed anyway, so a single tug pulled the cardboard flaps apart to reveal the contents.

"I thought you just did construction," I said, realizing after that the implication might be rude. "Not that there's anything wrong with that. I didn't mean that you *just* do construction, but I just assumed you didn't go to college."

"I didn't," Jace said as he continued to unpack his shirts, finally turning away from the bed after placing the final black button-up on the comforter. He groaned. "But I got in. I didn't go."

"Why not?"

"Why does it matter?" Jace whirled around to face me, looking at me like he'd expected a response. I was not about to give him one. I could already tell it wouldn't matter what I said. "You act like you're so misunderstood, like you're too edgy to hang with the rich kids but too privileged for anyone else to understand you. I was at the top of my class, too. I wasn't valedictorian like you, but that's because the two girls ranked above me got into three Ivy Leagues a piece. That doesn't really matter when you went to the kind of rich-kid school I did. I took all the advanced classes, the rich and famous people visited our school regularly to do their inspirational speeches, and practically everyone in my class had their family name on some building on campus. They all went to prestigious colleges after we graduated, except for me. I was tired of keeping up with the social game of all when I didn't care to begin with. So, again, does it matter?"

I wasn't going to argue with him because I completely agreed. It didn't matter. College wasn't what made people successful; what they did with their knowledge and abilities did. Hell, college wasn't everything and while I was making great grades and enjoyed my classes, I didn't know what I was going to do with my English degree after I graduated. Despite letting everyone believe otherwise, I wasn't going to law school. Everything to do with college was so boring to me. I barely remembered my classes after I'd finished with them. I remembered when I finished writing my book at three in the morning and the way I cried because the story meant so much to me. I remember that I was sitting at the clinic to get antibiotics for a sinus infection when I got my first five-star review. It's my only five-star review. It's one of my *only* reviews.

That's what bugged me so much about this whole college thing, my family, how everyone treated me like I was supposed to graduate and solve the world's problems. None of that excited me as much as writing stories. I thought writing deep, literary fiction was the best of both worlds, would make people take me more seriously. I even thought about telling my family when I published the first book in my journalist series. That was before I realized how colossal of a failure it was. Did it matter how important it all was to me if no one else gave a fuck? Even worse, as much as I loved writing stories, what if I really was bad at this? It felt like I was destined to be bored but successful, or a failure but happy.

"You're right," I said. "It doesn't matter."

Jace's mouth was slightly open as though he'd expected me to have a totally different response.

"What?" he asked, all anger in his expression replaced with surprise.

I shrugged. "My dad does business with people who make a lot of money, but didn't go to fancy colleges or grow up rich. College isn't everything and I don't even know why I'm there."

"So, this is about you, huh?" Jace asked and turned to fully face me.

"What's that supposed to mean?" I asked and crossed my arms.

He scoffed. "It means you're exactly the kind of girl I said you are."

Every nerve in my body was like a live wire now. I could almost hear the buzzing of anger in my ears as I took a step forward. "Say it."

"I already did," he said with a shrug. "You may have a totally different wardrobe, but you still live in the Barbie Dreamhouse."

"No," I said with a groan. "What do you *really* want to say?"

Jace paused, pursing his lips like he was seriously considering what to say. He let out a deep sigh and said, "You're exactly the type of spoiled, rich brat everyone thinks you are." The room was quiet for a moment. Jace rolled his shoulders to rid himself of the tension, taking another step forward so we were no more than a foot apart as he stared straight at me. "You're the kind of girl who grew up doing whatever she wanted and when you fucked up, you got taken out for ice cream because you cried about it when you should've gotten told off and your ass kicked."

I raised my hands to shove him away but stopped myself with my palms just inches from his chest. The corner of his lips turned upward almost like he had challenged me to push him anyway.

"Just because my parents didn't hit me doesn't mean I got to do whatever I wanted either," I said. Maybe I should've pushed him. "Sounds like yours hit you and look how you turned out."

Maybe it was a little harsh to assume, and my stomach even dropped a little after the words left my mouth, but Jace only seemed more amused. He was smiling now, the tension in the room a little lighter.

"Sounds about right," he laughed.

"So, you're admitting that I'm right?" I said and flicked his chest. Before I could lower my hand, he grabbed it. It wasn't rough. He wasn't even holding me that tight, but it felt like something shifted within me. My heart skipped in my chest, and all I could do was look up at him and wait for what he had to say.

He smirked again. "No," he said and tugged on my wrist so that I was nearly pressed to his chest. "It sounds exactly like something a spoiled little baby doll would say who's never had the brat spanked out of her."

"Didn't realize you were such an expert," I said, extending my fingers on the hand he was holding so I could pat his cheek. He lowered our hands to his chest.

"Expert on what? Brats, spanking, or spanking brats?" Jace asked, raising his eyebrows. "Keep up the attitude if you want to find out which, baby doll."

He was so infuriating, but I didn't pull away. I didn't understand why I didn't step away. Forget pushing him away, I should've slapped him across the face and kicked him out of the damn cabin. I didn't though and it felt like butterflies were gathering in my stomach. I hadn't realized I was squirming until I saw his eyes lower to take me in, feeling them rove over me before he lifted them to look at me again. Everything about the way he looked at me and the subtle tick of that smirk was a challenge. God, this was stupid. I'm stupid.

"What attitude?" I asked and stepped forward so our hands were pressed between us.

His lips crashed onto mine, the kiss deepening almost immediately, rough like the kiss was just another challenge of how much I would take. It was possessive, like he was making good on his promise that I would "find out which." My heart raced at the thought of what he might do, that I didn't just wonder what he might do, that I was excited to find out. He tugged me against him by my hips and then one hand slid up my back, finding the nape of my neck and winding into my hair. The other slid past the opening of my robe, slinking around my back and over the curve of my ass. I gasped when he squeezed, using the break in the kiss as an opportunity to tug my head to one side by my hair so he could press his lips to my neck.

"Stop!"

He was feet away a second later, a loud hiss filling the room. Both our hands were steaming, like my winter powers were rejecting his summer powers.

"I'm sorry," I said in a shaky exhale.

He shook his head, holding his hands up. "No, it's fine. You said stop. We'll stop."

"No, this," I said and motioned between us. "This. Us. Whatever that was … This can't happen. Fire and ice aren't compatible."

"Looked more like fire and ice just makes things extra steamy," he said, that onery smirk back that made my stomach squirm again.

"You are an asshole, and you are rude, and you … I don't like you," I said, pointing a finger at him.

He just smiled wider and shook his head. "Whatever you say, baby doll."

I opened my mouth to tell him off again, tell him to stop calling me that, but all I could focus on was that smile and the way those toned arms had felt around me. I groaned and left the room, forgetting until I felt my robe flutter around my calves that I'd been wearing my pajamas and had bedhead the entire time.

I closed my bedroom door and let out a deep breath. As I got ready for the day, the only thing I could think about was Jace Blackthorne.

Chapter 9

Amazingly, I spent the entire day writing. None of it was normal. I never wrote like this. I also never wrote out of order, but that's all I had to go on for this romance novel. I wrote down all the scenes that had been driving me crazy and making it hard to sleep. At best, I'd stop fantasizing. At worst …

I chose not to think about the worst of it and I just wrote, ignoring the little voice at the back of my head that said I was being frivolous and that my English professors would be ashamed of me for writing such mindless smut. But it didn't feel mindless. It felt deeper than anything I'd ever written before, and I hadn't even written the main plot yet. Already, the romance, the relationship, the two lovers felt more real and intense than anything I'd ever come up with before. The truth was that it felt a little overwhelming to come to terms with.

Maybe I was just a bad writer after all.

Maybe frivolous romance wasn't so frivolous after all.

Maybe it was all the patriarchy and men just sucked ass.

Jace Blackthorne came to mind immediately and clouded my imagination with the way he had smelled like pine and vanilla when his lips had crashed onto mine. Then there was the way he looked even better when a little disheveled like before he got ready for the day as he ate breakfast in the kitchen, and fuck me if my brain didn't always go to that moment he walked out of my bathroom completely naked.

By the time I was finished and had to take a break to keep from combusting, I'd written several scenes and had chosen names for my main characters. I still didn't know what the book was about, not really. The spicy parts were living up to my promise though, even if they were a little too close to home for me.

My phone only buzzed twice before I answered and held it to my ear.

"Hey," I said, breathing such a sigh of relief that Callie waited a moment before she spoke.

"You good? You sound winded."

"Yeah. I'm good for once," I said and let out another sigh. "I am finally getting somewhere with this book."

I heard the sound of men laughing in the background. "Well, that's good, because we record our next podcast episode tomorrow and that's the one I need your sneak peek for."

Yes. I knew that. I was trying to forget it.

"I'll have it ready by the time you edit the episode," I told her as another round of laughter came through the phone. "Where are you?"

"Home," Callie said almost like she was annoyed by the fact. "My brothers are all here and I swear, I forget what country boys are like sometimes."

"Yeah. I can't relate. Sorry," I said with a laugh.

"It's fine. I just wanted to see how things were going. You've been radio silent for a bit and I was starting to worry," she said. I heard her yell for her brothers to be quiet. The background sound died out, but the sound of door shutting told me it was because she left the room and not because her brothers did as she asked.

"Yeah. Well, it's been weird since I've been home," I said. I wasn't really sure what to tell her or what I wanted her to know yet. She knew about my family. She knew that I wasn't excited about Madison's wedding. I was excited for her to be married to Jared, but I could care less about her pink and frilly wedding.

"Something tells me there's more to this than just your sister," Callie said as though reading my mind.

I groaned. "Yeah, but I'm not going to tell you."

"Why?"

"Because I'm not going to tell you."

"Bullshit."

"My dad did this charity thing and took in a college friend's son and he's annoying as shit."

Dammit. I don't know what it was, but Callie always managed to get the worst of me, which meant she always got the truth.

"Is he hot at least?"

Did she have to ask that? As if I wasn't already struggling to forget how I'd met the guy ...

"He's an asshole, but he's remodeling the cabin for free, so I guess it's fine. I don't know, he does his own thing, and I do my own thing. You know what really bothers me though?"

"What?" There was shuffling on her end, like she was rummaging through a drawer.

"I'm in charge of decorating this whole Airbnb for my sister's bachelorette."

The shuffling sound stopped, and I heard the distinct pop and hiss of Callie opening a can of Cherry Coke. "When is it?"

"We leave tomorrow," I said. I'd almost forgotten how soon the event was. I'd been trying my best to ignore all the wedding planning and I'd mostly kept myself out of it. I ignored most of the group texts when they came through. I didn't know all the girls going, and I didn't care to, but they were active enough in the texts that sometimes I had to leave my phone in another room so I could get some alone time.

Callie let out a hum of consideration. "It'll be fine."

"Easy for you to say."

"Shut up. You know it will be," Callie said and laughed. "Just put on some of that screaming music you play at our apartment and pretend all the pink bows are actually black."

I laughed at the suggestion. "Thanks for that. Maybe I'll survive after all. So, we record the podcast episode tomorrow morning before I leave. Does that still work?"

"As long as you get the sneak peek to me before Tuesday," she said.

Tomorrow was Friday. We would finish recording by eleven. I would leave for the Airbnb in Denver afterward. The bachelorette party was Saturday and Sunday. We'd all be driving home on Monday and I planned to record the episode when I got back. It was doable. Busy, but doable.

"Yeah. I got it," I told her and switched the phone to my other ear.

"Okay. I just called to check in. Are you sure there's nothing else going on?" she asked.

She was close enough to me that I was sure she sensed something was off. I wasn't going to tell her the messy details though. "Yeah. It's all good. I'll see you tomorrow?"

"Sure! See you tomorrow."

We said our final goodbyes and hung up.

I'd been ignoring Jace. I hadn't seen him since we'd kissed in his room. We'd caught glances of each other. It was hard not to when you lived together, but aside from a brief look on the way to the living room, or the way Jace slid the extra helping of spaghetti across the kitchen counter to me, we hadn't spoken about the kiss.

I was getting my recording equipment set up at my desk when my phone rang, and I almost ignored it. I was getting ready to record a podcast episode after all. I was working. I had all the reason to ignore her, but I knew there'd only be more fallout if I didn't. So, I answered and put the phone on speaker while I finished setting up.

"What's up?" I asked, trying and failing to soften my tone.

"Hey! Oh, hi! I just—I didn't think you'd pick up. You never pick up," Madison said. I held my breath against the retort I wanted to say. "I just wanted to let you know that I got a DD for the weekend! Well, Jared got the DD. Margot reminded us last night that there's another guy in the family, well kind of in the family, that is free for the weekend. So, we have a DD and you don't have to do the setup by yourself."

"What are you talking about?" I asked as I finished connecting my microphone to my laptop.

"Jace!" Madison screeched the name into the phone in such a way that it felt like it had pierced my soul in more ways than one. First, why did she always have to be so damn stereotypical? Secondly, what the fuck?

"Jace? Jace Blackthorne is the designated driver for the bachelorette weekend?" I asked.

"Yes! Margot didn't tell me, but you know how she does that thing where it's so obvious she's trying to make everyone happy?" Madison asked, pausing long enough that I wondered if she wanted me to answer. Just as I started to, she began speaking again. "Well, I could tell that she knew you were upset about having to do all the setup for the weekend alone and I didn't really want anyone in the wedding party to have to be the DD for the weekend anyway. The whole point is all of us having fun, so I talked with Jared about it and before I knew it, he'd taken care of the whole thing! He's the best, I swear. So, anyway, Jace agreed to be the DD for the weekend and he's driving you to the Airbnb today to help set up the place, so it's really a win-win. You don't have to do it all alone and no one has to worry about driving the entire weekend. It's great, right?"

Fuck.

"Yeah. Great," I said, not even bothering to try to hide my frustration. Madison squealed like a little girl anyway, completely oblivious as always.

"Okay. Good. I just wanted to let you know," she said and let out a sigh of relief. "I'll see you there. I'm going to try and act surprised. I promise!"

God, this was the worst.

She hung up before I could say a word and I noticed a moment after that Callie was already logged on to record the podcast episode. I tossed my phone on my bed behind me, hoping it would absorb any sound of the text message I was sure would come through from the excited bridal party. I took a deep breath and entered the call with Callie.

I HAD TURNED up the radio the moment Jace tried to start a conversation in the car, putting an end to that and ensuring the rest of the ride to the Airbnb was silent aside from the classic rock music that blared through the speakers of the rental car. The rental was a cute two-story town house. I knew immediately upon walking in that we'd be doubled up in the rooms and that was including the living room. Since we were first, I claimed a room upstairs by placing my suitcase on the bed before I reluctantly went downstairs to begin unloading all the decorations from Jace's car.

He'd already brought in several boxes, setting them all on the living room coffee table. There were just two boxes left in the car by the time I got downstairs. Jace took the larger of the two before leading the way inside. I sat mine on the couch next to his, dragging my feet as he began unpacking all the pink items.

"I'm not very artsy, so I hope you have an eye for design," I said.

Jace snorted. "Stop acting like you aren't an expert and tell me where all this goes."

I opened my mouth to deny the fact, but I realized as he held a string of pink garland in front of him that I did in fact know where it fit best. I told him to hang it over the entrance to the back room, watching as he stepped onto a chair to pin the garland to the wall. My phone buzzed again for the millionth time, prompting me to set it aside. I went to unpack the rest of the boxes on the couch and the first one I opened contained several bottles of booze. I took a bottle of tequila to the kitchen, passing Jace as he stood on one of the chairs from the dining room.

"What's next?" he asked, the sound of a chair creaking behind me as he climbed down from his perch. I didn't turn. I opened two cabinets before I found one that contained glasses. No shot glasses, but I found a few short tumblers that would work. I pulled a pair down and unscrewed the tequila.

"Shots," I told him and poured a mouthful for him and another for myself. I screwed the cap back onto the bottle and turned to face him with both glasses in hand. "If I'm going to survive the weekend with my sister, then I'm going to need shots."

Jace took the glass from me. He even let me clink mine against his, but he didn't drink when I did. "Why don't you and Madison get along?"

I paused as the tequila burned down my throat. "She's my sister. I love her, don't misunderstand, but we are just into different things. I'm excited for her. Jared is great and the McAdams are great and she's doing great things with her clothing business. It's great, but we're just different and she knows that."

"I don't think she sees it that way," Jared said, not raising his glass any closer to his lips.

I groaned. "You don't get it."

"No, I do. I just think ..."

God, here we go again.

"What? What do you think?" I asked.

Jace tipped his head back, so he looked at the ceiling for a moment. When he recovered, he sat his glass on the counter and slid it to one side. "Not everything is so serious."

"Wow. You say that like I don't know it."

"Calm down. I know that you know that," he said, somehow maintaining that amused smirk as he looked back at me. "I just mean that you're kind of high-strung and not everything has to have a deeper meaning. Sometimes you just do things for fun, you know?"

"I can have fun," I said, setting my glass into the sink before turning back to him. "You act like I've never had a drunken night out or a one-night stand."

Jace blanched, looking back at me with that challenging look that made my stomach do flips. "One-night stands?"

"Yeah?" I asked, hoping he believed me and didn't notice the way I struggled to look at him. God, if he could hear the way my heart was hammering in my chest right now.

"You kiss like a virgin."

I gasped. "I do not."

"Does it bother you, baby doll?" he asked in that condescending tone.

"No, because I don't kiss like some novice," I groaned and turned toward the sink again, my hands finding the dish soap. I squirted a dime-size amount into the glass and started to scrub it with the sponge that was sitting on the counter. I could feel him approaching behind me, every nerve in my body annoyingly aware as he reached around me to set his glass to my right. It was still full, his shot of tequila untouched.

"I'm the DD and I'd kick my own ass if something happened tonight," he said as he lifted his hands from the glass. "Dump it."

My hand reached for the glass, lifting it to my lips. I tossed back the shot, draining the glass without even a grimace before he could say a word. I pressed the empty glass to his chest along with the sponge.

"And you said I couldn't have a good time," I told him, patting the side of his face before I started for the living room to unpack the rest of the decorations.

Chapter 10

"This is perfect!" Madison yelled.

She was the last one to arrive at the townhouse. She stood in the entryway with a look of shock on her face as she took in the room. Jace had done all the work, though I'd directed the placement of all the décor. The room was filled with pink bows, tablecloths, pillows, and several sparkly backdrops hung along the walls for photo-ops. Winnie Maxwell and a few other bridesmaids had already taken their turns posing for photos in front of all the displays. I sipped from my cocktail, standing a few feet away from Jace who looked over the group like he was taking his job a little too seriously. You'd think someone had hired him to be a bodyguard instead of the designated driver for the weekend.

"This is seriously amazing," Madison said, finally moving into the room to pull Margot into a hug before she came at me. I was never much of a hugger, but I knew this moment was hers and not to ruin it, so I let her tighten her grip around my waist for a second longer than I normally would.

"Did you see the signature drink?" I asked and pulled away. Margot had brought all the supplies. It was some kind of vodka drink with strawberries. The entire glass pitcher of it was a bright pink with edible glitter swirling around the ice.

"This is a Sinclair Soda," Margot said and pointed to the pink drink. "It's a spiked pink lemonade."

"You know I like things sweet," Madison said, taking the glass Margot had already prepared for her, a strawberry sitting on the rim of the glass.

"This one is a McAdams Mule, which is just a Moscow Mule," Margot said and poured herself a glass.

I was halfway into my first McAdams Mule and I fully intended to go back for another. I reviewed the agenda for the night, which Margot had printed on fancy stationery in gold-foiled ink. We were starting here at the house with gifts and some games before heading out to a couple of different bars. There was a place with a dance floor, then a bar that Madison said was perfect for Karaoke, and then we were going to bar to watch a drag show to end the night. It would be a fun night on any other day, but I was dreading the attention we'd garner. Everyone was dressed in pink, glitter already sparkling from the living room rug and couch thanks to two of the girls' dresses. Madison wore a white mini-dress and a tiara with the word "Bride" in pink gemstones across the front.

"Games or presents first?" Lola Carter spoke. She was one of two girls I didn't know, one of the girls whose dress was shedding so much pink glitter that it would be easy to keep tabs on her throughout the night. It took me a moment to recognize her name from the giant binder Madison had given me at the airport. She'd included character profiles on everyone in the wedding party from our ages and college majors to our favorite songs and Starbucks drinks. Madison had included handwritten notes next to Lola's and Remy's names in my binder. *Not members of the lodge.* It was her way to letting me know that neither of them were witches.

"Presents!" Margot said before Madison could answer. "I thought we could all use a round of drinks before the game."

Madison gasped, blushing pink. "Oh! So, it's *that* type of game, huh?"

I wish I could've sunk straight into the cushions of the couch as I sat down, right past the throw pillows and all the way to the floor with the dust bunnies. This was going to be a long night.

"Who's the guy?" Lola asked, loud enough that Jace could hear from his barstool.

The redhead sitting next to me, Remy Johns, lowered her voice to ask the group, "Is he the stripper?"

Winnie swatted her knee. "That's Jace Blackthorne. He's the DD. He'll be here all night."

I noticed the way Remy glanced his way, not looking away even though Jace was staring straight back at her in amusement. Annoyance burrowed into my gut. The moment came to an abrupt end as Margot slid the coffee table full of gifts closer to Madison.

"Bet you can't guess what I got you," Lola said and held out a Victoria's Secret bag with pink tissue paper sticking out of the top. The entire room filled with gasps and giggles.

Thankfully, the party was small, so it didn't take long for Madison to open all the lingerie. Satin, tulle, and enough panties to last a girl a month were strewn over the floor along with all the wrapping paper. Margot introduced the next game while Winnie and Remy collected all the lingerie into the largest giftbag.

"I asked Jared all these questions yesterday. He wrote down his answers and gave them to me in this envelope," Margot said, holding up a sealed pink envelope as though the room needed proof.

"So, what are these cards for?" Remy asked, holding up her stack of pink notecards.

Winnie pointed to her cards with her pen, tapping them with the penis-shaped topper on the end. "We're going to write down our answers to the questions. The goal is to try and match whatever Jared wrote down."

"That's it," Margot said with a nod.

I looked down at my stack of pink cards, counting them. Ten. Ten questions.

"What's the prize?" Lola asked.

Margot smiled and reached into a cardboard box at her feet to pull out a trophy. It was in the shape of a heart and in the middle was a picture of Jared McAdams. The room collectively sighed, laughed, and fawned over how cute he looked. Margot sat the trophy on the coffee table and opened the pink envelope.

"Question number one," she announced and cleared her throat. The entire room waited in silence, penis pens at the ready to scribble our answers onto our notecards. "Where did Madison and Jared have their first kiss?"

Hell, if I knew.

"Everyone ready?" Margot asked a few moments later. "Turn your card on three. One, two, three!"

Everyone turned their cards toward the room. I'd guess that it was at the cabin. The rest of the girls, including Madison, answered that it was at last year's gala. They were right. Madison's face flushed pink, and she smiled wide when Margot announced that Jared had said the same. One for the bridal party. Zero for me.

"Next question is," Margot said as she pulled the next card from the envelope. "What does Jared think is Madison's best feature?"

"Oh! It's got to be her butt," Lola squealed. "He strikes me as a butt guy."

Madison gasped and covered her mouth while the rest of the room laughed. I sat my cards on the couch next to me and stood up, downing the last of my mule and going back to the kitchen for a refill.

"You don't want to find out what Jared's favorite sex position is?" Jace teased as I filled my glass.

"Don't be gross," I said and sat the pitcher down. I took a big sip from the glass as the room filled with wild laughter again. Madison was bright red in the face as she told a story. I wasn't interested enough to get the details. "Remy is single."

Jace snorted. "Were you planning on asking her out?"

"Why, are you hoping to watch?" I asked, spitting an ice cube back into my glass.

I could feel the heat radiating from him.

"Stop talking about me like I'm some sleezy fuckboy just because you're pissed off," he said, watching as I lifted the pitcher to top off my glass. "And slow down on the liquor. I don't want to carry you out of a bar later."

"Calm down," I said with a sigh. "I didn't mean—I just meant that I saw the way she was looking at you and I thought I'd let you know that she's single."

Jace took a deep breath, looking over the girls at the other end of the room. "I'm not here for her. I'm just looking out for everyone tonight and making sure they have a good time."

"Sure," I said, my eyes lingering on him for a moment too long. The way he looked over me was less intimidating and more assessing, like he was gauging my mood. He probably was. He'd been right every time so far and he'd called me on it every time. It was strange how easily he seemed to understand without the need for me to say a word. It was also really fucking annoying.

"Do you want to talk about it?" Jace asked, lowering his voice so only I could hear. It wouldn't have mattered anyway with the way the rest of the party was laughing.

"Talk about what?" I asked and looked back at him. A pit formed in my stomach and my heart skipped from the way he looked at me. I felt the heat rise to my cheeks and I knew there was no hiding the truth. We hadn't talked about our kiss since it happened. I'd tried keeping my distance from Jace entirely since that day in his bedroom. "There's nothing to talk about."

"We have to talk about it eventually," Jace said.

"It was nothing, so there's nothing to talk about."

He didn't speak. I watched as Madison won the game. She took the trophy from the coffee table and posed with it on her hip as Margot snapped photos. She kissed Jared's photo in the middle of the heart, getting a round of applause.

"Why are you over here?" Jace asked.

I turned to face him. "I came to get a drink."

"No." He said and shook his head. "Why are you *still* over here?"

God, maybe I could toss a drink on him at the bar when no one is looking.

"Marlee, you bottle up all of your emotions. I get it. It's hard to deal with your feelings, especially when you have a sister like that who could be a whole one-woman Broadway show. Then there's Margot who has a wall of soccer trophies to show off and manages the entire family with enough anxious energy to power a small city. Your mom is so career focused and has the emotional capacity of a boulder. Your dad adores you, but he's fucking oblivious to the way anyone else feels, let alone his youngest daughter who is so afraid to be vulnerable that she doesn't let anyone in at all."

"Wow, you really have me all figured out," I sneered, keeping my eyes on the girls as they stood up from their seats. The real reason I didn't glare at him was because I'd have to do it through the tears.

"All I'm saying is that there are a lot of people who care about you, and you keep pushing them away. Push any harder and no one will be there at all," Jace said. I turned when he took my glass from my hand, reaching around me to dump the contents in the sink. "And be nice to your sister."

"Marlee, come on!" Madison groaned from the door. She was holding my black crossbody purse, the rest of the group all ready to leave for the first location.

Jace stood up from his barstool and caught the set of keys that Lola tossed to him.

"I have a minivan we will all fit in," she said with a shrug.

"Whatever the bride wants," he said, garnering a round of cheers as the party moved outside.

Chapter 11

"MAKE sure you wear your tiara, Madison!" Remy said from the seat behind me in the minivan. "People love to buy drinks for bachelorette parties."

"They can get it line. I'm buying the first round," Jace said, glancing at Remy in the rearview mirror for a second. I caught the smug smile that crossed her face while the rest of the group cheered. Margot passed another card to me, this one a game of Bingo. She'd already explained it to us. The goal was to check off every square on the board by completing the dares, most of them requiring talking to strangers at the bar or doing something embarrassing like certain dance moves.

Margot slid the door open to my right and I climbed out, waiting for the last of the group to file into the parking lot outside a large building. I could almost hear every word of the pop song that was playing in the bar.

"Let me know when you're ready to go," Jace told Madison, handing over a hundred-dollar bill. Madison gasped and turned to the rest of the girls, fanning herself with the money as she backed toward the building.

"Come on," Margot said as we walked through the double

doors. The music was loud and there were multicolored lights roving throughout the room. The pop music came from a live band on a raised stage at the far end of the room, the space in front of them filled with dancing college students. Margot turned to me and said, "Have a drink and come dance with me."

I thought about what Jace had said. I would never admit it, but he was right. I was awful to Madison most of the time and as cringy as this whole "best day of the rest of my life" theme to her wedding was, she deserved to be happy and have the day she wanted. It wasn't like I wasn't having fun. I was. I liked a night out with friends. I even squeal like Madison does when I go out dancing with Callie in New York. Those nights were the best and thinking about them made me relax a little. We'd dance until we got sweaty, moving to the beat of whatever song played until someone interesting caught our eye and danced with us. I could relax for a night out with my sisters, but the thought of dancing with another man had me thinking about the way Jace gripped my hips as he kissed me.

"Let's get a drink," I told Margot and grabbed her hand. I towed her through the crowd, leaving Madison, Lola, and Remy to take over the dance floor.

"I was worried about you for a second back there," Margot said, flagging down one of the bartenders. "I'll take a rum and Coke."

"Same for me," I told the bartender, waiting until she'd started filling two glasses to speak. "I'm fine. I just needed a minute to get to know Lola and Remy. It's the first time I've met them. It's just weird," I said.

"Oh. I thought it had something to do with Jace," Margot said, thanking the bartender when she brought our drinks. Margot stopped two steps away from the bar, looking back at me curiously. "You okay?"

"Yeah. What would Jace have to do with anything?" I asked and started walking, following her lead back to the dance floor.

"I don't know. You just kept looking at him, so I thought

maybe he'd made you mad or something. You didn't look mad though."

"Well, how did I look?"

"I don't know. He was looking at you the same way. It was weird, like you two were in some kind of silent war." Margot laughed and took a sip of her drink. She was less anxious than she'd been back at the townhouse. Two glasses of Sinclair Soda would do that to you though. It made brushing off the comment easy and soon she was distracted by the dancing. A few more girls joined us for a couple of songs and I noticed early into the night that a group of guys wearing fraternity shirts were watching us. I caught the tallest one of the group staring and he smiled, waving before one of his friends pulled his attention back to their game of darts.

Jace made himself scarce, appearing just long enough to provide us with a fresh round of drinks. The crowd surrounding us changed several times, but we stayed on the floor dancing long enough that the singer of the band gave us a shoutout at the end of one of their songs and after a few more he took a request from Madison. I recognized the song from the radio, but I'd never heard the explicit version before. It became apparent who in the crowd had come with a date thanks to the sensual ways they moved together.

Remy let out a cheer and when I looked up, she had Jace by the hand and was leading him toward our group. He was talking to her, waving a hand like he was trying to refuse her advances, but he followed her anyway. His eyes roved over her as they joined the group, Remy turning to face him.

"Show us what you got!" Remy cheered as Jace began to sway to the music. She took a step closer, draped an arm over his shoulder, and rolled her hips against him. Lola cheered them on. Margot and Madison were too busy dancing with two girls who had joined our group a few songs ago.

Once the chorus of the song hit, the room filled with cheers and the sound of people screaming along to the lyrics. Remy turned around, leaning forward just enough so she could grind her ass against Jace's hips. He went along with the movement, running a hand down her back as he swayed. His eyes met mine for a second and he paused. For a second I thought he might take a step back, but my stomach twisted into knots when I saw the corner of his mouth curve upward. He winked and then he vanished behind Remy when she straightened up, turning around to face him with both arms draped on his shoulders now.

I had to look away, finding that same tall guy staring at me from earlier. He waved again and I gave him a weak wave back. Then, he pointed to me and then to the bar before starting in that direction. I glanced back at our group. Remy and Jace were still dancing, though not as close now that Lola had joined them. Margot and Madison held hands, laughing as they danced.

I turned and started toward the bar, finding the guy halfway down talking to a bartender.

"And put whatever she wants on my tab too," he told the bartender, nodding toward me as I joined him.

"Um, a mojito," I said. The bartended nodded and turned his back on us to get to work. The guy turned beside me so he could face me, showing off a pair of bright blue eyes and his fraternity letters.

"My name is Tyler," he said and offered his right hand. I almost laughed at the formality, but I shook his hand instead.

"Marlee," I said and leaned against the bar.

He smiled. "So, your friend's getting married?"

"Sister," I corrected, looking back at the girls to see them exactly where I'd left them. Jace was still dancing with Lola and Remy, though I noticed she'd attracted a few more men to the dance floor. They danced with the group, though not as closely as Jace had.

"Are you the maid of honor?" Tyler asked.

I turned as the bartender returned with our drinks. Tyler handed him a tip before he moved to the next couple over from us. "No, thank God. Weddings aren't really my thing. They're kind of cringy."

"I cried at my sister's wedding last year," Tyler said with a laugh.

"I bet you did," I said, watching as his smirk dimmed a little.

"What's that supposed to mean?" he teased.

"Just that you look like the kind of guy who would try a line like that on a girl he just met at a bar," I said and raised my glass in a toast. He was stunned, pausing a moment before smiling wider and pressed his glass against mine.

"Good eye," he said with a laugh. "But I did cry."

"Sure."

"At least, like, one tear was shed," he said, dragging his index finger over his cheek to mimic the sentiment.

Tyler was a senior at CU Denver, and he already had a job lined up after graduation. He was graduating with a marketing degree and planned to move to Colorado Springs to work for a start-up. I told him what I told everyone. I was studying English and planned to go to law school. We talked a long time about New York City. He'd never been, but he had a cousin who lived there. He asked me if the rats really were large enough to drag a slice of pizza through the subway and I told him they were, although I didn't usually stick around long enough to make friends with the city's smallest dwellers.

"Marlee!"

I looked away from Tyler to see Margot hurrying over. "We're getting ready to go."

"Okay. I'll be right there," I told her, noticing the rest of the girls walking toward the entrance behind her. She left and I looked back at Tyler, opening my mouth to thank him for the drink when something entirely different came tumbling out of my mouth instead. "We're going to a place not far from here. I don't remember the name, but I guess it's kind of a Karaoke spot."

"Yeah! I know that bar," he said. "Sounds fun."

"Do you like to Karaoke?" I asked, motioning toward the door with my thumb.

He smirked and sat his glass on the bar. He looked back at his friends who were replacing their darts in a Solo cup at the machine. "I can't promise I'm a good singer, but I can try my best."

"See you there," I said and started toward the door. My heart picked up pace with each step. I hurried after the group, catching up with them at the main doors. The girls were busy talking about a couple of guys who must've come over to dance with them. Remy commented about how hot one of them was.

"For a second, I was worried you had run off," Jace said as I waited for the girls to climb into the van ahead of me.

"I'm just doing what you said," I told him, patting his chest. "I'm going to have a good night."

He smiled, but the little twitch at the corner of his lips told me my comment had exactly the effect I'd been hoping for.

Chapter 12

THE KARAOKE BAR wasn't as big as the last place, but it had several rooms behind glass doors where groups were seated, singing the lyrics to songs on a projector screen. The room we got had a stripper pole on the stage, which Remy and Madison immediately went to. They took turns spinning around the pole while they sang a duet. Everyone had a good buzz going so even Margot who normally declined to get on stage, happily belted the lyrics to a Dolly Parton song.

I was starting to wonder if Tyler was coming when the glass doors to our room opened and he came in with his friends. One of the guys lifted a bottle of champagne.

"My mom always told me never to come to a party empty-handed," Tyler said as his friend went to the stage. Madison and Lola squealed in surprise when he popped the cork, holding the bottle away from himself as it bubbled over the top and onto the stage floor.

"She sounds like a lovely lady," I said, my heart fluttering when he pulled me to his side.

"Very, but not as lovely as you," he said and leaned closer.

My heart was pounding the closer he got. I had to rise onto

my toes to kiss him, the room around us so preoccupied with whoever was singing that no one said a word as his arms tightened around me. Tyler pulled back and smiled down at me.

"How about another drink?" he asked.

"Please," I said and let go of him. My stomach twisted as he kissed my temple and promised to come back before he went through the glass doors. I looked up to see Jace watching me, his face so tight that all I could do was smile back at him. I blew him a little kiss, and no sooner had I lowered my hand, he'd crossed the room to join me.

"You know, you were right. I should've loosened up and had a good time earlier," I said.

"You're drunk."

"Hardly," I scoffed and punched his shoulder, knocking myself off balance while he stood there like a brick wall. "I've only had two drinks."

"Two drinks since we've been out," Jace scoffed. "You had at least two back at the house."

I opened my mouth to argue, but the truth was that I'd had a few drinks back at the Airbnb and now I couldn't remember how much I'd had throughout the night. "Well, I feel fine. You should be more worried about the rest of them."

Madison nearly tripped over the stripper pole, holding onto it and sliding to the floor of the stage while Lola and Remy stood off to the side, laughing. Jace didn't look concerned at all as he glared back at me.

"I'm not concerned about them," he said.

"Why not? You just saw how drunk they are. At least I'm not falling over myself and pole dancing."

"They aren't trying to go home with a stranger they met while intoxicated," Jace said, lowering his voice. "You're drunk enough that you can't give consent. You aren't going with him."

I felt like I was going to burst. It was so confusing. I wanted to scream at him and cry all the same. I wanted to cry into his shoulder and shove him away. It was overwhelming and all I could think about was how I needed to forget about the way he felt the other night, the way he kissed me, how he wound his hand into my hair and tugged ...

"I'm going to the bathroom," I said, feeling the words catch in my throat.

"I'll show you the way," he said, his voice gentler than before, but the intent was clear.

"I can walk myself to the damn bathroom, Jace," I grumbled, already halfway to the door. I could hear him following me as I turned the corner down the long hallway, heading straight for the only place where I could truly be away from him. Only, even behind that thick wooden door I couldn't get rid of the pressure in my chest and the thoughts of him kissing me. I leaned against the door and noticed there was another one directly across from me. I felt my muscles relax as I realized what I was looking at; there were two entrances to this restroom.

Excitement built in my chest, propelling me across the tile floor and out that door. It opened into the main room where the bar was and where I immediately spotted Tyler ordering drinks. He straightened up when he saw me coming. I pulled a twenty from my purse and tossed it on the counter next to the untouched drinks.

"How about we go somewhere more private?" I asked.

Tyler smiled and tucked his phone into his pocket. "I'm parked in the first row."

I laced my fingers with his and we started toward the entrance. I didn't feel any better after I climbed into the passenger seat of his truck. It felt like my whole body was still buzzing with energy and I couldn't tell if it was from the confusion I'd felt during my argument with Jace or if it was just nervous excitement about what I was doing. I'd never gone home with someone before. Hell, I'd never had sex. Did Tyler expect that?

He stopped next to the curb of a two-story house and before I could register it, the door opened and he stood just outside.

"Are you okay?" he asked me.

"Oh! Um, yeah," I stammered, grabbing my purse from the

floorboard and stepping out onto the sidewalk. "So, you live here?"

"Me plus a couple other guys. I think just two of them are home right now though," he said, glancing up where one of the second-floor windows was lit. The shadow of a man walked past. "Are you sure you're okay? You seem nervous."

I chewed on my bottom lip for a moment. I could ask him to drive me back. The bar was only a few minutes away from here. Better, I could let Jace think I'd gone home with him and have him drive me to the Airbnb instead. Maybe they were both stupid ideas.

"I'm fine. I just don't do this very often," I said and smiled up at him.

He extended his hand to me, and I took it, feeling the churning in my stomach settle a little when he kissed the back of my hand. He led me to the front door. He had to jiggle his key in the lock, the thing was so old. He held the door open for me. The floors looked original and they creaked beneath my feet as I walked inside. A noise to my right caught my attention and I turned to see the dark hair of a man.

"Ty, there's pizza here in—" The man stopped when he saw me, a piece of pizza drooping from his right hand as though he'd planned to take a bite the second before he'd noticed me. He smiled and sent Tyler a knowing nod. "Didn't know you were bringing someone."

"We'll be upstairs," Tyler said and started pulling me toward the stairs.

"Oh, I wouldn't," the guy called out, tossing his pizza back into the cardboard box and standing up. "Reed got stoned and took a massive shit in the upstairs bathroom."

"Emory!" Tyler snapped, motioning to me. "No wonder you're single."

"Sorry. I've had a couple beers, and I forget my manners sometimes," Emory said, sending a look of apology my way.

"We'll be in the game room," Tyler reluctantly said. My stomach was churning again as he led me past the stairs to a cracked door. There was a couch inside that sat in front of a TV. The coffee table that sat between the two held three gaming controllers and a dirty bowl that looked like it had been there a couple of days.

"Sorry for the mess," Tyler said and picked up the bowl. "My roommates are disgusting."

"It's okay. Not going to lie, I expected worse," I told him, watching as he sat the bowl on the TV stand next to an empty beer can. He took my hand again and led me to the couch. He sat down and pulled me onto his lap.

"I swear I'm not like those guys," he said, running a hand along my leg from my knee to the hem of my dress. "We're fraternity brothers. That's all."

A chill ran over my bare skin and not the winter witch kind I was used to. Tyler was nice. I barely knew him though and something about this house …

"What makes you different than them?" I asked, brushing his hand away when it snuck beneath my dress.

He smirked. "I actually call girls back the next morning."

"I have to get up early tomorrow. We're only here for the weekend," I started. A second later his lips were on mine, and he shifted our weight so I was on the couch beneath him. I rolled onto the floor before he could go any further, scrambling to my feet and nearly turning my ankle in the damn heels Madison insisted I wear for the night.

"I'm sorry. We'll go slow," Tyler said and held a hand out to me.

"I've never—No. I think I'd better just go back. We're supposed to go to this thing next," I said, taking another step backward when he stood up.

"I'm sorry. I mean it. I didn't mean to make a move so quickly. I just thought you were more into me, I guess," he said, lowering his eyes from my face. How did he not know that I was into him? I'd asked him to follow us to the Karaoke bar. Still, the guy looked like I'd just call him fat and ugly.

"You're so hot," I blurted, gaining his attention again. My face flamed. "I mean, I am into you, Tyler. I didn't mean anything—"

"We'll go slow then," Tyler said, taking a cautious step forward. When I didn't move, he took another until he was close enough to cup the side of my face. He brought his lips to mine, moving gently, brushing my cheek with the pad of his thumb. Then I felt his fingers slide up my leg, taking the hem of my dress with them.

"Stop," I told him and stepped away, tugging my dress down. He groaned and ran a hand through his hair, forcing a sweet smile when he caught me looking. It was the smile I'd been looking at all night and I could see how fake it was now. My stomach rolled and I tasted bile at the back of my throat.

"I'm sorry. I've got to go," I told him and turned for the hallway.

"Let me drive you back," he called, footsteps hurrying behind me and sending another wave of panic dancing up my spine.

"No! Don't follow me!"

He didn't. The only sound was my heels clicking against the hardwood and I rushed to the front door, tears already sliding down my face as I threw open the door. I pulled my phone out from my purse and found Jace's contact with shaky fingers.

"Jace?" I asked, barely stifling my sob.

"I'm around the corner," he said.

"Okay," I whispered, taking off my heels and relishing in the feel of the frozen concrete against my bare feet. I took a couple calming breaths, letting the temperature and my powers meet to soothe my nerves. Jace rounded the corner in Lola's minivan a second later, the breaks screeching when it came to an abrupt stop. He got out of the car, leaving it idling as he came running around the hood toward me. He looked me over and once he was satisfied that I was all right, he pointed toward the van.

"Get in the car."

I took a final sobering breath and ran for the passenger-side door. I tossed my heels and my purse on the floorboard and climbed in, looking up to watch as Jace rolled up his sleeves and went through the front door of the house.

Chapter 13

I HELD my breath as I waited. One minute. Two. Jace wasn't gone long before he left the front door, shaking his right hand as he hurried around the front of the van to climb into the driver's seat. The van pulled away from the curb and when a pair of headlights fell across him, I noticed the blood streaked across Jace's right hand.

I closed my eyes, trying to cope with the anger that settled into my gut as we drove. When we got the townhouse, I got out and immediately went inside. Jace followed closely after me, locking the front door behind us and tossing Lola's keys on the entryway table.

"If that guy did more than touch you—fuck that. I should go back and kick his ass again," Jace growled.

"I am so stupid!" I wiped my cheek with the back of my hand, coming away with a smear of mascara. "I didn't even like that guy."

"Why did you do it?" Jace asked, looking back at me like his emotions were ready to spill over the same way mine had. Why did he piss me off so much? And why did I like it?

"Why did you dance like that?" I asked and pointed toward

the door. "I told you Remy was into you, and you acted like you didn't care."

"I didn't," he shot back. "I don't."

"Then why did you dance with her like that?" I yelled.

"Because you were watching," he snapped, stealing all the air from the room. "Why did you invite that guy along?"

More tears spilled onto my cheeks. He had to know. It felt like he knew. I shook my head, unwilling to say the words aloud.

"You hide the most honest parts of yourself from everyone, but you can't hide them from me. And you don't have to, baby doll," he said and took a few steps closer. "I can keep a secret and I'll be a pawn in your game as long as you want to play it. Because as much as you drive me crazy, this is the closest I've felt to someone in a very long time."

I took a deep breath, my heart heavy. "What are you waiting for?"

"I don't know," he answered with a laugh of disbelief. "This is all just a game to you and I'm just playing along in hopes that you'll hit me with a "Simon Says' before one of your teasing remarks."

He spoke every word with such seriousness. He felt exactly the way I did: conflicted, annoyed, and unable to think straight because we both existed and found a reason to argue rather than letting the other one in deeper. Well, *I* found a reason to argue.

"Well, maybe it's your turn," I said.

He smirked. "You didn't say Simon Says.'"

I felt the smile tug at my lips. I groaned and brushed away the last of the tears from my cheeks. With a final look, I turned and hurried upstairs.

THE REST of the girls were so hungover the next morning that it was hardly a party anymore. We ate fresh fruit and snacked on plain saltine crackers, exchanging simple chitchat until it was time for everyone to leave. Jace didn't bring up last night's conversation. He barely talked at all as we drove back to Crescent Peak.

"What is he doing here?" I asked, sitting up a little straighter when I spotted Jared McAdam's truck parked in front of the cabin.

Jace groaned. "I have an idea."

I didn't get a chance to ask for an explanation as he parked in the driveway. He got out of the car as Jared approached and it wasn't until I got out of the car that I saw how angry Jared was. He ran the final few steps, pulling his right arm back and punching Jace in the face.

"Jared!" I rounded the car to put myself between the two men, but the fight was already over.

"I deserved it," Jace told me, saying the words loud enough for Jared to hear.

"You deserve more than a single punch. I should kick your ass," Jared said, rubbing the knuckles of his right hand.

"I would too if I were you," Jace said.

"What the hell is wrong with you?" I asked, looking back at Jared as Jace recovered from the punch.

Jared straightened up and rolled his shoulders back with a sigh. "He left the whole bachelorette party. Madison called me drunk from the back of an Uber an hour after she told me she'd be back at the Airbnb. He didn't answer any of my calls and I know he sent at least one of them straight to voicemail."

I glanced back at Jace as he attempted to staunch his bleeding nose. Jared would run straight to Madison with the truth, I knew that, but Jace didn't deserve to take the fall for this when I'd been the asshole.

"I snuck off … I was scared and Jace came and got me. It's my fault," I said with a sigh. Jared opened his mouth to speak but paused. The anger in his expression faded, eyes filling with regret that only made the guilt gnawing at my stomach worse. For such a big guy, he really was a giant teddy bear. His eyes flicked past me toward Jace and I could see the anger fade in seconds. Jace gave up on controlling the bleeding from his nose and used the hem of his shirt to mop up the last of the blood on his chin.

"I'm sorry," Jared said. "I didn't know."

"I get it," Jace said and flattened his stained shirt over his stomach again.

"Yeah. I see that now," Jared said and reached out for a handshake. Jace gave him a fist-bump instead. Jared sent me an apologetic look before he leaned in and kissed the top of my head.

"Are you okay?" he asked when he drew back.

"Yeah. Fine. Hey, Jared," I started, ready to beg before I remembered who I was talking to. Jared was as loyal as a golden retriever, a man of his word. Unless he thought Madison needed to know, he wouldn't say a word, especially with their wedding just a few weeks away. "Don't tell Madison about this, please? I'm fine. Nothing happened. I was just … stupid."

Jared offered a small smile and nodded. "You know where to find me, if you need anything."

I tightened my arms around my middle as I watched him walk back to his truck. He gave a final wave before starting back down the hill. I groaned and turned to face Jace, but he was already halfway to the front door with his duffle bag over one shoulder and my suitcase rolling behind him. I followed him all the way up the stairs and to the hallway outside our bedrooms. He left my suitcase outside my door.

"I'm sorry," I said, getting him to pause after he'd opened the door to his bedroom. He let out a deep sigh and tossed his duffle bag on the floor of his room. He shrugged out of his leather jacket and tossed it on top of the luggage before turning to face me. He looked annoyed.

"I'm good, baby doll," he said and tugged his long-sleeved shirt over his head. "You don't make it in a gang if you aren't able to take a few punches." He balled the fabric between both of his hands.

"It's more than just that. I'm sorry for—" Anxiety churned in my gut and all I could focus on was the way his forearms flexed as he twisted that bloody shirt. His biceps tightened with the motion and my eyes roved over his shoulders where the tattoos started. I'd seen him with his shirt off before, but I hadn't been focused on the top-half of him when he walked out of the steamy bathroom when we met.

Jace's entire torso was covered in tattoos, black ink that swirled and gathered across his chest. I didn't get long to admire the work before I realized he was watching me. I opened my mouth again to speak, but I wasn't sure what to say. I couldn't really remember what I'd been talking about before.

Jace snorted and shook his head. "Back to your games."

"Fuck you," I said, nearly tripping over my suitcase when I backed into my bedroom. I dragged the suitcase through the door after me.

"Whatever you say, baby doll," Jace said with a smirk.

"Don't call me that," I said and snapped the door shut.

Chapter 14

I HADN'T LEFT my room since the fight with Jace, and I tried focusing on recording my sneak peek for the podcast instead. My microphone was on my desk next to the keyboard, the red light blinking that it was connected and ready for the recording that was supposed to launch my next book. Callie had made a few posts since our last podcast episode hyping up my announcement and our listeners kept commenting and sharing the posts. I was a disaster.

I'd already cried twice. Once because I was angry at Jace and felt stupid about getting him punched. I felt confused because I liked the way he stood up to me and I liked when we bantered even though he also pissed me off. I was worried that he'd finally had it with whatever stupid game this was and would keep to himself from now on. The second time I cried was because there were now thirteen drafts of this shitty sneak peek, and I sounded like an idiot in each one of them.

I was pretty sure I'd ruined everything and all I could do now was stare at that stupid, blinking red light on my microphone and try to rationalize why the thirteenth recording was good enough to send to Callie. She needed the recording today. She'd even texted me an hour ago to remind me. I told her I'd send it before five so she could finish editing the episode and get it scheduled to go live tomorrow.

Shit. My script was shit. This book was shit.

There was a knock at the door that made my heart jolt in my chest.

"What do you want, Jace?" I called out, expecting him just to shout through the door like he had earlier when he asked if I wanted lunch. Nope. Instead, the door opened and he came right in like he was ready to face off. I stood up from my desk to face him, my stomach filling with butterflies as he stopped just a foot away.

He was still shirtless, but he'd showered since this morning. He wore a pair of black athletic shorts that hung low on his hips, yet another tattoo peeking out from the hem along his left thigh. He was close enough that I could see the tattoos across his chest now, and see that they were a series of smaller tattoos and words all woven together. There was a pair of sharks, several different variations of waves, a sun, and words I didn't get a chance to read before I was distracted by his scoff. He took another step closer, and I backed into the desk, throwing my hands behind me to catch myself. I was practically sitting on the keyboard now and he was dangerously close—close enough for me to smell that smokey vanilla scent on his skin.

"I'm done playing games," he said firmly.

"You said you didn't care about games," I said, lifting my hand to pat his chest. After making contact with his skin, I couldn't bring myself to put any more space between us. I exhaled and let my fingers slide over one of the waves tattooed on his chest. My other hand was in his before I realized it. He raised it to join the other, pressing it against his chest and taking a step closer so he was standing between my legs.

"If you see something you like, you better say something," he said, letting go of my hand so he could brush my hair behind my ear. "If you want me, take me, baby doll."

I gasped. God, those words, the rough tone of his voice ... I lowered my eyes to my hands against his chest and allowed myself to slide them along his collarbone and up his neck. I cupped his face. I didn't want to push him away, not anymore. Not when every second like this only left me with more fantasies of him. Still, the moment was too perfect, and I couldn't help myself.

"You didn't say 'Simon Says.'" I quipped, flashing both my middle fingers before patting his cheek twice. He gripped one of my wrists before I could pull away. My heart gave a jolt, everything stopping between us with my tiny gasp. He was just inches away, his deep exhale tickling my nose.

"Don't ever say another man's name while your hands are on me, baby doll," he said, his voice a warning growl. It sent shivers over my skin in the best way, a feeling I'd never had before, not this intense. It made it hard to take the snarky tone I wanted, and my next question came out in almost a whisper.

"Or what?" I sat up a little straighter, willing the razor-edge back into my tone. "I'm not your girlfriend."

That challenging smirk spread across Jace's face and he said, "No, just my pretty little problem."

"I bet you think you can solve that problem, don't you?" I asked, gently pressing my knees against his hips, ready to hook my legs around his waist and pull him closer once he said the words.

"If you ask nicely," he said. The thoughts that immediately flooded my head made my face heat and he only smiled wider.

Was it technically losing the fight if I gave in?

"Kiss me," I said, my words sounding less like a command and more like a plea. My heart skipped in my chest. Heat washed over my body as he laid his hands on my knees and slowly slid them up my thighs as he leaned in, raising one of those hands to my chin so he could tip my gaze up to meet his. He paused with his lips just inches from mine and gave a single laugh.

"You didn't say 'Simon Says,'" he said and patted my cheek before pulling away. "Maybe next time, baby doll. I don't negotiate with brats."

He left the room, and it felt like I'd just run a marathon and was detoxing from the adrenaline. The need I felt was the worst part, urging me off the desk. I shut my laptop and turned off the microphone, not caring that I might be late getting the recording to Callie. I hurried from the room in time to catch him at the end of the hall.

"So, I'm *your* pretty little problem, huh?" I called down the hall, stopping him at the top of the stairs. He turned to face me.

"I've never pretended otherwise. I've been honest, so yeah. You are *my* pretty little problem. When you mouth off it drives me fucking crazy because not only are you the most frustrating person I've ever gone toe-to-toe with, but fuck if it doesn't turn me on at the same time. So, yeah. You're *my* problem, baby doll."

I might have been losing the fight, but I was sure now that I'd just won the whole damn war.

"Take care of the problem then," I said, not stopping until I stood close enough to shove him by his chest. "Simon Says."

My back was pressed against the wall a second later and Jace's lips came down on mine, claiming them as he lifted me into his arms. I wrapped my legs around him and parted my lips to deepen the kiss. His hand wound into the hair at the base of my neck, the other holding me up by my ass. I slid my hand around his bare shoulder and let the other venture down his stomach toward the waistband of his shorts, struggling to slide past the elastic.

He kept me pinned against the wall with his body, moving both my hands to his shoulders and slipping my sweatpants off my hips with ease. I gasped as he gripped my ass again, letting the fabric slide down my legs to the floor to fall in a heap. I arched against the wall as he slid my underwear to one side, desire flooding the space between my legs as a single one of his fingers found its way there.

"I've never done this," I breathed, moving my lips from his to his throat.

"No one-night stands for the college girl?" he asked, lifting his head to look at me with those devilish eyes as his finger traced around my center. His expression changed, falling a little before his eyebrows rose with the question he didn't need to ask. I just shook my head, face flaming.

"Not here," he said and before I could protest, he tossed me over his shoulder by my hips. I let out a squeal of surprise, glad when he held tight to my legs before going into his room. He tossed me onto the bed, looking down at me as my heart thundered in my chest.

"You still want me to take care of that problem?" he asked.

I nodded and parted my legs for him. "Simon says."

He smiled and moved between them, using one hand to slide off his shorts while he traced his thumb back and forth across my cheek.

"I promise to be gentle," he said as he adjusted himself, smirking before adding, "at least the first time."

I bit my lip against the smile pulling across my lips. I wrapped my legs around his hips, pulling him closer. He resisted and I understood why when he finally settled between my legs. It took a moment to adjust to the feeling and he gave me the time, brushing the hair from my face and kissing me until I angled my hips to take him deeper. He moved slowly, gently rolling his hips and only picking up the pace once I moved my hands to his ass. I held him tighter, feeling the satisfied smile spread across my face when I dug my nails into his skin, eliciting a groan from him.

"You and your damn games," he growled before nipping at my bottom lip.

"I thought you were going to fix your pretty little problem," I challenged, my stomach twisting at that mischievous twinkle in his eye.

"Oh, I'm going to fuck the brat right out of you, baby doll," he said, making me squeal when he pulled my hands from his hips and placed them above my head. He didn't hold them, and I wasn't about to keep them there. I pulled his face back to mine, kissing him as he quickened his movements, slamming into me over and over until I couldn't focus on kissing him.

"There's no one here but us, baby doll," he said as I bit my lip against my cries, caught up in a wave of pleasure just like the waves tattooed across his chest. "Let me hear you."

I'd never imagined it could feel like this. Every inch of my body had relaxed, and I felt like I was floating, held aloft only by Jace's strong arms and entranced by his moans. He let out a deep breath and rolled to his side, flashing me that smile that made my core tighten again.

He pulled me to his side as the sensation slowly faded, leaving me feeling squirmy and tired all at the same time. He kissed my temple and started to trace soothing patterns along my thigh, making it easier to come down from the floaty feeling and relax against his bare chest. He was warmer than I was used to, and I was sure it was a summer warlock thing, my own personal sun, like sitting in front of a fire as a blizzard raged outside around us. I tucked my head into the crook of his shoulder and let my eyes close for just a second.

Chapter 15

IT WAS dark when I woke up, barely remembering where I was or why I'd suddenly sat up in bed. Jace was still sleeping next to me, his arm falling away from my side. I climbed out of his bed and darted across the hall to my room, pulling open my laptop before I remembered that I was naked. I pulled on my pajamas before I started the email to Callie, attaching the fourteenth shitty recording I'd made. I groaned as I hit send. It really wasn't that bad. It was good enough. It would have to be. There was no going back on the idea now and it wasn't like it was fully formed anyway. Even the recording had been pretty basic with just a few tantalizing phrases thrown in to catch our listener's attention.

I still had to write this book.

I slumped into the desk chair for a second, exiting all the tabs on the computer and disconnecting my microphone. I stared at the background for a second. It was live video that played on a loop to make it look like it was snowing across the screen. It made me glance at the bay window across the room. Sure enough, snow floated past the glass in the dim lighting from the sunrise.

I lifted my laptop from the desk and moved to sit in the window, propping the laptop on my legs and opening my blank

Word document that I hoped to fill with the pages of a sexy story that would fly off the shelves in another six months. I opened my notes beside the document and stared at the pages of scenes I'd written. They weren't all real. Only a few of them were inspired by moments between Jace and me, but as I thought about those and last night ...

I let my fingers dance across the keyboard, allowing my brain free reign to draft whatever came to mind into my notes. As a snowdrift gathered beneath my window, I wrote a few more steamy scenes and another that didn't feature sex at all. That was the scene I needed all along.

I moved back to the blank Word document and started the first chapter, setting the scene for the whole book as I detailed my protagonist's first day at her new job. She was a stripper at an exclusive nightclub, only she was a novice. She'd never done this before, never so much as kissed a boy, and she got the job because she desperately needed the money. Not only that, but she needed an entirely new life, one away from her previous life and as far away from her abusive father.

The entire chapter came to me, and it felt like my fingers never paused over the keys, typing the tantalizing scene as she dressed in the lingerie, took the stage for the first time before a crowd of men, only to be invited into a private booth with the club's wealthiest customer who never engaged with anyone, especially not the dancers.

I fell into the story and the world so quickly, letting myself be pulled under and I typed whatever came to mind. I was completely uninhibited, at the mercy of the little blonde midnight dancer on the run and the high-power billionaire who was tired of the games of the rich and willfully ignorant. I'd written enough of my sexy thoughts down since getting to Crescent Peak that it didn't take much of the morning to get several chapters into the story. I wasn't pulled away until near noon when my phone rang.

"Callie," I said, ready to gush about how I'd finally gotten somewhere with this book. She cut me off with a gasp instead that sent my heartrate skyrocketing.

"God, Marlee!" she yelled, completely wrenching me out of the dinner party scene I'd written for my characters. "This sneak peek is so good! I mean that. It's so spicy and I can't wait to launch this podcast episode."

"Thanks," I said, still trying to recover from the panic. "The ideas finally came together and I've been writing the book all morning. I can't believe how much I've gotten done. I've never written anything that's come together this easily."

It technically hadn't come together easily, but once the inspiration struck it was game over. It wasn't a total lie, but now I hoped that the sneak peek I'd sent matched the story I'd written. It was pretty vague, so I was surprised at how excited she was to release it.

"I'm glad, because it's all people in the comments of our podcast Instagram can talk about and that's pretty impressive. I'm releasing book two in a few months, you know? I just pushed out the book cover and people are more excited about your sneak peek than the shirtless guy on the cover of my book," she said with a laugh.

I opened my mouth to respond, but paused when my phone beeped. I looked down to see that Madison was calling. Shit. There was no way Jared would tell her about coming over to punch Jace yesterday, so this had to be about something else. If she was calling me, then she actually needed to talk to me.

"I have to go. We'll talk later," I said.

Callie groaned. "Okay, but the episode will probably be live by then, so make sure you get on your author social media accounts and share it like crazy. It's great promotion."

"Will do," I told her before ending our call and accepting Madison's.

"Thank God. I thought you'd let me go to voicemail," Madison said.

"I was sleeping."

"At noon?" Madison scoffed into the receiver. "You've probably written a whole essay for one of your classes by now."

Normally, I'd have a retort ready, but she wasn't wrong, and I wasn't offended. If only my girly oldest sister knew what I was up to. God, she would die.

"Anyway, I called because the Winter Solstice Gala is Friday and I have your dress ready," Madison said and let out a sound between a groan and a whine.

"What?" I asked, already annoyed that I'd have to see her today.

"It's just not my favorite dress. I could've done better," she said.

Jesus, she'd made her own wedding gown plus the four bridesmaids' dresses and she insisted on each of them being different so she could "showcase her talents" and fit everyone's style. When she told me she was also making Margot and my dresses for the gala, I really started to question her mental state.

"I'm sure it's fine, your designs are always great. I know it's always the coolest stuff in my closet," I told her, closing my laptop and slumping against the windowsill. There was no coming back from this conversation. I'd come back to my billionaire romance later.

"Marlee!" Madison groaned. "*Cool* isn't my brand. I don't want to be trendy and cool; I want to be timeless with a unique flair."

"Well, no one ever notices me unless I'm in the stuff you make, so whatever your brand is it's eye-catching," I said, hoping it would be enough to calm her down and wrap up the conversation. She didn't complain, so I decided to move things along myself. "How about I come by in like twenty? I just need to shower really quick and I can meet you at the mercantile."

"Fine, but make sure your hair is dry and put on makeup. I can work without your hair styled, but you won't get the full vision if you don't have makeup on."

God, she was annoying. I stood up and tossed my laptop onto my bed a little more aggressively than I'd intended.

"I will. Don't worry," I said, forcing the sweet tone in my voice as I gathered a pair of sweatpants and a sweatshirt from my floor that I'd worn just around the cabin before the bachelorette trip. Knowing the type of dresses Madison made, I could probably get away without wearing a bra under the sweatshirt. "Give me twenty minutes."

I hung up and went to the bathroom. I took a quick shower, deciding not to stall and wash my hair just because I knew I'd regret it if I made Madison any more stressed out than she already was. Jace wasn't lying in bed in his room across the hall when I opened my bedroom door, but I wasn't ready for the conversation I knew would follow last night's events. I hurried downstairs and upon hearing the sizzle of bacon from the kitchen, decided to leave out the front door instead of going through the garage like I normally would.

I climbed into the driver's seat of my Jeep and backed into the street. It didn't take long to get to the McAdams' Mercantile and for dread to set in my gut. I didn't hate shopping and dressing up the way Margot did, but at least she got along with our solder sister. Even worse for me, she wasn't here to be a buffer. I parked out front of the red barn and went inside, finding Madison ready with a black garment bag.

There wasn't a word of small talk, not even a "hello" or "why the hell are you ten minutes late?" Madison ushered me into a changing room to try on the dress, which I found out was a simple one-shouldered gown that flowed to the floor. The only added detail was the high slit along the right leg that went higher than I really cared for. It didn't matter. It was her creation and I was just a live mannequin. It was more comfortable than I'd expected it to be and after showing it off for Madison—she made me walk the length of the store on my tiptoes and promise that I'd wear heels with the dress on Friday—she let me walk out of the mercantile with the gown tucked safely in the garment bag without much fuss.

I made a mental note to call Margot when I got home and ask her to check on Madison.

All said and done, I'd only been gone an hour and Jace was still in the kitchen when I got back. He peeked his head around the corner when I closed the front door, moving into the living room with a wooden spoon in hand, which he used to point toward the garment bag in my arms.

"What's that?" he asked.

I could tell he would follow if I didn't answer and honestly, we needed to talk.

"It's a winter witch thing. You wouldn't understand," I said as I crossed the living room.

"Winter or summer, I'm still a warlock," he said as I passed him on the way for the kitchen. "Try me."

He playfully swatted my ass with that wooden spoon, and I whirled around, tugging it from his hands and smacking his bicep with it.

"We need to talk," I told him and tossed the spoon onto the kitchen island with a clatter. He rubbed the spot where I'd hit him, smile fading. After a moment, he nodded.

"You're right," he said and went to the stove to turn off the heat that was blazing beneath a pot. "You want to start?"

I didn't hesitate. "Last night was amazing. I'm not going to pretend like it wasn't and like you aren't—" I had no words to describe him, simply motioning toward his white T-shirt and those damn sweatpants that looked hotter on him than a pair of sweatpants should. "You're sexy and you're really good at, well, you know. I'm not looking for anything serious though and I don't think you and I would ever work as a couple anyway."

"What's that supposed to mean?" he scoffed and motioned between us with his index finger. "Are you saying I'm the problem?"

Shit, this exactly was the problem. He wasn't the issue at all. I wasn't really sure I was either, but he drove me absolutely insane, and he'd already told me about how much I pissed him off. Whatever this was—a hate-fuck, lust for a bad boy with a great ass, or me looking for inspiration for this damn book I was writing—It didn't matter. We'd end up tearing each other to shreds if we attempted to do this for the long-term.

"I'm saying that neither of us can stand the other," I told him. "So, thanks for the great sex, but that's all this can be."

"The movies say this conversation should be the other way around," he said with a smirk. "One hundred bucks that you end up in my bed by Sunday."

I groaned, but the challenge made my stomach flip. Disappointment settled in my chest at his words, because a part of me hoped I'd find myself on my back a lot sooner than that. I wasn't a quitter though and I sure as hell wasn't the girl to back down to a challenge.

"You're so annoying," I told him and went to the bar to drape the garment bag over one of the barstools.

"Sounds like you don't have a hundred dollars."

"Oh, I do," I told him and climbed into the barstool beside the dress. "And I think it will be a lot easier for me to win that bet than you. I hope you can survive the blue balls though."

"That's nice of you to consider my balls," he said as he pulled a pair of paper bowls down from one of the cabinets. He started to spoon stew into one from the pot on the stove.

"Well, from the way you talk, it sounds like I own them, and I was brought up to take care of my belongings," I said with a shrug, only hating him more when I saw the humor on his face as he turned from the stove. He stuck a plastic spoon into the bowl and walked toward me, setting the bowl of stew on the counter before sliding it toward me.

"And you say I'm annoying, baby doll," he laughed and then nodded toward the garment bag. "So, what's in the bag?"

I sucked in a deep breath, not finding a witty come-back. I could've told him no. I wasn't sure why I didn't. "Madison always makes our dresses for the Winter Solstice Gala. It's a winter witch thing."

"I get the idea. We have a party for the summer solstice, too," Jace said, going back to the stove to spoon a helping of the stew into his bowl. "So, what? Your sister made you a dress for a fancy party. What's different about this gala?"

I don't know that I'd ever really thought about it. I knew there were other kinds of witches. Winter. Summer. Spring. Autumn. We existed across all the seasons; our powers amplified at the peak of our phase of the moon. My powers were stronger this time of the year and I could feel them grow almost unbearably strong the closer to the winter solstice that we got, but I'd never thought about how other witches and warlocks celebrated their own heightened powers.

"You can come, if you want," I offered, kicking myself even before the words had tumbled out. "Not with me. I mean, we aren't going together. We can drive together, but no promises."

He smirked. "I'd love to. No promises."

"I'm not teaching you the solstice dance though," I told him, remembering Madison's story about teaching the dance to Jared. It was romantic, but not for me. I'd never even engaged in the tradition, even when I was old enough to join.

"No promises I'll be going home with you, baby doll," he said and raised a spoonful of stew to his lips. "But I'd be lying if I told you I didn't want to be between those legs again."

Fuck my expression for betraying me. I was sure my face was bright red from the way it ached now.

"Let's make it two hundred then," I said and extended my hand to him.

He sat his bowl on the counter between us, that wicked smirk back. He took my hand and instead of shaking it, he raised it to his lips and placed a kiss against my knuckles. He never lowered his eyes from me, and I felt that intense gaze threatened to shatter me.

"Deal," he said and let go of my hand.

Fuck him.

Fuck me.

Chapter 16

I SPENT most of the week shut in my room as I wrote my new book, cranking out chapter after chapter each day until I felt like I was more than halfway into this project. Once I felt stuck, I moved locations. I'd been to the coffee shop, back to my bedroom, to the banquet hall of the winter witch lodge, and then to a corner of the bookstore once I learned it was still open.

Dottie's stock was dwindling, but she told me that the new owner would keep whatever she didn't sell and that was encouraging. It made me happy whenever I looked up from my draft to see her smiling as she talked to customers. She told me the first day I'd come in that the new owner told her not to worry about all the bookshelves. She told me they planned to continue the business for a while, so she could retire without needing to worry about the last of her stock. When I'd asked if the new owners were planning to run the bookshop, she'd lost a little of her spark. She told me she wasn't sure if the new owners were going to run a bookstore and that boxes were already arriving for whatever the new business was going to be after she retired.

Whenever I started to think about it, I would turn back to my draft. Things were going well. I'd gotten halfway into the book in just a few days, and I was impressed with what I'd written and how I'd crafted it. I was used to obsessing over the details and the word choices, but this book was flowing so naturally that even my concerns for the quality were quieted by my sheer excitement. I was enthralled enough by the book that I'd told Dottie the entire plot and she loved it, lamenting that she couldn't dedicate space on her bookshelf to it thanks to the sale of the store. I promised her that I didn't mind, but a part of me was sad that I'd never see the cover sitting on display in the very shop that had inspired me when I was just seven years old.

Jace and I kept our distance and part of me wondered if it was due to the bet. The way he smiled at me when I caught him at work on the bathroom remodel or bent over the stove making dinner ... I found myself writing outside the cabin these days more than I was in the cabin and part of me hated it. I was beginning to wonder why I'd found him so frustrating to begin with, only able to think of those strong biceps and the dirty things he whispered into my ear.

"Coffee?" Dottie said, sitting down a full mug on the coffee table before I could answer.

"You don't have to do that for me, Dottie," I told her, eyeing the steaming mug.

She waved her hand in dismissal. "It's just Folgers, nothing fancy."

"Thank you," I told her. She smiled and went back to the register when the bell above the front door sounded. A pair of older women walked in, not even glancing my way before they started toward the non-fiction section to the right. I lifted the mug to my lips and was reminded why a cup of plain Folgers could taste just as good as any of the fancy artisanal coffee shops I frequented in New York City. There was something homey about it, familiar, and so casual that make me feel comfortable in the store all over again.

I'd silenced all notifications on my phone, and I even told Callie not to message me unless there was an emergency. I told her I was deep in my writing cave and that everyone knew not to disturb a hibernating bear. I'd come out when I was ready, preferably with a finished draft. At the rate I was writing, I'd have that before the spring semester started and realizing that warmed me from the inside out in ways even a cup of Folgers couldn't.

I finished writing my paragraph and decided to reward myself for a moment with some music, slipping my headphones over my ear to muffle the sound of shoppers. The rock music pulled me out of the sexy club scene I'd been writing, but it was worth it. I hadn't taken a break from writing since inspiration struck earlier this week and as I let the lyrics of the song pull me under, I felt exhaustion set into my muscles.

I closed my eyes and leaned back against the couch cushions, and I didn't attempt to stop myself when I felt sleep closing in. I dreamed I was sitting at my desk in the cabin, my microphone propped in front of me as I attempted to record my book teaser for the podcast. Jace barged in just like he had that day, dressed only in his boxers this time and when I jumped up from my seat and whirled around to face him, I realized I'd stripped down to my bra and panties.

I started to come out of the dream when I remembered where I was, opening my eyes and expecting the image to fade. But it didn't. I could still hear Jace's rough voice in my ears. My heart jolted in my chest and I almost dropped my laptop, knocking it into the coffee cup instead. A woman at a bookshelf of fantasy novels glanced my way, oblivious to the voice in my ears telling me how I was his *pretty little problem*.

No. There's no way.

I sat my laptop on the seat beside me and used the sleeve of my sweatshirt to mop up what little coffee had splashed onto the table. My fingers shook as I lifted my phone from my lap to pause the podcast. Our podcast. The most recent episode.

Shit!

I backed the audio up a little, hitting play and listening to the last of Callie's rant about the casting for the next screen adaptation of yet another Jane Austen novel. Our intro music played with Callie's voice layered over it, introducing the teaser for my upcoming book. The music faded and a second later I heard my own gasp. It only got worse from there.

"I'm done playing games."

"You said you didn't care about games."

I could hardly focus on what we were saying, not that I needed to know. I'd been there. I remembered the way my heart fluttered in my chest and heat pooled between my thighs. Panic rose into my chest now as I listened to the whole intimate moment perfectly recorded on that damn microphone like I'd carefully staged the damn thing. God, Callie probably thought I'd hired a voice actor or something. It even sounded like I had, like we were doing a live-action version of a scene from my book. I thought it was bad enough that I'd been using inspiration from my fantasies about Jace to help write my book. This was an entirely different kind of offense.

I turned off the podcast and went to our shared social media account. Callie had posted the sneak peek as a separate recording, and I listened to the entire scene again as I scrolled through all the comments saying how sexy it was and how they had already pre-ordered my book. It had more likes, comments, and shares than anything we'd posted recently and with a click of a button I was taken to a screen that displayed several pages of videos where people had remixed the video or taken the audio and attached it to videos of couples kissing. There were even videos of our listeners reacting to the audio live, their faces blushing just as much as mine probably was now based on how hot I felt. Fuck, we couldn't even take down the post now because so many people had already shared it and copied it, every one of them tagging M. A. Jenson or mentioning M. A. Jenson or showing a screenshot of my book on pre-order with my pen name in bold on the temporary cover.

My eyes burned and I could feel my lungs ache as I attempted to control my breathing. I shoved my laptop and headphones into my backpack, exiting the podcast on my phone and pulling up the messaging app as I left the bookstore. I started to text Margot, then Callie, then Margot again. I delete each message before I'd even finished typing them. I thought more about the whole fucking mess, from all the confusing feelings about Jace to this fucking podcast episode that I was sure had well outperformed even my drunk book announcement. There was only one person I knew would understand. I couldn't believe I was considering it. I couldn't believe the relief that filled me when she picked up.

"Hello?" she asked. "Don't tell me there's something wrong with your gala dress."

"Madison, I need you."

THE CHILLY AIR tickled my witchy senses and calmed my nerves as I stood on the doorstep of the McAdams' farmhouse. Madison had already started her gala routine, her nails perfectly manicured and her face dewy from the sheet mask she peeled off as she answered the door for me. She must have known how serious this was because she didn't complain about the interruption, just pulled her pink robe tighter around her and led me into the entryway.

"Where is everyone?" I asked her, slipping off my coat and hanging it on one of the many hooks along the wall.

Madison motioned for me to follow her as she started into the kitchen. Two mugs were perched on the countertop, one already filled and topped with whipped cream and mini chocolate chips while the other sat empty. The coffee maker next to the mugs slowly dripped hot liquid into the glass carafe.

"It's just me. Everyone else had to work at the mercantile today," Madison said and lifted the full mug to her lips. Hot chocolate. Madison's daily fix. She lowered the mug back to the countertop and checked the coffee maker before looking up at me. "You never call me, you know?"

"I know," I said with a sigh, considering the guilt before I decided it wasn't guilt I felt at all. "You never call me, you know?"

Madison rolled her eyes. "I know. You and I are just two totally different people. I figured it wasn't worth trying to make you like me if all we were going to do was argue about our differences anyway.”

“I like you,” I said in defense, going to the coffee maker as soon as it started to beep that it was finished brewing. I poured some coffee into the empty mug and stared down at my reflection in the dark liquid. “And maybe we aren’t all that different.”

“What do you mean?” she asked.

I groaned and lifted the mug from the counter and moved around her for the opposite side of the kitchen where the tiny table was. I remembered sitting here last year, the Sinclair and the McAdams families, staring out the giant windows at the Christmas tree farm. I sat my mug on the table and sank into one of the chairs. Madison took one on the opposite side, watching me curiously. For once, she looked nervous.

“Jace told me that it didn’t matter that I didn’t fit in with our family and all of Mom and Dad’s rich friends, I was still every bit a part of that life. He said I’m just a spoiled rich girl playing pretend,” I told her. He hadn’t said it quite like that, but the message was the same.

“Just now?” Madison asked with a gasp.

“No, a few days ago.”

“So, what happened today?”

I looked up from my coffee at her, watching her curious look fade and that incredulous expression spread across her face. “You may think I’m an airhead, but I know when something’s up.”

“It’s a long story,” I said in a sigh.

“You didn’t drive out here to see your least favorite sister just to tattle on Daddy’s new pet project,” she scoffed.

I groaned. “Gross! Don’t call him that.”

“We all know Dad took him in to make himself feel better after Mom pissed him off,” Madison said and stood from the table. “Come on. Grab your coffee and come with me. You can tell me the long story while I curl my hair.”

I followed her to a room at the end of the hall that she shared with Jared. Her white gown for the gala tonight was laid across the bed. It was a halter dress with extra fabric I was sure she’d designed so it draped just so to highlight her curves. Madison went to the vanity in the corner where her curling iron sat plugged in. She plopped down on the stool and used her finger to section her hair into a small piece.

She raised the iron to her hair and said, "All right. I'm listening."

I hesitated for just a moment before the whole store came tumbling out, starting with the failure of my first book and the start of the podcast. I told her about Callie and her overnight success of a first book, the envy burning even worse in my gut when Madison told me she'd heard of the book. Of all people to pay attention to what books were popular, I'd never imagined it would be my oldest sister. She kept quiet after that as I told her about the podcast and my drunk post on our shared Instagram, the way my untitled book had blown up at the sheer mention of "smutty romance" and the fact that *the* Callie J. Cody was recommending it.

Angry tears pricked my eyes when I got the part where Jace came into the story, telling her about seeing him naked in my room and how he drove me crazy despite how attracted I was to him. She'd finished her hair by that point and sat, watching me in the mirror as I walked around the room behind her. She gasped when I told her about fight in my bedroom and ending up in his afterward. Her jaw dropped when I told her what I'd discovered today, prompting her to turn from the vanity to face me.

"No!"

"Yes!" I threw my arms up in frustration. "It happened and I'm such a dumbass!"

"No, I mean I didn't know you had it in you," Madison said, motioning for me to move closer. I was stunned. What the hell was she talking about? Didn't know I had what in me? She stood up and pulled me to the stool by my wrist, pushing on my shoulders until I sat down.

"I just told you that I didn't mean to send that recording," I told her as she started to brush my hair.

She laughed. "Not that. The book. We all know you're smart

and going to do great things—blah, blah, blah—but I can't believe you're writing a *romance* book. Oh my God, Marlee! You're an amazing writer. I can't imagine what kind of book you'd write when you let yourself show some real emotion for once."

I opened my mouth to let my insults fly but stopped when I saw her genuine smile in the reflection of the mirror. The last time I saw her this excited was at the coffee shop with Margot when she told us about her plans for her wedding. I'd always been so concerned about not being like Madison, not being dramatic and so outgoing that I drew attention to myself the way she did. I always thought I was just the kind of person who held onto their emotions until they were ready to express them, but maybe I'd actually just thrown them in a cage and locked the door. Hell, I think I'd lost the key along the way.

"What do I do?" I asked.

Madison let go of a piece of my hair and let the curl fall away from the iron, framing my blushing face. "Just tell him the truth."

Jace knew about the podcast. He knew I talked about books on the internet, so it might not be that earth-shattering to tell him I write them, too. It was the podcast teaser I was a little more concerned about and the fact that this book only existed because I saw him naked. And kissed him. And touched those amazing biceps.

Damn it. I needed to get a grip.

"It's not that easy," I told him.

"Well, no. Telling him isn't easy, but solving the problem is that easy," Madison said as she continued to curl my hair. "He likes you. It's obvious. He even told you, from the way it sounds, so you should just tell him the truth. He might even think it's kind of hot that there's a recording of the two of you. Tell him and then play it for him. I bet he freaks, but in a good way." She giggled.

I swore I'd leave as soon as she finished with my hair, but I didn't. I let her do my makeup and after she decided that my gala gown needed a little more drama, I was finally out the front door with a pair of her sparkly heels that were easily six-inches tall. The gala was just a few hours away and Jared came in the back door by the kitchen as we were returning our empty mugs to the sink.

"I didn't know you were all getting ready here," he said, smiling at me as he kicked off his boots.

"Just Marlee," Madison told him as she rinsed our mugs under the faucet. "Don't leave those dirty boots there! You know your mom will kill you."

Jared laughed and lifted his boots from the tile floor. "Yes, ma'am."

He patted my shoulder as he passed for the front door, surely leaving his work boots along the wall where the rest of the family's shoes were. Madison put our mugs in the dishwasher before she turned to face me with a sigh.

"You should tell Jace," she said, keeping her voice low so Jared couldn't hear. "And you should tell him tonight while he's too distracted by how good you look."

I felt a blush creep into my cheeks. "You are so—" I was going to say that she was boy-obsessed and shallow, but maybe she wasn't being shallow and maybe she never really was. Maybe she'd just fallen in love more times than I had. Thinking about Jace made me feel dumb and embarrassingly mushy inside. Even worse, the idea that maybe I wasn't being stupid and I was just falling in love made me want to run as far as possible from it all. I still could. I didn't have to go to the gala tonight. Madison would kill me if I didn't make an appearance though, so maybe I could get away with dealing with it all for just an hour. Both of my sisters had snuck out of the gala early before, so they really couldn't complain about me doing the same this year.

"You know, if you don't let people in every once in a while, then you miss out on a lot of great things," Madison said with a weak smile. She adjusted my curls so they lay over my shoulders. "Like today."

She didn't have to explain further. I never dreamed I would admit it—and I still wasn't sure that I would if anyone ever asked — that Madison and I really did have a lot in common. She was just more expressive about things than I was. Part of me was jealous that it was so easy for her to be that transparent, to just give the world the middle finger and be exactly who she wanted. It was only just hitting me that I'd done exactly that when I showed up on the McAdams' doorstep. I told her what I considered to be my biggest secret and she didn't bat a single perfectly-curled eyelash. I was my high school's valedictorian. I'd received a large scholarship to Yale. But right now, I'd never felt like more of an idiot.

"Thank you," I said, hesitating before I pulled her into a hug.

"Don't worry. I won't tell a soul," she said in my ear, pulling away before she added, "especially not Mom and Dad."

"I think I'd be more concerned if Margot found out," I scoffed, making her laugh.

She led the way to the front door, pulling my coat down from the hook. "Mama Margot would probably just stress you out more. You know how she is."

"Oh, I know. She's freaking out about all the wedding details, by the way," I said, not sure what I expected her to say. I knew this was a big deal to Madison, but somehow I knew that despite the dramatics and her obsession with all the tiny details that she was keeping her cool. If it was anything like what writing this book was for me, she was enjoying it. As stressed as I was about revealing this new story to the world, the process of writing it had been exactly the release I needed. It was both terrifying and thera-peutic how much of myself I was discovering through each page. Madison had seemed more herself after opening her clothing company and I felt a little like that too now that I was nearly finished writing this book.

Madison smiled, holding the sparkly heels while I slipped into my coat. "I knew she'd be more concerned about Mom and Dad's drama ruining the whole thing than I would be. That's why I put her in charge of it all," she said and handed me the shoes.

Damn. She was a lot smarter than we gave her credit for.

"I'll see you at the gala," I told her and stepped onto the porch. "Thanks for helping me get ready and for the heels."

She sent me a pointed look. "Just don't mess them up because

I'm going to walk down the aisle in those. Remember that I still have your bridesmaid's dress." She shut the door and left me with a pit in my stomach.

Did that bitch really just give me her wedding shoes? Was this a setup?

"What the fuck, Madison?" I called out, hearing her laugh through the wooden door.

Chapter 17

I PARKED behind Jace's rental car in the driveway instead of parking behind the POD, which would probably be there until he moved out again and was onto the next thing in his life. I pushed the thought from my mind and focused on the night ahead. I planned to drive us to the lodge in my Jeep. I'd stay long enough to show off my dress and tell everyone who asked that Madison had designed it. Past that, I could leave if I wanted.

I took Madison's sparkly heels from the passenger seat and started for the front door, stopping just inside to slip out of my snow boots.

"I was starting to wonder about you," Jace said from the living room couch. "Most girls need half the day to get ready for a ball."

"It's a gala and it's not as big a deal as you'd think," I told him. He didn't say a word, too busy scrolling on his phone. "You should shower if you want to be ready in time."

Finally, he looked up from his phone. I saw the double-take, the way his eyes lingered on my face. I ignored the heat rising to my cheeks and pretended to inspect the heels in my hands.

"Whatever you say, baby doll," he said and stood up from the couch. He slowed his pace as he went to the stairs, almost as though he expected me to say something. I kept my eyes on Madison's shoes as he passed, realizing how fast my heart was beating once he was at the top of the stairs.

I waited a moment to follow him, glad to see his bedroom door was closed as I made my way into mine. I'd done all the time-consuming parts of getting ready with Madison. All that was left was to slip into the one-shoulder white gown and the sparkly heels she'd loaned me. Then it was my turn to scroll my phone on the living room couch while I waited on Jace.

I looked up when I heard him clear his throat. He stood at the bottom of the stairs in a tuxedo. I'd seen so many men in tuxedos, but I'd never seen a man look like this. It was strange, like the style shouldn't fit him given what I knew, but it did. He looked powerful, like a mafia boss ready to order the most expensive bottle of champagne at a party and prepared to pull a gun on the first man who looked at him wrong in the same breath. He smirked and I realized I'd been staring a second too long. He nodded at me.

"You look good too, baby doll," he said.

I stood up from the couch, moving to slip my phone into my pocket and remembering as it hit the carpet that I didn't have any pockets.

"Shit," I groaned. I bent over to reach for it, but Jace was already there. He lifted it from the floor and held it out to me. I hesitated before I took it, slipping it into purse. "Don't call me baby doll."

He smiled. "Whatever you say."

I expected him to finish with that pet name I loved to hate. He didn't. It only made my stomach twist tighter with anxiety. Damn this man.

"You look nice," I told him, making eye contact for just a moment before I went to the front door.

"You look too good not to have a man on your arm," he said as I turned the doorknob. I pulled the door open and stepped aside, motioning for him to go ahead of me.

"Good thing there will be a room full of them once we get to the lodge," I said.

He laughed and said, "There she is." He led the way onto the porch, waiting as I locked up before we made our way through the snow to reach my orange Jeep. I climbed into the driver's seat and started the Jeep, barely giving him time to click his seatbelt into place before I backed into the street.

We were quiet the whole way up the mountain. Jace didn't seem surprised when the lodge came into view, and I was sure it was his upbringing. He'd probably grown up with something comparable. Maybe there was a country club of sorts or a beachfront resort where his summer coven resided. I knew they celebrated the summer solstice the way we did the winter solstice. Their traditions were likely different, but the principles were the same. One night out of the year, my powers were at their strongest. The same was true for him and I found myself wondering what it would be like for him to take me to celebrate with his coven. Maybe instead of a tuxedo and a white gown he'd wear a pair of swim trunks and I'd wear a bikini. We'd watch the stars align as we lay in the sand, maybe wade into the ocean so our hands could wander below the surface unnoticed by the crowd on the beach.

"Anything I should know before we go in?" Jace asked.

I was pulled out of my thoughts. I cut the engine, and I glanced his way. My eyes roved over him again, taking in that strong jaw and that waiting expression. I almost asked him to save a dance for me before the dome light in the Jeep faded and we were left in darkness.

"I think you'll be fine," I told him and unclicked my seatbelt.

He stayed at my side as we made our way up the stairs toward the entrance, following an older couple past the giant grizzly bear ice sculptures that manned the main doors. Jace held one of the large double doors open for me and we stepped into the lobby. Neither of us bothered with a coat for the night—not that either of us needed one given our powers to regulate our body temperatures—so we skipped the line for the coatroom and went straight into the main room where people were already mingling. I recognized most of the people who were making their rounds, not interested in talking to anyone except for maybe Madison and Jared who stood next to the bar with another couple who were gathered around Madison's extended hand, staring at her engagement ring. Margot and Dax were one of the few couples dancing near the front of the room, and maybe the only people in the room who didn't have a glass in their hands.

"Are we late?" Jace asked.

I turned from the crowd to look at him. "We missed the opening of the gala where they talk about the winter solstice and why it's important and stuff like that."

"Glad I missed that shit," Jace scoffed and looked at me. "It's the night you're strongest, right? It's the time of the year I'm at my weakest. You could freeze me solid, and I would struggle to defend myself against you. It would be easy for you."

Shit. I don't know how he does it, but even while talking about being at my mercy he made me feel like I was under his spell. It might be the night I was strongest, but I felt totally powerless beneath his gaze. His lips twitched upward like he knew it, too.

"Well, you haven't missed all our traditions. The solstice dance comes next," I said, backing away from him. "You can watch. Maybe you'll learn something."

My stomach turned and not in a good way as I left him. I glanced around the room to make sure my parents hadn't spotted me—like they would *actually* pay attention to what I was doing if they had anyway. I went to the buffet and snagged a glass of champagne from the end before I started toward the most congested corner of the room, slipping between a pair of couples to hide myself among the crowd. I downed half the glass before I took in my surroundings.

At first, I thought I was looking at Dax, but he was kissing a blonde girl that was definitely not my sister. I realized as he pulled away that he was Daren Krune, Dax's younger brother, and he caught me staring a moment later. He slipped his hand into the blonde girl's and led her toward me.

"Hey! This is Georgia," he told me, nodding toward the girl. She extended a hand to me as though I was more important than I actually was.

"Hi, I'm Georgia. I'm Daren's girlfriend," she said, shaking my hand.

"This is Marlee Sinclair. You met Madison earlier, the bride. This is her little sister," Daren told Georgia, practically yelling into her ear over the loud music before he looked back at me. "Georgia is from a winter coven in Fairbanks. You should see some of the spells she can do."

The way Daren looked at her told me he wasn't talking about magic. Typical Daren Krune. It was hard to believe he and Dax were related. I loved Dax and he was perfect for Margot, but I really fucking hoped they eloped someday, so I didn't have to deal with Daren at a wedding. I wouldn't be surprised if he showed up at Madison and Jared's wedding reception with a different girl at his side.

"It's good to meet you," I said before downing the rest of my champagne flute. "I'll see you around."

I turned around and started back toward the table only to walk straight into something solid. Someone solid.

"Oh! Sorry," I said, looking at my empty glass before inspecting him to make sure I hadn't somehow spilled champagne all over his tux.

"I'm fine. No problem. I think we both managed to stay dry," the man said, looking back at me with a pair of handsome blue eyes. "My name's Grant. I'm visiting from Fairbanks."

It was easy to put it together once he introduced himself. Grant and Georgia were siblings. Both blond with blue eyes, from Alaska, probably strong enough witches thanks to the long winters to take on most of our little Crescent Peak coven.

"Hi, Grant from Fairbanks," I said and allowed him to take my empty champagne flute. "I'm Marlee from Heritage City. Well, New York City now."

I saw the way he paused when I mentioned New York City. He looked past me long enough to wave Daren closer, passing him his champagne flute before looking back at me.

"Come with me to get another round of drinks. I'd like to know more about what you do in New York," he said as he backed toward the buffet, the crowd seeming to part for him without needing to be asked. I followed him, taking another glass of champagne when he passed one to me from the buffet.

It was quieter away from the crowd of college kids home for Christmas Break. Like Jace, Grant was a few years older than I was, already graduated from college, and worked in Alaska as an ecologist. I caught Madison's curious glance when she and Jared were finally free from the latest couple to accost them. When she noticed me staring, her eyes shifted across the room where Jace was leaning against the wall a glass of champagne in his hands. He raised it in a toast to me, but I could tell he wasn't amused.

Good.

"Would you like to join me for the solstice dance?" Grant asked. The music had stopped, signaling to the room that it was time to pair off for the dance. The coven elders were always first, symbolizing the passing of magic from one generation to the next. They formed a large circle as the room quieted in anticipation. Grant moved to my side to watch. I made eye-contact with Jace again across the room, the moment lasting for just a second before the orchestra began to play and my view of him was obscured by the dancing couples.

They rotated and twisted, the dance growing more sensual as the couples did lifts and turns. It felt like snakes were sliding around in my stomach as the music swelled and the couples finished dancing, the women walking away from their partners in the circle. It was our cue. All of the younger women took their places, towing their partners behind them to maintain the circle. I held Grant's hand as we joined the group, eager for the orchestra to start just as much as I was eager for the whole thing to be over.

The music began at a slow pace again and Grant and I moved in our own little circle, our right forearms touching once, and then switching to do the same with our left arms. We rotated again as the music built into a crescendo, repeating the movement for a second time before the tempo increased, pressing our palms together this time instead of our forearms.

The music quickened and Grant took my hand, spinning me around before letting go. The group was now two circles, the inner ring of women rotating to the left while the men stood in wait for us to return to them. I followed the girl to my left, my heart racing in my chest as I looked at each man's face as I passed, feeling like it might beat right through my chest when I saw Jace standing in that outer ring. A gasp caught in my throat when I felt his fingers bush against my hip as I passed him, not relaxing even when I made it back to Grant for another round of lifts and spins.

It was the men's turn to rotate, and I stood stationary this time, waiting for Jace to appear in front of me and when he did, I lifted my hand just enough to meet his fingers. The ring was moving too quickly to fully grasp his hand, so my fingers slipped from his as quickly as they had tangled with them. Grant returned to me seconds later for the final turns, holding my waist as we spun a final time before he lifted me into the air. I lifted my arms above me and looked around the circle of woman, feeling my back slowly slide down Grant's chest as I searched and finally found Jace directly across from me.

Jace's partner was in her own world, completely disconnected from him as he watched me. He didn't even finish the dance, keeping his eyes on me while Grant slid his hands over my hips and up my arms, taking my right hand for the final spin. I turned, moving to the outer ring with the rest of the women and exiting the dance floor. Instead of looking back at Grant, my eyes went straight to Jace, who was staring across the dance floor at me instead of looking at his partner. He smirked and I finally turned, finding my way to the glass doors for the outside deck.

I inhaled the icy air, nearly losing my balance in Madison's ridiculously tall heels and startling a group of teenagers huddled near the railing. They spun around, eyes wide, one of them holding a flask and the other a vape pen.

"If you leave now, I'll pretend I never saw you," I told them once I'd caught myself against the handle of the door. They barely let me finish before they stowed their goods and rushed back inside the building. I groaned and took their place at the far railing, looking down at the untouched snow below.

"I introduced your dance partner to mine. I hope you don't mind," Jace said.

I whirled around, not needing to take more than a few steps. He was already reaching for me, his hands guiding my face to his so my lips could smash into his. I pulled him closer by his belt, feeling immediately how ready he was to move this to a more private location.

"Let's get out of here," I said, breathless from our kiss.

"I want to show you something," he said, pulling my hands from his belt and lacing his fingers with mine. "I *need* to show you something."

"Okay," I said, starting to think the worst when I saw the anxiety in his expression. Was there more to his past than what he told me? Was he still connected to that gang? "Show me."

Chapter 18

"You know where the bookstore is?" Jace asked as we reached the Crescent Peak town square. I couldn't contain my groan.

"What do you think?" I asked, giving my sarcasm free reign. I glanced away from the road just long enough to see his smile.

"Just find a spot close," he said, pointing to one of the many empty parking spots along the road in front of the store. The coffee shop across the street was still open and hosting live music from the look of it. Based on the out-of-state tags on the cars parked down the block, all the tourists in town were in that tiny shop.

I did a U-turn so I could park next to the curb in front of the bookstore. It was late enough that everything but the coffee shop was closed. I got out of the driver's seat and moved to the front of the Jeep, expecting Jace to come around the hood to meet me so we could cross the street together. He reached out for my hand instead, not moving from the curb.

"Where are we going?" I asked, carefully walking around the front of the car to take his hand. If it weren't for the tourists, I'd just take my heels off and walk barefoot. The icy sidewalk wouldn't bother me, but it would definitely draw attention from the non-magical residents.

Jace laced his fingers with mine and held up a gold key with the other. "Just let me explain when you see it."

My heart sank as he led me along the sidewalk, rounding the bookstore for an alley that was even more iced-over than the sidewalk. I let out a squeal when he scooped me off my feet, cradling me against his chest so I didn't need to attempt the final stretch to the metal door halfway down the alley in my heels. He turned the key in the door, and it gave a grating squeal when he opened it, revealing a screen door that looked like it was original to the building.

"Is this ...?" I didn't finish the thought as I took in the room. Concrete floors with drains. Four large metal containers that looked like they might be filled with liquid judging by the spouts mounted on the front of them. There was a long counter on one wall and two sinks, but no other equipment to suggest it was a kitchen like I'd originally thought.

"I could lose my license for this, but it wouldn't be the first illegal thing I'd done in my life," Jace said as he approached one of the counters. "This is probably the least of my offenses, anyway."

"What is this place?" I asked as he opened a cabinet above the counter to pull down a short glass. It wasn't quite a shot glass, and I realized a moment after what it was. That's when it hit me what this place was. "Is this a brewery?"

Jace filled the small glass with dark liquid, a small layer of foam on the top. Dottie told me that she wasn't sure what the new owners of the bookstore were planning, but that she didn't expect them to keep it as a bookstore despite taking on the last of her stock. Jace turned from the large containers and offered the glass to me.

"Mine," he said as I took the glass. "My brewery."

I was stunned for a moment, thinking through the last few weeks and how I'd missed that this man had bought and started a whole brewery just down the road. Jace didn't spend his entire days at the cabin, but it wasn't like I'd expected him to. He had a whole shelf in the fridge full of craft beers from Denver. I just assumed he had good taste, but I wondered now if he was just comparing notes. I lifted the tasting glass to my lips and sipped. It was a dark beer, a stout, but it had a bit of a cream taste to go along with the normal bitter coffee taste that so many dark beers had.

"What do you think?" Jace asked.

"Of the beer or this?" I asked and motioned to the room around us.

He smiled. "Well, all of it. I haven't been totally honest with you. It's not like I lied."

I hummed in agreement as I looked around the room. There was enough equipment in here to suggest he'd been working on this for a long time. Maybe not, though. He had a lot of money, despite being cut off from his father. He could afford to drop millions on a new business. Knowing that, the timing with Dottie's announcement that she was retiring, and then there had been that big delivery truck that wanted to stop at the cabin …

"You bought the bookstore," I said. I didn't need to ask.

"Before you get mad that Mrs. Petty is closing up shop, let me give you the full tour and explain," he said, extending his hand again.

I reminded myself that he'd agreed to take on Dottie's stock. He wasn't kicking out the bookstore for the brewery. At least, he wasn't right away. I downed the last of the beer and sat it on the counter behind me before I took his hand, letting him lead me through the next door that led into the bookstore.

"I'm not changing anything here," Jace said.

I scoffed. "Really?"

"Well, I'm consolidating things, not replacing the greeting card section once it's gone," Jace said and motioned to the back of the room. "There's already space along this wall, so I'm putting taps here and a bar. This space will be a kind of lounge area." Jace pointed to the opposite wall where the greeting cards were displayed.

"Sounds cool," I said when I couldn't come up with a nicer

way of expressing how disappointed I was that the new business wasn't another bookstore.

"Just, keep an open mind. I'm not done," Jace said and led me toward the back of the store. "I want to open up this space to make it more obvious that there's another floor."

I had no idea there was an upstairs until now. Behind a wall and what I thought was the door to the employees' entrance was actually another hallway. There was a wide staircase, and I followed Jace to the second floor.

"There are bathrooms on the right. To the left is the new apartment. I knocked down a few walls and moved enough around in the original living space that I basically rebuild it," he said.

Apartment? The stretch of hallway looked new and I recognized his craftsmanship in the woodwork. The bathrooms were marked with hanging metal signs on the right and to the left was a little sign with Jace's name and the building address etched on it. The door along the wall was complete with a metal knocker in the shape of a hammerhead shark, the same species of shark that was tattooed on his chest.

"What's at the top of the stairs?" I asked, looking up the final flight.

"The best part," Jace answered and gave my hand a squeeze. He led me up the final stretch and through the door. We were on the roof, but it was much fancier than just that. The entire space was surrounded by glass so patrons could still look out and see the town square around us and all the twinkling lights. Heaters stood tall around the perimeter, enough to keep the whole space warm on a cold winter night. There was a covered awning with a raised stage for live music and enough tables, chairs, and outdoor couches to make the space inviting for a large crowd. I could see how even on a busy night the rooftop would still feel intimate. The sun had already set, but I could still see a sliver of light in the distance. The stars were already shining down on us from above, adding to the serene environment and easing the frustration of what this place was becoming.

I'd been so absorbed in the space that I hadn't realized Jace had moved away from me until the roof was suddenly illuminated by patio lights. They hung above the glass railing around the roof, a warm but dim glow that added to the romance of the intimate space beneath the stars. My eyes burned and I wasn't sure why. It was confusing. Everything since I got off that plane in Denver had been confusing, but it was freeing and terrifying at the same time. I had started to take a deep breath when I heard the pop of a cork from behind me. I turned around to see Jace sitting on the edge of the stage with a bottle of champagne. He tossed the cork back into a basket that had two glasses peeking out of the top.

"You planned on me coming here with you," I said.

"I hoped," he answered and sat the bottle aside. "You're free to do what you want and who you want. You make me crazy, Marlee, but I think it's a kind of crazy I need in my life and I'll take you however I can get you and when you'll have me. So, yeah. I hoped you would dance with me tonight and come here and listen to me talk about this totally different life I want to build for myself that's completely mine and can't be torn away by my family's greed. I think you want that, too, even if it doesn't include me. I think you want something that's honestly yours: something reflective of who you are and not what you think other people should see."

I laughed, the sound bursting from my lips before I could contain it. It made my eyes burn because I wasn't being held back at all. Madison was right. I'd spent so long on the run from anything real that I wasn't used to having what I wanted. And now that I knew what it felt like, to write a book I was truly passionate about and to be with someone who made time slip away, I wasn't sure what the future held for me. Yale didn't seem as exciting or prestigious as when I'd started there, and the academics just felt unfulfilling. Fuck, our tiny apartment was stifling on a good day.

"Come here, baby doll," Jace said gently.

I shook my head and looked back at the railing where the dim light from the sunset had been just moments before. It was hard to see past the lights from the rooftop now.

"Now," Jace said, his tone sharp enough to send a jolt through me and to sever the last of whatever stubborn resolve was keeping me on the run from what felt good and easy. I swiped at the moisture that had spilled onto my cheeks, and I turned to face him, the firm yet understanding look he sent me enough to propel me across the space to join him.

He pulled me to his chest and I groaned into his neck, fighting against the tears.

"Fuck, I'm such a dumbass," I said.

"You're not a dumbass," he said with a laugh as he broke our hug, pulling back just far enough so he could brush the tears from my cheeks with both hands. "I should've told you sooner."

"It's not that. I haven't been totally honest with you either," I said, pulling his hands from my face.

"You didn't have to tell me. It didn't take long for me to find your books," he said, pulling his hands free from mine and pushing my curls away from my face.

What even was this night? I had to pause and digest what he'd said before I fully understood it. He knew I was a writer. Not just a writer, but he knew I had books. Plural.

"Shit," I groaned and stepped away from him. "It's stupid."

"It's not stupid, but I see why you might think that," he said with a laugh, turning to pull the champagne flutes from the basket. "You were valedictorian, a scholarship recipient to Yale, your family's bragging point ... It doesn't take a lot to see why you'd hide your work, but it's obvious you care a lot about it and that's really all that should matter. It's honest and that's all I care about."

"Really? You don't care that I'm writing some vapid, smutty book?" I asked.

"For such a strong, smart, independent woman you talk about basic human emotions like they're not the driving force behind our entire world," Jace said with a laugh. "There is nothing vapid about writing deep, real emotions and there's nothing wrong about writing sex, especially when the entire world is either having it or wishing they were.”

“Sure,” I said, suddenly not so concerned with the public opinion about romance novels now that he was close enough to kiss. The corner of his mouth hitched into a smirk, officially sending all thoughts from my head.

“Tell me you aren’t thinking about it right now,” he challenged, brushing my hair behind my ear.

Damn it.

“I’m not.” I kept my eyes on him as I reached behind him for the open bottle of champagne. I didn’t bother with a glass, taking a sip straight from the bottle.

“Whatever you say, baby doll,” he said and held out an empty glass for me to fill.

“It’s impressive what you’ve done here,” I said as I filled his glass. “But you haven’t shown me the entire place. You said you rebuilt the whole apartment.”

He lifted his glass to his smiling lips, taking a sip. I’d be lying if I didn’t admit that I wondered what that sweet champagne tasted like on his lips. I pushed aside the thought by taking the remaining glass from the basket and filling it for myself.

“For someone who isn’t thinking about it, you’re pretty eager for a trip to my place,” he said.

I held the full glass in my right hand and the bottle in my left as I backed toward the door, hoping this didn’t backfire and I tripped over Madison’s stupid-tall heels along the way.

“I just want the full tour,” I said and stopped at the door. My hands were too full to open it myself. “I want to see for myself what you were doing when you should’ve been finishing the bathroom back at the cabin.”

Jace laughed and pulled open the door. “If I had finished it sooner you wouldn’t have that memory of me naked in your room.”

Bullseye. It was so close to the truth that heat rushed to my face, and I knew he saw it when I paused to look back at him. I focused on the stairs ahead and how close we were for the landing.

"Let's just get to your new apartment and we'll see if that memory was worth it," I said.

Jace let out a low hum. "You said you weren't thinking about it, baby doll."

"I'm not," I lied, glad when I finally reached the landing and the long hallway. I didn't wait for him and went down the hall, turning to face him when I reached the apartment door.

He smiled and I swore he was walking slower on purpose. "You know, I haven't shown you my office downstairs. You really need to hear the whole business plan to get the full tour."

I downed the last of the champagne in my glass so I could shift it to my other hand without worry of spilling, freeing my right hand so I could pull him closer by the front of his shirt once he finally reached me.

"Just open this damn door," I said and kissed him, pulling away as I felt him relax. "You can take me on the desk later."

He smiled and I felt his arm slink around my waist. Instead of pulling me closer, I heard the click of the lock behind me. I let go of his shirt so he could straighten up to open the door.

It was obvious that the place was brand new. It smelled like wood from the fresh flooring and leather from the new couches to the right. It had all the markings of a rich man, all the furnishings top-notch straight out of designer magazines. The space was small and homey though, not lavish the way someone of his upbringing might desire and yet this apartment already looked lived-in somehow, like the kind of place built and decorated for the long-term.

Jace crossed the small living room for the kitchen in the back. Everything branched from this one room, open-plan other than the short hallway that led to a bathroom on the right and a bedroom on the left. The walls of the living room were the original brick, rustic next to the black leather furniture and wooden floors. I joined him in the kitchen, setting my empty glass and the champagne on the granite countertop. Jace filled his champagne flute and sat it and the bottle down to take my hand.

"You've seen the apartment. Well, almost all of it," he said and motioned to the room around us. "Would you like to see the bedroom?"

That challenging look would be the end of me someday. He said I drove *him* crazy ...

"Tell me you aren't thinking about it," I said.

"Just go to the fucking bedroom before I carry you there," he said, his lips crashing down onto mine a moment later.

Chapter 19

We never made it to his office.

I was pressed to Jace's side, wrapped in his thick comforter-not that I needed it. Jace was warm and I was sure it was a summer warlock thing.

"Do I feel cool to you?" I asked him, raising my head from his bare chest to look at him. "You feel warm to me, but not uncomfortably. It's like sunbathing. I was just wondering if it was the same for you, if I felt cooler to you."

He smiled and nodded. "Like the other side of the pillow."

I sat up in the bed, relishing in the way his eyes dropped to my naked chest. I reached for his white dress shirt on the foot of the bed and slipped it onto my shoulders. "I'm going to get champagne," I said and fastened one of the buttons between my breasts.

"I'll come with," he said as I stood up from the mattress.

"No, put something on the TV," I told him a moment too late. He was already out of the bed and dragging his boxers up his thighs. "I'll come back with the bottle, two glasses, and we can snuggle."

"Not a chance," he said and followed me to the door. "I'd follow that ass anywhere."

I squealed as he patted my butt, chasing me out of the bedroom and into the living room. I turned around and he pulled me closer. I rose onto my toes to kiss him but pulled away with a smile before I could let it go any deeper.

"Champagne," he said.

"I can think of a few things I'd rather put to my lips right now," I said and reached for the elastic of his briefs.

He pulled my hand away and sent me that challenging look I was growing to love. "You are a greedy brat."

"I think you like brats," I said and slipped my hand from his. Rather than going in for another kiss, I poked him in the stomach. Not hard. It was enough to make him gasp and buy a little time so I could make it to the kitchen ahead of him and put the counter safely between us. There was an onery look on his face when he reached the kitchen.

"Champagne?" I asked and slid the bottle toward him.

He hesitated, those eyes a warning that I was one snarky comment away from finding myself pinned beneath him again. My face burned with my blush. He took the bottle from the counter and began to pour a glass.

"You writers really do have a way with words," he said and slid a full glass across the counter to me.

"It's easy to paint a pretty picture when there's already one right in front of you," I said and lifted the glass from the counter, watching as his eyes flicked to mine.

He smirked. "I doubt I live up to the book boyfriend you're imagining as you write your next bestseller."

I hesitated with the glass at my lips for a second. My heart skipped right out of my chest. He hadn't listened to the latest podcast episode. This wasn't just a joke; he honestly didn't know. I could see it in the casual way he filled his own champagne glass now. He even looked up at me with a smile.

"Ouch," he scoffed. "Your book boyfriend that good, huh?"

I shook my head. "He's fictional."

"So, I can never compete," he said and raised his glass in a toast.

"Eh, you do all right," I said and clinked my glass against his, forcing a smile past my guilt. I should have told him. But at that moment, he sat down his glass and rounded the end of the counter to reach me with that challenging look on his face.

"Just all right, baby doll?" he asked as he slid his hands around my waist.

"At least," I teased, the knot in my chest only easing a fraction at his touch. I gasped when he lifted me onto the counter, the granite cool against my bare skin. He pushed my knees apart so he could move closer, hooking his finger into the top of his dress shirt where I'd fastened it between my boobs.

"I don't want anyone else but you," he said, the playfulness in his expression fading and only worsening the tension in my chest. "Tell me you don't want anyone else but me, Marlee."

My body ached. The guilt. The shame. The fact that I couldn't imagine wanting anyone else right now or ever. Jace Blackthorne was insufferable in so many ways, rough around the edges, and in some ways, he was no different than the rich family I wanted to distance myself from. Still, he could go toe-to-toe with my quick remarks, wasn't offended or turned-off by my intellect, and he didn't think my writing was stupid. He might even see my work as valuable.

That's what hurt about keeping my secret the most.

Tears stung my eyes as I said, "I only want you."

He lifted me from the counter, and I wrapped my legs around his waist and my arms around his shoulders as he carried me back to the bedroom, the champagne we'd come for forgotten on the counter.

I DIDN'T WANT to leave Jace's cozy apartment, but my laptop was at the cabin, and I needed to finish the rough draft of my book. I *wanted* to finish the rough draft of my book. Miraculously, I wasn't far off from typing "The End" on the Word document. I waited as long as I could before I had to leave for the McAdams Mercantile for a bridal party meeting.

I parked my orange Jeep next to Margot's blue Jeep, which was parked next to Madison's pink Jeep. It looked like the perfect commercial, the vehicles in a perfect line as the snow fell heavily around them. It didn't matter that the winter solstice was over now. The winter weather made my powers sensitive, like I'd chugged an energy drink before the drive and needed to take a long walk.

I went through the double-doors of the red barn. There was a group of older women looking at the wall full of Christmas wreaths and a family of four wandering through Madison's clothing section to the right of the doors. I caught the attention of the man behind the counter, recognizing him from the familiar tall build. Jared's uncle Mark.

"They're in the workshop," he told me and motioned for me to follow him. He led me to the back doors where the deck was, pushing one open so he could point out the little shed halfway between us and the main house. "You might want to knock first. Madison has been so serious about keeping the dresses a secret that I thought she was going to launch across the dinner table last night when she found out that I went in workshop for more wreaths."

"Thanks, Mark" I told him. The snow crunched under my feet as I crossed the deck, and my boots sank deep into the white powder once I reached the yard. I trudged the final stretch toward the little building and knocked hard on the door, hearing a few screams of surprise within.

The door opened and I was greeted with laughter. Madison cracked open the door just enough so she could tug me inside before locking it behind her. "I don't want anyone seeing the dresses."

I almost pointed out that there was no chance of that with the workshop being so far away from the mercantile. No one was going to stumble upon our little party and a party it was. I didn't realize there'd be champagne or more gifts. It looked like Bachelorette Party 2.0 minus all the penises.

"Is it too tight on my ass?" Winnie asked from the opposite side of the room.

The walls on all sides were covered in pegboards that held spools of ribbon and twine and other instruments for wreath-making. At the back of the workshop was a section with bolts of fabric and a desk with a sewing machine. Winnie stood next to the desk in her bridesmaid dress. They were all the same shade of light pink but created in different styles Madison had designed unique to each of us. Winnie's dress was a mermaid style that hugged her hips. She turned away from us slightly so we could better see the silhouette.

"I made it that way to show off all your curves," Madison said, leaving me at the door to join the group around the worktable in the middle of the room where a bottle of champagne and six glasses sat.

"I just wanted to make sure," Winnie said and turned to face the room again. "It doesn't feel too tight at all, but I didn't want to put it all out there for everyone when it's your wedding day. They should be looking at you and not all this." She gestured to her hips with both hands.

"I'm sure she has a plan for standing out," Margot said, joining Winnie to help her unzip the back of her dress.

"Marlee, you got here just in time," Lola said and gestured for me to join them. "We've already tried on our dresses and had a final fitting. It's your turn."

I took a tentative step farther into the room. "I've already tried mine on."

It was true. I'd tried it on before when Madison was still figuring out all the designs. It had been months ago, but the dress was mostly done. She had my measurements from the past several years of the Winter Solstice Gala and she rarely needed to adjust the sizing once the construction was sound.

"Then model it for us!" Remy called from the stool directly in front of me. She whirled around quickly enough that the stool wobbled, and I thought she might fall off. I was a little surprise at the satisfaction that pulled at the corner of my lips, glad that she mistook the smile for excitement. "Come on! This is the first time we've seen all the bridesmaids' dresses!"

I let the smile spread, catching Margot's concerned look as I rounded the worktable to join Madison and Lola at the back of the room. Madison held up a pink dress, though blush was probably a better way to describe the color, and waited for me to undress. I glanced at the room of girls and was glad to see that they were all too busy talking and drinking champagne to notice me.

"Just do it for a second, okay?" Madison asked, pulling my attention back to her and the dress. "One minute tops so I can see how you'll all look together."

"I didn't wear a good bra for this," I warned her as I popped the button on my jeans and pushed them down my thighs.

"Then just take it off," she said with a shrug.

Fine. Whatever made her happy.

Whatever you say, baby doll.

I turned toward the back wall for a little more privacy and stripped off my top, letting my bra slide down my arms before I draped both over the sewing machine to the right. I took the dress from Madison and stepped into it, the fabric soft as it slid up my hips. I adjusted the spaghetti straps on my shoulders and then the fabric that draped over my biceps as Madison zipped up the back. She fluffed the fabric at the bottom, so it flowed better from there it gathered at my waist.

I turned to face her and she gasped and took a step back. "You look gorgeous!" Her eyes roved over the dress before they stopped halfway to my face, her smile fading and turning to surprise that chased away all the cool flutters of magic that ran through my veins.

"Oh my God," Lola said, prompting me to turn toward them before I thought about looking at myself in the mirror. I watched as everyone in the room stared at me, realizing that there was something wrong with me and not the dress.

"Is that ..." Remy started, pointing at my chest.

Fuck. Was my tit out? Could you see my nipples through the fabric or something?

Nope. Worse.

I turned toward the full-length mirror in the corner. It was obscured behind Madison before, but she'd moved to the table for her champagne glass, leaving a clear view of myself in the mirror and the dark splotch on my right boob. A hickey. I had a hickey, a dark one at that, and it was high enough on my cleavage that the only way to cover it was to wear a crew-neck top.

Lola's mouth hung open and her cheeks were bright pink. Remy looked impressed, like she might start cheering me on once she'd stopped laughing at me. Winnie looked from me to Madison like she might have to step in to prevent a fight. Margot was looking at me in that motherly way I hated. Shit, I could practically hear her giving me all the bullshit advice that her therapist had fed her over the last year, words that gave her comfort, but I knew would only piss me off and make her worry about me.

"It's fine. The wedding is a few days away and if it's still around by then it will be lighter. The makeup artist can cover it," Madison said, her voice getting progressively more pinched as she spoke like she was fighting the urge to either burst into tears or scream at me.

"No way!" Remy cheered, making me jump and sending a shock of silence through the room. She sent me a devious look from across the room. "That's why you snuck off at the bachelorette party."

Damn it.

"I didn't sneak off. I told Jace I was leaving," I said, feeling heat rush to my face as I said his name.

Remy shook her head and pointed an accusing finger at me. "No, you left with that guy at the Karaoke bar, that frat guy you spent the whole time with at the first bar we went to."

I opened my mouth to deny it, but it dawned on me what she was saying. She thought I'd hooked up with Tyler. Could a hickey even last that long? It had been over a week since the bachelorette party. Too much time must have passed for me to answer, because Remy was laughing again and Lola and Winnie joined in a moment after. I glanced at Madison to see she was smiling too, though the brief knowing look she sent me told me she knew the truth.

"It's not a big deal. I won't see him ever again," I said, trying my best to ignore the disapproving look on Margot's face. Shit. Mom and Dad would probably be less appalled about me losing my virginity than my sister.

"Is that why Jace stood us up?" Lola asked, less of a question and more of an assumption as she put the pieces together. God, I could see the gears in her little blonde head working overtime. "He left us at the Karaoke bar to go and get you after you went to hook up with that guy?"

"His name was Tyler, and he was—" I was going to say that he was a douchebag, but I needed to keep up the ruse and I caught myself. "Okay. It was fine." I shrugged.

Remy let out a laugh. "Just fine? He wasn't even good?"

"He was fine," I said again and turned toward the wall, stretching my arm as far as I could in hopes of reaching the zipper on this damn dress.

"I bet Jace was pissed," Lola said with a teasing tone in her voice. I almost looked over my shoulder at her, but Madison appeared instead.

"I bet he was," she grumbled behind me and unzipped the dress in one smooth motion.

"I don't want to talk about it," I whispered to her and let the dress pool around my ankles. I lifted my bra from the sewing machine and started to fasten it around myself.

"Probably. We were having a great time at the first place," Remy said. I focused on flattening my shirt down my stomach. "Maybe I'll text him and see what happens."

I whirled around before I could help myself. "You have his phone number?"

Remy looked at Winnie beside her before looking back me like I was the one who'd gotten plastered and forgotten that whole night. "Yeah. He gave it to all of us for the trip. Did he not give it to you? Wait, isn't he staying at your family's place?"

"He is. I forgot he did that," I said, joining them at the work-table and reaching for the only empty glass left on the table. I poured it almost to the rim of the glass and took a sip.

"That's because Jace wasn't the guy you were focused on that night," Remy said, getting laughter out of everyone but my sisters. "Me, on the other hand ..."

"I think we need to move on to what's left in the binder," Madison declared, moving into place to my right and dropping the thick wedding binder onto the table. I thought about how I could show her how grateful I was, but I didn't need to. She rubbed the small of my back as she turned to the pre-rehearsal dinner tasks section of the binder.

As everyone else in the room easily moved on to the reason for why we were meeting, I was left wondering which was worse: making Remy think that Jace was single or telling them all just how much I loved him.

Both options left me feeling shitty, because it didn't change the fact that he didn't know the whole truth about me. And I wasn't sure if he would forgive me for just how much of him I'd shared with our thousands of podcast listeners.

Chapter 20

I was having a difficult time writing. After the bridesmaid meeting, I'd spent part of the day helping Madison confirm wedding details while Jace was busy prepping the brewery to open. We 'd been spending our evenings together, both of us ending the nights in my bed. But things weren't as busy as they could be. I'd written my last book under a more stressful timeline, and I managed it without breaking a sweat, but I just couldn't get past Remy's comments about Jace and how my guilt about the podcast teaser had led me to another lie. Now, it wasn't just Jace I was keeping things from; the entire bridal party thought I'd hooked up with Douchebag Tyler and that Jace Blackthorne was single. I know I should've told them we were together. Jace was my boyfriend. I was his girlfriend. Exclusive. But somehow, I didn't feel like I fully deserved him until I told him the truth.

But I just couldn't burst our happy bubble right now, not when things were so fucking good.

"Hey, can you pack a suitcase in the next twenty minutes?" Jace asked.

I turned from my computer screen at my desk to look at him leaning in the doorway. "What? Why?"

He groaned like I was wasting time. "I want to take you somewhere."

"Overnight?"

"Yeah. You can get away for one night, right?"

Yeah, I guess, if I didn't care about what Madison or Margot would think if they needed me for wedding stuff in the meantime. "I'm supposed to be around to help with wedding shit."

"Like what?" Jace asked, moving farther into the room. He paused so I could answer and when I didn't, he spun me in the desk chair so I was facing him. "They don't need your help with place cards or centerpieces or whatever there is to do for this rehearsal dinner. What *you* need, baby doll, is to relax. You've been tense as fuck the last few days."

I let out a deep sigh. He was right. I was tense, but not because of the wedding.

"What I *need* is to finish writing this book," I told him.

He placed his hands on both armrests of my chair, leaning in far enough to kiss my forehead and send a jolt through my heart. "And what do you need to finish writing this book?"

Time. I needed time to write this book—maybe just an hour of actual writing, if my brain would shut up about Remy. I needed to forget about the bridesmaid meeting and the way Jace danced with Remy at the bar before everything happened and we started seeing each other. I needed time to write this book. I needed to unplug myself from everything in Crescent Peak. Maybe I did need to get away with Jace.

The way he looked at me now made me think of all the fantasies that had inspired me to write words on the page in the first place, how I'd written thousands of words in a single sitting about a story I never dreamed I would ever write, much less enjoy writing.

I needed Jace, time, and some really dirty sex.

"A writing retreat," I said as the idea came to me.

Jace paused for a moment before nodding. "I can do that."

"Okay."

"Is twenty minutes long enough to pack a bag?"

My heart fluttered in my chest. "Plenty."

Twenty minutes was all we needed to pack our things and get out of the house. Jace refused to tell me where we were going, but I started to narrow it down the longer we drove. No rural adventures. Good. I wasn't an outdoorsy girl at all. We were either going to Denver or one of the suburbs, maybe doing a fancy dinner tonight. I packed a causal outfit and a cocktail dress just to make sure I was prepared for either.

"You really aren't going to tell me?" I asked him as we cruised down a busy street between a block full of tall buildings.

"Nope."

"What if I needed to pack something special and I didn't do that?"

He scoffed. "You aren't that type of Barbie doll. I know what I'm getting myself into with you. I'm sure what you packed is fine."

"Just tell me where we're going, please?" I asked again.

He smirked and shook his head. "You're going to have to trust me and just do what you're told for a change."

"You know I'm not good at that."

"Trust or doing as you're told, baby doll?"

I held up a middle finger even though he was too busy with the traffic ahead to get the full view. "I don't let anyone boss me around, especially men."

"I'm well aware." Jace laughed.

We kept going through the bumper-to-bumper traffic until he pulled into the pore-cochère of a tall hotel. It was hard to tell on the outside, but the suits the men and women wore who were manning the valet podium told me this place was expensive. We pulled in behind a Rolls-Royce, which was parked behind two BMWs that were polished to perfection despite the messy winter weather we'd been having.

"We're staying here?" I asked. It wasn't like I'd never stayed at a fancy hotel like this, but it wasn't the kind of place I'd ever go to on a whim. Getting a room here last minute would be hard without a name like Blackthorne.

"We aren't checking in yet," Jace said and put the car in park. I got out before he got the chance to come around and open my door. He sent me a look of disapproval as I rounded the front of the car. I stuck my tongue out at him and he smiled, turning only when a little man in a valet uniform approached us.

"Mr. Blackthorne," he greeted with a handshake before turning toward me and bending into a half-bow. "Miss Sinclair."

A bow? A fucking *bow*? What kind of people usually stayed at this place?

"I called about a service," Jace started, getting a wide smile and an enthusiastic nod from the man.

"Of course, sir. We will take your bags up to your suite and park your car. Your driver is in the BMW at the front there. Julie will escort you there," he said, pointing to the dark SUV at the front of the line of cars. A woman in a suit joined us, her hair slicked back into a dark bun at the nape of her neck. She smiled and motioned for us to follow her.

"Are you not cold?" I asked her, noticing as she started to walk that she wore a knee-length skirt with tights and a pair of black heels. Neither Jace nor I were dressed in many layers, both of us sporting our leather jackets by coincidence. Our powers allowed us to temperature regulate, however, and non-magical people would've been freezing in just what the valet wore.

"There are several heaters around the entrance and the valet podium. I start to sweat if I wear too many layers," she answered as we walked, her heels clicking on the concrete as we went.

I saw Jace attempt to move around me for the handle of the BMW. I put a little skip in my step and gripped the handle before he could, his fingers grazing mine. Satisfaction bloomed warm in my chest as I stared back at him, watching the humor ease his frustrated expression.

"Bitch," he said teasingly under his breath. He ran his fingers from my right arm, along my lower back, and to my left before he left me to go to the opposite side. I slid into the back of the BMW as the driver got in the front seat. Jace climbed in next, pulling the door shut and leaning forward to speak to the driver.

I expected him to finally announce what the plan was for the day, but he flashed his phone to the driver instead. I tried catching a glance, but he'd purposely turned the screen away from me and the man behind the wheel laughed when he caught on.

"So, it's a surprise, huh?" the driver asked, his eyes flicking up from the screen at me.

"I call it torture," I said, getting a booming laugh out of him as he turned toward the steering wheel. Jace sent me that challenging look I'd grown to love as he sat back in his seat.

"You just can't let go of control, can you?" he teased.

More like I didn't want to risk looking stupid.

The idea came so fast to the front of my mind that I was shocked by the truth of it. Was that why I couldn't tell Jace the truth, why I hid that I was an author, why I was still fighting against that part of me that said I was stupid for writing this sexy little romance book? Was I just afraid of people thinking I was stupid?

No. Worse. Everyone knew I was smart. No one had ever questioned that. No one had ever accused me of being fun or emotional or dramatic ...

I was afraid that I couldn't be both.

It felt like there were two sides to me and I was afraid that no one would accept that both were entirely me.

Ouch.

"The parking at our first stop isn't great, so I will stop next to the entrance to let you out," out driver said. "I'll find a place to park. Text or call the number on my card and I'll pull around to pick you up when you're ready for the next stop."

The next stop?

We were in an artsy area judging by all the murals painted on the sides of the buildings and the modern boutiques that lined the block. I hated shopping. There was no way Jace would take me shopping, right? I was a little worried that he'd missed that little detail about me until our car pulled next to the curb outside a brewery.

"I'll text you when we're ready," Jace said and took a business card from the driver. I was still taking in the building, so I didn't rush to get out and let Jace play the gentleman and open the door for me. He held my hand as I stepped onto the pavement, still staring at the building that was made to look like a log cabin on the outside.

"Stop number one?" I asked as he led the way to the glass door. The door handle was a piece of metal in the shape of an evergreen tree. He opened the door and let me walk ahead of him.

"Welcome to Two Pines!" a man not much older than us called from behind the bar. He was dressed in a dark purple button-up with the sleeves rolled to his elbows. He had dark hair and a mustache straight out of the '70s. "Oh! Are you Jace Blackthorne?"

"Yeah. We talked on the phone," Jace called back, passing me to head for the bar. It had a concrete bar top and the wall behind the man was covered in pine planks. Little chalkboard signs hung in neat rows on the wall with funny names for the beers like Ale Always Love You and Polygamy Porter (Because You'll Want More Than One) and my go-to at any brewery, a stout, which the sign designated as Black Bear Stout. Next to each sign was a number that was cut out of a piece of metal and mounted to a round piece of wood that looked like it had been sawed off from a tree branch.

"From Crescent Peak B—"

"Hold up!" Jace said, lifting up a hand to cut off the man. He looked apprehensively back at me before extending his hand. I stopped studying the room to join him at the bar. "I want to keep the name of the place a surprise."

"More surprises?" I asked. I let go of his hand so I could climb onto the barstool beside him. "I'll take the number three, the Black Bear Stout." I held up three fingers to match the metal number hanging on the wall.

"Slow down," Jace said and wrapped his fingers around all three of mine. He sat them back on the bar. He looked from me to the man behind the bar. "We'll take a flight. We're here to try it all."

The man smiled and clapped his hands together. "I'm glad you could come in early. I can take you through our operations later if you'd like." He turned his back to us to start our order.

I swiveled in my barstool to look at Jace. "You brought me all the way out here for a brewery?"

"I know you like craft beers," Jace said, sliding a hand up my thigh and back to my knee.

I laughed. "You really know the way to a girl's heart."

"Oh, it gets better," he smirked. "We're doing a brewery tour. So, take things slow, baby doll."

I felt the smile tug at my cheeks. I was glad when the first flight arrived, so I had a tiny glass of beer to hide behind.

Chapter 21

IT WASN'T a surprise that my favorite beer at Two Pines was the *Black Bear Stout*. I'd called it from the beginning. The *Two Pines Pilsner* was a close second though. We went to two more breweries, neither as good at Two Pines, before our driver took us back to the hotel.

"Thank you, Rodrigo," Jace said to our driver as he pulled to a stop. Jace was already out the door before Rodrigo could reply. He turned in the driver's seat to smile at me and offer to drive us again while we were in town.

"Just text my card. I mean it," he said and waved his index finger at me. "You two remind me of me and my wife before we got old."

"Go home and kiss her for us," I said and patted him on the shoulder, only turning when Jace opened my car door.

"You got a good buzz going, don't you?" he said as he took my hand. I didn't complain about the gesture and let him help me out. Once we got checked in and up to our room, a gentleman was the last thing I'd want him to be. So, I would play along for now.

"I'm fine," I groaned and adjusted my purse at my hip. "I'm barely buzzed. I just had a nice time."

He hesitated for a moment before placing a finger under my chin. He raised my lips to his, letting the kiss deepen for just a moment, long enough to make me ache for more, before we were forced to move out of the way of an SUV. We'd barely gotten through the door before a woman with long, curly hair met us. She was dressed in the same brown and deep red tones that the valets wore, only instead of wearing a suit she wore a brown dress that tapered at her knee.

"Mr. Blackthorne. Ms. Sinclair," she greeted with a big smile. She passed a pair of keycards to Jace. "Your suite is on the thirty-first floor. It's the top-most floor for our guests. The thirty-second floor hosts one of the best restaurants in the city and I took the liberty of confirming your reservation for seven tonight. Is there anything I can do for you?"

I was glowing, I was sure. I wasn't the kind of girl to be picky about a date. I loved the casual scene. I was low maintenance, for sure, but a fancy dinner with a view over the city and Jace Blackthorne seated across from me was perfect.

"Thank you," I said before I realized she was expecting me to answer her question.

"We will call down if we need anything," Jace said, slipping his hand into mind and giving it a squeeze.

"Of course," the woman said with a sincere smile.

Jace and I walked hand-in-hand through the lobby, passing a long fireplace that sent a wave of warmth over us. Jace pressed the button to call one of the several elevators down to the lobby.

"I can't wait for you to see the suite," Jace said as we waited, the elevator dinging and a little screen above the silver doors counting down the floors.

I scoffed. "More like you can't wait to get me alone in that suite." I turned to face him, reaching for his waist until that final ding sounded and the silver doors split to reveal an empty elevator. Jace smirked down at me before taking my hand and tugging me into the little space.

"Slow down, baby doll. We have a few hours before our reservation and you wanted a writing retreat," he said and pressed a kiss to my temple. "Finish writing your bestseller. Consider it motivation for what I have planned for you after dinner."

"More surprises?" I asked. I felt too light and floaty to bring on my usual snark. This entire day had been perfect, straight out of a romance novel and I was suddenly so excited to see this suite and unpack my laptop.

The elevator hummed to a stop and the bell rang around us, the silver doors opening to a long hallway that only had a few doors. My God, this suite must be massive. Jace swiped his keycard at the first door on the left and held the door open for me. The suite *was* huge. There was a foyer with an armoire and a painting of a mountain range at sunset. The short hallway opened into a large area separated into two living rooms, one with a kitchenette to the left and one with a fully stocked bar to the right. The entire room was flanked by floor-to-ceiling windows that looked over the city and to the mountains on the horizon. It was beautiful. It was so beautiful I didn't do more than glance at the bedroom through the door next to the bar area.

"I thought about the larger suite," Jace said and joined me in the living room. "It had the same view, but with a balcony and a hot tub. I didn't think we needed the extra bedroom though and I was sure you wouldn't mind."

I opened my mouth to make a joke, but I couldn't think of one. This was all too perfect and my brain was already focused on the task at hand: reviewing where I'd left off in my manuscript so I could continue until I wrote "The End" at the bottom.

"Thank you," I said and wrapped my arms around his shoulders. I rose onto my toes to kiss him, and he pulled back before I could get carried away.

"I'll be in the lobby," Jace said and started for the front door. "I'll be back in time to get ready for our date. Get comfortable and finish the damn book." He smiled and paused in the doorway as though waiting for the smartass remark I didn't have ready. I had nothing. Nothing would ruin this moment and my worries about this book being too unserious had left my mind entirely. Love was one of the deepest emotions I'd ever felt, and I was sure it was true for anyone else. If love was something felt so deeply by a world full of people, then there was no story more universal than that of two people falling in love. Nothing more honest. Nothing more real.

I found a spot on the gray couch by the windows and had no problem falling back into my manuscript and no trouble finding my way to that happily ever after on the final page.

WHEN JACE RETURNED I was in the shower, which added another forty-five minutes to my dinner-date prep and cut out the time I planned to spend trying out the complementary spa basket left on the bedroom vanity. I'd have to test those in the morning. We finished getting ready together in the bathroom, Jace gelling his hair into place in a style I'd never seen him wear and only made him look every bit the millionaire's son that he was.

"Zip me," I told him and turned to face the bed, ready with my purse in hand aside from that important detail. I heard the zipper as it slid up my spine to rest at the nape of my neck. Jace pulled me against his chest by my hips and left a trail of kisses up my neck. "I'm really not that hungry."

He laughed. "We're going to celebrate you finishing your book. I want to hear all about it."

My stomach twisted as I thought about what that would entail. Was a fancy dinner a good time to tell him the truth? What if he was mad enough at me to leave me? What if we had a big argument and we had to share this fancy suite and spend a whole car ride home together?

"It's so different than what I normally write," I said slowly. I'm sure he noticed my nerves and I didn't really care anymore. Everything today had been exactly what I needed and the best day I'd had in such a long time. I knew I was taking a risk in ruining it all, but I couldn't do this anymore. I had to tell him.

"Tell me about it over dinner," Jace said and started through the bedroom door and into the main room of the suite. I almost asked him to stop for a moment so I could go ahead and get it all over with, but he'd promised celebratory champagne, and I could use a little liquid courage.

We left the suite and went back to the elevator. The ride upstairs to the next floor was short. The doors parted to reveal the foyer to a room of crystal light fixtures and black round tables. The waitstaff were all dressed in black as they made their rounds to the tables of finely dressed patrons.

"What's the name on the reservation, sir?" the hostess asked.

"Blackthorne," Jace answered, wrapping an arm around my back and tugging me closer to his side.

"Right this way," the hostess said with a smile. She led us into the room, which was bathed in sunlight from the tall windows surrounding the restaurant. The light glittered off the crystal chandeliers, reflecting off the dark floors. The hostess led us to a corner near the bar at the back of the room, telling us that our waiter would arrive shortly as she laid my napkin in my lap. She poured two glasses of water from the glass bottle she'd brought with her before setting it in the middle of the table and starting back toward the front of the restaurant.

"This place is gorgeous," I said, still taking in the room. It was quiet for as many people as there were. Even the instrumental music was soft. Jace's smile was illuminated by the crystal lamp sitting next to the bottle of water.

"This is how I grew up," he said, his smile not touching his eyes as he glanced around the room. "Fancy restaurants for business deals, the lectures on what not to say and what to say beforehand, and the rotation of suits. I swear, I grew out of them quicker than it took the tailor to fit them for me."

I didn't laugh when he did. "I don't need fancy dinners."

"I know that."

"Then why did you do all this for me?" I asked and pointed to the giant chandelier hanging in the center of the room.

He smiled and let out a deep breath. "Because it's obvious no one ever has and as much of a brat as you are, you deserve this and so much more."

My eyes burned. Damn it. I'd spent so much time getting ready and trying to do my makeup like Madison would.

"The brewery tour was better," I said, barely getting the words past the lump in my throat.

He laughed, a deep sound that seemed loud in the quiet space. He didn't stop when he saw the nearest couple look over at us. They seemed amused and I couldn't help but find the humor in the scene. I dabbed at the mascara I could feel gathering beneath my eyes.

"You asshole," I said and slapped his hand where it rested on the table. "You shouldn't make your date cry."

"I didn't know the Wicked Witch could show emotion at all, much less cry," he teased, dipping his finger into his glass and flicking a bit of water at me. "Don't melt!"

"I'm a *winter witch* and believe me, a little water won't make me melt," I said, conjuring a little ice cube between my index and thumb. It was a risk, doing magic in public, but people had stopped staring and the room was growing darker as the sun set on the mountain range outside our window. I leaned on my elbow, holding the ice closer for Jace to see.

He smirked and leaned toward me, keeping his eyes locked on mine. My stomach did flips. When he lowered his eyes, it was too late to attempt to mask my shock. His lips came down around my fingers, taking the ice cube into his mouth, eyes flicking up to mine in that onery, challenging way.

"I'm a summer warlock and, baby doll," he said, his hand brushing mine on the table. "I think you melt for me."

Well, shit.

"I'm going to clean up in the bathroom," I said and stood up from my seat, relieved that we were far enough into the corner of the room that the nearest table couldn't overhear. "I bet there's mascara smeared under my eyes."

Jace stood up like the proper gentleman I was sure he'd been raised to be. Before I could pass him, he placed a hand on my bicep. He turned my face to his and kissed me. I parted my lips, letting his tongue meet mine along with the half-melted ice cube. He passed the cube to me before pulling away with a smile.

"Are you a puddle yet?" he asked.

I swatted his chest. "Wouldn't you like to find out."

I left him for the bathroom, my heart keeping pace with each quick step I took across the room. Damn, why was this restaurant so big? It felt like minutes before I was safely in the women's restroom, dabbing a wet paper towel on my face, more to calm myself than to clean the few mascara streaks beneath my eyes. I forced myself to walk slower when I made my way back to him, feeling a little more relaxed when I saw the champagne sitting on the table next to a little charcuterie board.

Jace stood again as I approached and he waited until I'd taken my seat to take his. He'd already filled our glasses. He raised his glass and I lifted mine from the table, pressing it to his with a soft clink.

"To finishing a bestseller," he said.

"We can always dream," I said and took a sip.

He lowered his glass from his lips, studying me for a moment. "Will you tell me about it now that you've finished it?"

I hesitated. I took another drink to buy some time, but it didn't change anything. I wasn't sure I had expected it to. I took a deep breath, reminding myself that I swore to tell him the truth about the podcast, and started from the beginning of the story. I told him how the book started, how the characters met, fell in love, and how life threatened to pull them apart. I told him about how silly it felt to write about love and sex and how I knew that it was actually just relatable and honest and everything we all wanted. To be desired. To feel sexy as hell. To feel sexy as hell *and* desired by someone. The right someone.

Jace never once scoffed or took his eyes off of me as I talked. He looked interested. He was quiet for a moment after I finished. The room was nearly dark now.

"I think that's all most of us really want. It's all I ever wanted, to be loved for exactly who I am," Jace said softly. He gave a sad nod. "It's all I ever wanted from my dad and it's exactly what I got from my mom. That's what made it so hard to leave. It felt like I was leaving her memory behind and like I was accepting what I would never get from him. I know my dad loves me, but it's just not that kind of love. I think we all want that."

The words stung. My heart ached for him. Sure, he'd made bad choices in the past, but they were motivated by rejection. He just wanted his dad to see the great person he was and not the man he could show off at dinner parties. Maybe that's why my heart was racing now and why my throat was tightening. I was the perfect daughter, the one my parents would brag about to make the final sale, the daughter they would brag about to bolster their image at every social gathering. I wasn't beautiful the way Madison was or sporty the way Margot was, but I had all the potential to "quietly change the world around us" as my mother would tell people. I was different and my love for fairytales was always hidden away in favor of my intelligence. Dad would sometimes joke "I love you all equally, but third time was the charm."

What a terrible thing to say.

I looked out the window and slowly breathed in. The sun was barely peeking over the farthest mountain and movement in front of it caught my attention. Snow was silently falling outside the window, large flakes that looked like they were suspended, slowly wafting toward the busy street below. It was such a strange thing that one angle of the view was so peaceful and just a few inches down was a bustling reality I could barely tolerate.

Fuck, I hated New York. School was important, sure, and I would finish my degree. But I couldn't stand the idea of going back there. I didn't want to graduate into a life of sitting behind a desk and forcing myself to endure the pressure of changing the world behind the scenes. Facts and science didn't reach people the way true emotions and love did, like the love I had for writing and the real emotions I'd put into this book. I could tell it was better because of the simple fact that I fell in love writing it. I wanted to write stories that made people feel the way I felt now looking past the snowy sky at the sunset. I wanted to be exactly who I wanted to be without feeling the pressure to be perfect for my family. I wanted to express my emotions rather than bottle them all up. I wanted to be seen the way Jace saw me, be loved the way I felt I was when we were together.

But that wasn't what I told him.

"I want to be an author," I said and forced the thickness building in my throat to dissipate. "That's all."

I looked back to see him smiling. He sat back and reached into his blazer to withdraw a business card. He held it out to me and I worried for a moment that he was going to recommend the number for a good therapist. I took it and looked down at it to see a drawing of a crescent moon on one side. I flipped it over to look at Jace's name, business email, phone number, and the address of the brewery back in Crescent Peak. The name brought my heart to a stop.

Crescent Peak Books and Brews.

I couldn't believe it. I looked up at him and he smiled back at me, a michievious look that told me he'd been holding onto this secret from the beginning.

"I'm going to need a little help building the inventory," he said.

"I'm going to need you to get the check right now," I told him and tossed my napkin on the table. He laughed as he waved toward our waiter. I downed the last of my champagne as he handed several bills to the man, settling our tab with a generous tip before we hurried from the restaurant for the elevator across the hall, the back of my dress unzipped and my hands working on the buttons of his shirt before we could unlock the door to our suite.

Chapter 22

"THAT'S all for this week's episode, but before we go," Callie said, pulling my attention away from the frosted glass of Black Bear Stout I'd brought back from Two Pines Brewery. I'd set it out of view of the camera and planned on drinking it as a kind of reward for recording the podcast episode today. Whatever Callie was about to say wasn't in our script. "I wanted to give some huge props to my cohost, whose new book is seriously amazing. It's hot. It's deep. It is perfect for the reader who likes their books smutty, but with a high-stake plot. It's got a blurb that will make you immediately want to hit 'add to cart,' which is great because it is also available for pre-order now. And, it finally has a title, and I thought today's episode would be the perfect time to share it with our listeners."

Of course.

"I don't know," I said, glad that we never did these episodes live.

Callie shook her head on the screen. "The title is perfect! You have Hannah, who is on the run from her abusive husband, and she thinks she's going to start a new life with a short stint working at a nightclub. The Sunset Nightclub, where fantasies come true after sunset. Instead, she is pulled away from a handsy man by none other than the millionaire owner of the nightclub. The official blurb is linked in the show notes, so check it out and make sure you pre-order the book," Callie said before locking eyes with me through the screen. She wasn't just excited about the book. She was cheering me on and I could tell she really believed in this book. I sent it to her once I'd finished my draft and the first thing she said when we hopped on the video call was that she finished it in one sitting and loved it.

I took a deep breath. "The title of my next book is Sunset Millionaire, and it will be released in May. Make sure you have subscribed to the podcast and all my socials, so you don't miss the updates. I have a cover reveal coming soon!"

Callie squealed and I missed everything she said after. She jabbered on excitedly before giving our signature sign-off.

"I ended the recording," she announced and started to disconnect her headphones and microphone from her computer. "The episode doesn't go up for a few days, so I can always edit out the part about your book."

"No. I think I needed the push," I told her. It felt a lot like life was giving me a bunch of little pushes. Jace was here and as annoying as he was sometimes, he saw exactly who I was when no one else did. He was using his rich family's money to form the small business he wanted and start the simple life he's desired all along. He was keeping the bookstore that was so important to me, where I told Dottie first that I was an author and thanked her for letting me hide between the stacks on the days when the tension in my house was stifling.

"Happy to be of assistance," Callie said, reaching off screen and returning with a glass of whiskey in her hand. Neat. Always Glenfiddich. She raised it toward the screen, and I raised my beer. "To M. A. Jenson."

"M.A. fucking Jenson!" I laughed and took a drink.

MARGOT and I got to the lodge early to set up for the rehearsal dinner. I was so tired of Margot stressing about getting the table runners and floral displays just right that I was nearly ready to open one of the bottles of champagne that were waiting in the back of the room for toasts later.

Things got better as people started to arrive. Neither the McAdams nor the Sinclair families were large, so the party would be small. Madison had allowed the bridesmaids to invite their significant others and family members if they wanted, which was the worst part. Just as nearly everyone gathered in the room to mingle, my mom asking Margot about opening a bottle of wine, my dad and Lori Maxwell walked into the room holding hands.

I saw Margot stiffen next to our mom.

"Mom!" Winnie said, leaving Lola mid-sentence to go and pull her mom aside, smiling as she led her toward the long table set up at the back of the room. Dad smiled at me when he noticed me watching them, patting mom on the shoulder as he passed and getting a very annoyed look from her. He pulled me into a hug before stepping aside to take in the room.

"This looks great."

My dad had been more excited at the sight of Empower Field at Mile High the last time I went to a Denver Broncos game with him.

"It was a lot of work," I said, hoping he heard the bitterness in my voice, if not to let him know that I was annoyed with him then to remind him that this was a really big deal for my sister. He might not think all the pink and white was extravagant, but Madison had spent a lot of time planning and creating the details.

"I thought someone was enchanting the place to make it snow throughout the entire event," he said and turned from the long white carpet to look at me.

"It will," I said, looking past his shoulder to watch as Jared's Uncle Mark inspected the ice sculpture of a giant wedding ring that Winnie had crafted with her powers before the non-magical people arrived. "If anyone asks, we are telling them that it's some kind of new technology. Fake snow."

Dad chuckled as Dax appeared at his shoulder. I swore, the guy looked larger and more muscular each time I saw him. All his training for the Olympics was showing off.

"Are you excited that someone in the family will go to all the Bronco games with you?" he asked, clapping Dad hard enough on the back that it pushed him forward a fraction.

Dad laughed and turned to him, already launching into his favorite football team's stats. I sent Dax a grateful look and he winked.

After mingling for what felt like a painfully long time to me, we were finally interrupted by a shout from the back of the room. The officiant, Jared's uncle, called for the wedding party to gather in the hall to practice. I followed the bridesmaids and groomsmen out the double doors while the rest of the party took their seats in the audience.

Madison had planned everything so meticulously that we'd practically memorized the instructions by now. A rehearsal was hardly necessary. This might as well just have been a dinner and toasts. I would've worn something other than the nude heels Madison wanted us to wear during the ceremony, but Margot had already reminded me twice since we got here that it was important to practice walking in them.

I barely listened to Mark explain the process. He was mostly reading from his copy of Madison's wedding binder anyway. I stood silently, resisting the urge not to pick at my nails that I just had gotten done that morning in Heritage City with the rest of the bridal party. Then, finally, it was time to march into the ballroom and practice the ceremony. Margot was the maid of honor, and she walked arm-in-arm with Andrew, one of Jared's best friends from college. If it hadn't been for him taking the initiative, I wouldn't have thought to ask for my partner's name.

Gavin was one of Jared's friends from business school. He had dark, curly hair and he stood just a few inches taller than me. We were two of the shortest people in the whole wedding party, so of course we'd been paired together. He extended his arm to me as we approached the entrance. I waited until Margot and her partner walked over the threshold to wrap my arms around his and let him lead me down the aisle.

We parted at the end, and I stood on Margot's left. I zoned out as Mark practiced his speech and Madison and Jared rehearsed their vows. I didn't come back to reality until Margot left my side. She and her partner led the way back down the aisle and I met Gavin in the middle of the alter to do the same. I almost groaned when Mark announced that we would be doing it all again.

"I guess we weren't pretty enough," Gavin scoffed, smiling when he caught my attention. "I mean, it wasn't our walking. Pretty sure we all can walk a straight line."

"Should've done this after dinner and drinks," I said under my breath as we all got back into formation in the hall. "Probably would be more realistic."

Gavin laughed. "Probably."

"I just want to get this over with and get to dinner," I said as Margot and her partner started back into the ballroom. I wrapped my arm around Gavin's.

"Are you hungry or is the food at this place just that good?" he asked.

We stepped up to the threshold and paused, waiting for Margot and her partner to reach the first row of chairs. "I'm excited for Madison, but weddings just aren't my scene."

We started to walk, and I forced a smile when I noticed my parents watching. It was a strange sight to see them, with Lori Maxwell sitting between them.

"I thought the same thing," Gavin said as we reached the end of the aisle. He let go of me before I could look his way, wondering if he felt the same way I did or ... Surely, he didn't mean anything bad by it. He was close to Jared. He was happy for him. Right?

I watched him through the rest of the rehearsal, and he looked just as distracted as I felt. I wondered if I looked as annoyed to be here as he did. He kept shifting from one foot to the other, glancing from Jared to Madison and then looking at his feet. He cheered the loudest when Madison and Jared kissed, and I felt the irritation run over my skin like an itch I'd rubbed raw. I couldn't stand it anymore.

"I thought you were Jared's friend," I said as we approached the hallway. Gavin let go of my arm early and I walked ahead to join the rest of the group, ready to face whatever answer he had. He stared back at me in shock, his expression obscured by Winnie Maxwell as she stepped between us to grab my shoulders.

"Would it be better if my mom just left? It would be better, right? It's not like it's *her* daughter getting married," she said.

I glanced past her, but Gavin had already been swept up by the rest of the groomsmen who were busy clapping Jared on the back and saying something that had turned his cheeks bright red.

"I don't know, Winnie. Go ask Margot," I said and brushed her hands from my shoulders.

"You're right. I will," she said and left me to pull Margot away from Mark and Madison.

I went back into the ballroom to join the crowd. Everyone was gathering around the table, searching the little cardstock name-plates to find their places. I pretended I was busy looking for mine when I noticed Dad try to catch my attention with his arm wrapped around Lori's back. I was one of the first people seated, finding my place near the head of the table where Jared and Madison would sit. Thank God, Margot was sitting next to me. I assumed that Dax was assigned across from her and it wasn't until after the last of the wedding party joined the table that I realized he wasn't.

Andrew sat across from her. Dax sat on the chair to her right where I thought Mom would sit. Madison sat at the head of the table and Jared sat across from Dax. I did a headcount and figured out exactly who was missing, seconds before Gavin joined the table and apologized to the best man for taking so long.

"Shots in the hallway?" I asked him, ignoring the sharp kick to my foot that I was sure came from Margot. My comment had the desired effect. Gavin was taken aback and it took him a moment to reply.

"Phone call."

"Must have been an important one."

"It was," he said, keeping his eyes on me long enough to tell me not to push him.

He didn't know me though. I loved to poke the bear. I didn't think Gavin was the type to bite the way Jace was though, which was a shame. It was one of my favorite things about him.

"All good, Gavin?" Andrew asked, his eyes moving from me to him.

"Yeah. It's good. Let's hope it stays that way, and it doesn't progress," Gavin told him with a deep sigh.

Was that a threat?

"I'd like to start the toasts as the food starts coming out," Mark said as he stood up, interrupting me before I could make a threat of my own. Mark cleared his throat, waiting for the wait-staff to finish setting glasses of champagne in front of all the guests.

"Go easy on me, Uncle Mark!" Jared called out, getting a few chuckles from the guests.

Mark lifted his glass from the table and held it to Jared as he spoke. "Most of you know me as Jared's uncle. He's my only nephew, so it makes sense that I have a soft spot for him and get him in a bit of trouble at least as much as I get him out of it, so this story is one my sister has never known the full truth about until right now."

"Oh boy. To think I got away with it." Jared laughed, pointing at his mom, Joanne, down the table. She smiled despite the warning look she sent his way.

Mark went on to tell the story of a time when Jared came back after a night of drinking after a winning football game during his senior year. Rather than run to his mom about the whole thing, Mark made him help in the mercantile and they talked about the future and it was the first time Jared had told anyone he didn't want to go to a big state school to play football. He wanted to stay close to home so he could help at the farm and learn the ropes so he could take over some day. By the end of the story, everyone was quiet and even Jared's mom looked down the table at him like he'd sacrificed something important for the sake of family.

Hell, maybe he had. I didn't really know him super well. Did that make me a shitty person? Maybe I should know my sister's boyfriend better. In my defense, I'd learned early on in high school not to invest too much time into Madison's boyfriends—they never stuck around long. But this was Jared McAdams and I knew this was different. He was my brother-in-law.

I was a shitty person.

Jared's best man talked about all the amazing things Jared had done for him through college, while Gavin stole glances at what I could only assume was his phone judging from the light emanating from his crotch.

Asshole.

I was glad no one expected me to speak, because Margot's speech was the best of the bunch. She cried. Our mom cried. Dad looked like he might cry by the end of it. I was glad when it was announced that she was the final speaker and plates of roasted chicken, green beans, and mashed potatoes were placed in front of us.

"Thank God," I said, glancing around our half of the table in case someone heard the annoyance in my voice. Gavin seemed to be the only one. "I was getting hungry."

"I was thinking the same thing," he said, echoing the comment he'd made earlier and sending the pot boiling over.

"What did you mean by that?" I asked.

Gavin hesitated with his knife and fork poised over his chicken. Everyone else around us was too busy eating to notice. The table was actually pretty noisy. The group of us had been through enough rounds of toasts by now that we were on our third glasses of champagne.

"I don't know what you mean. I was just agreeing with you that I'm hungry."

"No, before that," I said and motioned with my knife toward

the hall. "The way you said that weddings weren't your scene? The way you look so bored to be here? You were late to the table because of a phone call, like there was something else so important at eight o'clock at night. You texted through all the speeches, aside from the one you pasted a smile on your face to give. What do you mean that weddings aren't your scene?"

He stared back at me in shock for a moment before he sat his fork and knife down and looked around us, confirming that no one was witnessing our argument. He adjusted in his seat so he could pull his phone from his pocket.

"*You* said that weddings weren't your scene. I said that I *thought* the same thing, as in, I used to think that," he said as he unlocked his phone. He turned the screen so I could see the wallpaper. There was a woman in a white dress with a wide smile on her face as she held up her hand beneath an arch of wedding guests holding sparklers against the starry night sky. Her hand was entwined with none other than Gavin's. He smiled in the photo, his eyes on the woman beside him.

My stomach plummeted and I wasn't the least bit hungry now.

"You're married," I said.

Gavin nodded. "I am and I took a phone call and all those texts because my wife is pregnant enough to have Baxton-Hicks. She would be here with me if it wasn't for that."

"Oh," I said, wishing that dinner was over and not just beginning. "How far along is she?"

Gavin shook his head. "It's pretty normal for a guy to roll his eyes about weddings and marriage, but you ... I was afraid to admit how deeply in love I was with Olivia and I almost waited too long. I always thought it was weak to express that much emotion. It made me feel so vulnerable when I told her that she was the only woman for me, but that's what I felt and I would rather have been stomped into the ground than not have told her. I was in deep enough by then that I knew what I'd be missing if I didn't tell her and I couldn't stand to miss a second."

I lifted my fork and knife from the table and focused on

cutting my chicken for a moment as I thought of what to say to take the attention off of me. A tear fell onto the piece I'd just cut. Then another. I looked up, ready to accept defeat and escape to the bathroom, but Gavin wasn't paying any attention to me. He was already mid-conversation with the best man, laughing about something he'd said like he hadn't just shattered the last of my ego.

Chapter 23

THE PLAN WAS to go back to the cabin after the rehearsal dinner, which I did, but I didn't stay there. I changed out of my dress and into my pajamas, making sure to grab my bridesmaid dress and the pinchy heels before I left for the brewery.

I didn't have a key, so I called Jace as I waited on the sidewalk out front.

"Open the door," I said.

"What door?" he asked. There was a bang as though he'd sat something down. "You mean—Front door or back door?"

"Front door," I told him, feeling heat rush to my face as the comment sprang to mind. "If you get to the front door quick enough, I might let you enter the back door though."

Jace laughed into the receiver before hanging up. A second later, I saw him run from the side door of the bookstore, jogging his way down the main aisle to reach the front door. He turned the key in the door and pulled me into his arms, locking it behind us as we kissed.

"I want to stay here tonight," I told him. "I don't want to stay in that place anymore."

"What? Why?" He pulled away from me, his hands resting on

my hips. He smelled like wheat from all the brewing he'd done that day. "Why don't you want to stay at the cabin? It's where all your stuff is."

"Yeah, but it's full of past memories that your new floors and granite counter tops can't erase and I just want ..."

A pit formed in my stomach as I thought about what Gavin had said earlier tonight. I could still remember every word of what he'd told me and he was right. If I didn't say it now, if I didn't tell Jace that I was fully committed to us, then I worried what I had to say next would shatter us.

"I love you, Jace," I said, letting the words fly from my mouth and feeling a little like I'd taken flight with them. "I mean it. I love you and I don't want to be held back by my past and all the things I thought I was supposed to be. I don't want to pretend that I'm just cynical and serious when I'm actually just so fucking unhappy. For the first time, I feel like I'm every bit the person I want to be, and I only feel one hundred percent this way when I am with you, and I don't want to go back to that place. I want to stay right here with you and with my future, *our* future if you want that too, and forget about all the things I'm supposed to want and just go after what makes me happy."

Tears slid down my face as the words came tumbling out. Jace kept his hands on my waist, his expression not nearly as affected as I'd anticipated. I thought he would be surprised, at least smiling as I told him everything. He looked a little like he might tell me off. It was like he'd expected me to say the words all along and was ready to let rip a savage "I told you so" and not start in with the serious tone he did now.

"You serious about this, baby doll?"

"Yes! Fuck, Jace! Of course, I'm serious," I said and shoved his chest.

He smiled, that challenging look that always melted me. "Good."

"Good?"

"Good," he said firmly, taking a step closer. "Because I knew I loved you when you were more offended at the idea of playing house with me than the fact that I was in a gang. And baby doll, all I've wanted to do since is play house with you."

He lifted me into his arms and I wrapped my legs around his waist, letting my lips crash onto his as he started for the back of the room. He didn't break the kiss until we reached the stairs and nearly tripped on the bottom step. I gave him a final kiss on the lips, shoved his chest hard enough to catch him off guard, and then flashed him two middle fingers before getting a head start on the way upstairs to the apartment. He chased after me and my heart raced, eager to face the consequences of my bratting when I reached the door.

"You're going to be late," Jace warned as he dressed for the day. He'd already laid out his dress clothes for the wedding later that day. Right now, he was dressed in a pair of joggers and a T-shirt with his brewery's logo across the front. I wore an earlier version of the logo he'd printed, the shirt stained with a drip of paint from the day he must've painted the apartment. It was just oversized enough to be baggy on me, but small enough that when I groaned and rolled onto my stomach in the bed that most of my ass hung out the bottom.

"Come on. Get up," he said. A slap rang through the room, and I rolled to my side, fully awake now as I looked up at him.

"Ouch!" I rubbed the spot on my ass where his hand had connected. Shit! I could see where his fingers had made contact with my skin. "You better be nicer to me or you can sleep in the brewery tonight."

Jace laughed. "After a romantic wedding?" He tossed my clothes onto the foot of the bed. Madison had designed the matching sweatpants and pullover. She asked the bridal party to wear the set to the lodge to get ready for the day. "You'll be begging me to get into bed with you."

"The other way around," I said and sat up on the edge of the mattress. "It's your bed and you'll be begging me to join you and if you aren't nice to me, then you can wake up in it alone tomorrow and on Christmas morning. Don't try me."

He moved in front of me, placing his hands on the mattress on either side to box me in. "Are all winter witches so coldhearted or is that just you, baby doll?"

"Are all summer warlocks so hot-headed or is that just you?" I countered, tugging on the front of his shirt. "You sure do like a good fight."

Jace scoffed. "*I* like a good fight? I've never met a girl so ready to take things outside."

"Don't act like you don't love it. You love fighting with me," I teased, nipping at his bottom lip.

"Someone has to keep you in line," he said, kissing me once before he turned his head to the side, preventing me from kissing him again. His brows were raised in warning. "I am older than you."

"Not wiser though."

"Get dressed, baby doll," he said with a smile. He patted my knee and straightened up. "You're going to be late. Grab your stuff. I'll drop you off and meet you there in time for the wedding later."

I climbed out of bed and slipped into my sweatpants. It was going to be a long day of prepping for the ceremony and making sure Madison didn't cry off all her makeup before she made it to the altar. At least I got to spend most of the day in comfortable clothes. Like most of the wardrobe surrounding the event, Madison made all our sweatsuits, and she somehow got them to look cute and form-flattering and not boxy and baggy like my favorite set back at the cabin.

"Want a Pop-Tart for the road?" Jace called from the kitchen.

I finished tying my sneakers and left the bedroom for the living room, glancing toward the hooks along the wall by the front door where my bridesmaids dress was safely tucked inside the black garment bag.

"The lodge is providing breakfast to the bridal party," I told him.

Jace tucked one of the silver packages back into the cardboard box before he opened the package left on the counter. "What about the groomsmen?" He dropped two Pop-Tarts into the toaster and pushed down the lever.

"They're having breakfast at the diner down the block," I said, slipping my purse onto my shoulder. I caught him watching me and he rolled his eyes a second later with a smirk.

Jace pointed at me. "Not a word."

"Who's late now," I said.

"What did I say?" Jace asked, sending me a look of warning as the toaster popped.

"*Not a word*. So, I gave you three," I said and backed toward the door. I took the garment bag from the hook on the wall and draped it over my arm. "Grab your breakfast and let's go."

"Such a little brat," Jace laughed as he wrapped his breakfast in a paper towel before joining me at the door.

The drive up the mountain to the lodge was too quick. I was excited for Madison, but did she really need me this early in the day? She had her whirlwind romance. Couldn't I have mine and stay just a little longer with Jace? Maybe drive farther up the mountain and find a place to park and make out?

Jace gave me a final kiss and practically pushed me out of the car, passing the garment bag and my heels to me before reaching into the backseat.

"One more thing," he said and lifted a tote bag from the floorboard and moved it into the passenger seat. "I thought you could use it today. Just don't go crazy and make me regret this, baby doll. I'd like a dance before I take you home."

I glanced at the bag as I pulled it onto my shoulder. The top was zipped shut and I had just enough to carry that I'd have to put something down to investigate the contents.

"Whatever you say," I said and blew him a kiss. Jace smiled before I closed the door and started up the stairs of the lodge.

I went through the double doors and took a right, following the long hallway to the end where there was a door labeled with Madison's name on lodge stationery. I opened it, immediately greeted by laughter and the smell of fresh fruit and cinnamon rolls.

The room had a wall of windows that overlooked the mountains, untouched snow at the bottom of the valley with tiny evergreen trees sprinkled throughout. There was a large TV mounted against the far wall above the granite countertop where the breakfast spread was set up. The girls were seated on a pair of couches in the middle of the room with a wooden table between them. I moved to the right to set my things with the others' on the long bench that sat beneath an abstract painting of a mountain scene. Once I sat everything down, I unzipped the tote bag Jace had given me and found twelve cans of beer at the bottom.

Thank God.

I lifted one out to see which brewery it came from, hoping he'd snagged at least one from Two Pines Brewery from our trip, but I didn't recognize the label. It was a little crescent moon above the modern font with the name of the brewery. Crescent Peak Books and Brews. I felt the smile pull at my lips as I turned the can to see that it was a stout. It wasn't just a stout. Sinclair Stout.

A quick glance in the tote bag showed me that there was a variety of beers, though there were more Sinclair Stouts than anything. I cracked open the top of one, drawing the attention of the group.

"What's that?" Remy asked. "Is that beer?"

"I'm not really a beer fan," Lola said and wrinkled her nose.

"Have you ever had a craft beer?" I asked and lifted the tote bag from the bench. I moved it to the coffee table and Winnie and Remy started pulling out the cans. Madison lifted one from the table, a knowing smile pulling across her face before she looked up at me.

"That's what's moving into the bookstore?" Margot asked, taking a can of an amber ale.

"The bookstore's staying, thank God," I said and took a deep breath. I couldn't help but glance at Remy before I said the words, ready to publicly stake my claim. "Jace is opening the brewery and he's keeping the bookstore for me."

The room went quiet. Margot's mouth parted in shock. Remy's surprise turned to a sincere smile and she was the first to move, opening a beer with a hiss and raising the can to me.

"Good for you," she said coyly. "I'm jealous."

I raised my can to her in return. "I would be too after getting to know him better."

Lola and Winnie both laughed.

"Getting to know him better, huh?" Lola giggled.

I felt my cheeks flame, but I didn't care. It felt good to admit the truth; I wasn't lying anymore. Anyone who took the time to get past Jace's rough exterior would see that on the inside he was as warm as the summer sun that strengthened his powers. And despite being a winter witch, I wanted nothing more than to watch that summer sunset from his hometown beach the way he'd watched the stars from the brewery rooftop that snowy night that changed everything.

Chapter 24

I savored that Sinclair Stout. The group's consensus was that Crescent Peak Books and Brews was destined to be a hot spot in town and even Lola—who swore she had never found a beer she liked—decided that the vanilla porter was the only beer she would ever drink. After a few jokes about breakfast beers and reviewing the timeline for the day, the hairstylist arrived.

Madison made the poor woman wait until the photographer got there twenty minutes later. She set up the portable vanity she brought while the photographer took photos of us in our sweatsuits, pretending to laugh and drink beer around the coffee table the way we had been a half-hour before she arrived. Once that was done, Madison made us all change into light-pink satin robes and fluffy slippers. We popped a bottle of champagne, the photographer snapping shot after shot of everyone squealing as the bottle in Madison's hands foamed down the neck and onto the floor.

There were more photos taken of Madison pouring glasses for everyone and then dozens more where we pressed our glasses together in a big circle. By the time we'd staged these moments the hairstylist was so bored that she sat in the corner scrolling on her phone. She looked relieved when Margot announced that she was the first on the schedule to have her hair done.

Remy and Lola immediately launched into their questions about Jace, Remy's questions a little more personal than I cared to answer. Winnie stood behind the couch, pretending not to be interested in the conversation as she flipped through the wedding binder.

"He's not the kind of guy everyone assumes he is given how he grew up," I told them, glancing at Madison who just smiled sweetly back at me almost as though to tell me *I told you so*.

"What do mean? He's the brooding bad-boy type. Is he actually a giant teddy bear?" Remy sat forward on the couch across from me.

"Well, yes, but he didn't grow up—" I wasn't sure how to explain it to non-magical people. It wasn't like the summer warlock and winter witch part was super relevant, but even though the covens didn't spend a lot of time with other kinds of witches, we all knew the most notable of the bunch.

Winnie Maxwell had sat the wedding binder on the back of the couch, fully engaged in the conversation now. Madison cleared her throat and did that thing where she straightened up, tossed her hair ever so subtly, and shrugged like whatever she was about to say was no big deal.

"Jace Blackthorne's dad is a millionaire," she said, barely giving Lola and Remy a moment to recover from their shock before she continued with her explanation. "He grew up with serious money, super exclusive private school, you know ..."

No. No one in the room besides my sisters and me knew what that was like. But Madison carried herself in such a way that if I hadn't been her sister, I'd have thought she was a millionaire, too.

"Wow!" Lola said with a laugh of disbelief. She was red with embarrassment. "It's not that I thought he was, like, some ex-con or something, but ... I mean, he has tattoos like one or a rapper or ... I don't know. I guess, I shouldn't assume."

"I'm sure he spent a lot of money to get them done by the

best," Winnie chimed in and moved from behind the couch to join us.

Remy had a devious look in her eye as she pulled her robe tighter around her and leaned in. "So, speaking of all those tattoos …"

It took me a moment to understand what she meant. My mind went to the black ink across Jace's chest. To be honest, when his shirt came off I wasn't normally focused on what his tattoos actually were. I rarely had time to study them before he pinned me beneath him.

"Um, so, I don't know," I stammered.

"Come on. You don't remember any of them?" Remy asked, pouting like I was denying her of the best part of the day. It wasn't like we were here to celebrate her best friend, my own sister, on her wedding day.

"Some memories are personal, Remy," Madison said in that teasing tone. I knew her better though. This was high school Madison and Winnie's smirk told me she recognized it, too. "I'm sure she's gotten a whole tattoo tour. It would be weird for someone else to fantasize about what tattoos he has where anyway, especially when he's a friend's boyfriend. Maybe she wants to keep that memory to herself."

I saw the excitement dim behind Remy's eyes. She smiled nonetheless and raised her hands in surrender. "You're right. I might not want another woman to know that much about my man either."

I'm sure she wouldn't.

It felt like forever, long enough that we were eating finger sandwiches and fruit for lunch, before everyone's hair was done. Somehow, the makeup artist took less time. Mom had joined us by that point to have her hair done while we rotated through the makeup chair. The photographer snapped photos through the entire process and then directed us to follow her back through the lodge. Lola and Remy were the only girls that complained when we were given fur shawls to wear on the way outside.

We were quick to snap pictures in the snow, taking pauses in between so Remy and Lola could warm up inside before we went back outside. Once we were done, Mom and Dad joined Margot, Madison, and me for family photos. The awkwardness that had hung in the air whenever we were all together had vanished at least for the time and I was sure the photos would turn out magical as the snow began to flutter around us.

Madison remained outside while the group of us moved inside, the groomsmen joining us a moment later. Down the hallway, Jared looked handsome in his black suit, rubbing his hands together nervously as he prepared for his first look at his bride.

"She went in the side door," the photographer said as she propped the front door open. "If everyone could stay off to the side when Madison walks down the stairs, that would ensure I get some good shots of her. My assistant is going to take photos of Jared to get the full effect."

Our group split in half, the groomsmen joining Jared in the hallway while my parents and the bridesmaids backed into the opposite hall. Jared followed the photographer out the front door and onto the front lawn. Once he was there, Margot went for Madison around the corner. Her white gown clung to her to show off her figure and sparkled like fresh snow. She moved in double-time to get into place and waited for Margot and Gavin to pull open the double doors to start walking down the steps.

We waited a full minute before the whole bridal party crowded around the front windows to watch as Jared pulled Madison into his arms and lifted her into the air for a kiss. The romance of it was undeniable and tears pricked my eyes.

"The right man doesn't complete a woman," my mom said from my left, her voice just low enough for just me to hear. "The right man complements a woman and everything she is."

She turned from the window to smile a me for a moment, something about the look making me feel anxious. It was like the start of a lecture, like when I was in high school and my mom gave me "the talk" before I went to my first homecoming dance. I could tell these words of wisdom had nothing to do with Madison and Jared.

"I didn't understand that when I married your father. I looked for a man who would fix these weaknesses I thought I had," she continued, scoffing at the mention of *weakness*. "He made me feel beautiful and desirable. He was my first boyfriend and after I met him, people noticed me. Suddenly, I was Peter Sinclair's pretty girlfriend and then I was his beautiful wife. That got boring fast though. I never wanted to just be pretty. I worked late nights through high school to save for college, stayed up studying for tests to get a good scholarship, and went to one of the best schools in the country. I was highly educated and I wanted most of all to be his *brilliant* wife so I poured my time into building my company. It grew beyond anything I could've ever dreamed and then I realized that I never really wanted to be Peter's pretty, brilliant wife. I'm not sure I ever wanted to be a wife at all."

She stared out the window for a moment, the silence stretching for a moment before I mustered the courage to ask what had bothered me for so long.

"What did you want?"

Part of me hoped she would say my sisters and me. It was a small part though because I knew she wouldn't. She'd never been a perfect mother, absent a lot of the time, but I knew she loved us. While my dad praised us for what we excelled at, my mom was the one quietly supporting us. She was one of the first to discover Madison's clothing shop and bought items every day without my sister noticing until she'd grown a clientele of her own to bolster her confidence. Dad liked to take the credit for connecting Margot with important names in soccer, but Mom collected all the details and videos that got her noticed by the masses. And for me ... I'd never really noticed what she did behind the scenes. Even now, I wasn't totally sure.

Mom turned to smile at me. "I wanted what I think we all want, to be noticed and appreciated for who we are without needing to do a thing to ask for it."

"Oh," I said, my heart skipping in my chest. The way she looked at me now, like she understood. She had to know.

"I know we've always worried about Margot, but you've always been my sensitive girl," Mom said with a little laugh. "You were always in your own world, quiet because that little brain of yours was so full of ideas. You used to play all by yourself. I know your dad and I have always talked about how you liked to play on your own, but you would create these worlds and a whole story like you were the star in your own play and the trees or the walls of your bedroom were your audience. No one was surprised when you got that scholarship and chose to study English, but I hope you don't ever feel like you need to do anything more than what you want to with your education."

Shit. My eyes stung. Now was not the time to cry. Maybe it was, but there was a whole day ahead and I hadn't planned for her to suddenly be so understanding and the parent I wish I'd had had a long time ago. Then it hit me. All the silent support she'd shown my sisters.

"Mom," I started, still working through how to ask. I wasn't even sure what she could've done to support me in my writing along the way. I wrote stories through high school. I even finished my first book by junior year, but I did all that work on my computer. It wouldn't have been obvious. As the seconds stretched, I wasn't sure what to ask, so I decided not to ask at all. "I'm a published author and my next book releases in the spring," I blurted.

She smiled, easing the thick knot that had developed in my chest. "Oh, Marlee, why do you think I gave you all those notebooks?"

That was it? The notebooks? I told her I wanted specific notebooks for school, but they stayed in my bedroom. The notebooks were more expensive by most school supplies standards, but they felt like real books and that made me feel like I was a real writer. At first, my dad complained because they always stayed home and he thought I was forgetting my schoolwork. I took them with me after that and then my sisters thought they were diaries. I was protective of my writing back then, so I let them believe that.

"All right!" the photographer cried out, snapping me from my thoughts. "Now, we want the whole wedding party."

Mom had left my side, moving back into the hallway.

"Are you okay?" Margot asked, patting my shoulder.

I smiled and let out a deep breath. "Yeah. I'm great. It's a good day."

We followed the last of the wedding party out the front doors.

Chapter 25

IT WAS a little awkward having my arm wrapped around Gavin's after what happened at the rehearsal dinner, but seeing his very pregnant wife smiling at him from a seat in the crowd as we walked past reminded me that he wasn't thinking about the interaction at all. There were so many other amazing things happening around us and a lot of what had been bothering us throughout the day wouldn't matter in a few hours. Taking my place next to Margot and seeing Jace in that perfectly tailored suit near the back of the ballroom sent all my fears from my mind and made me think about what my mom had told me: how important it was to follow our dreams.

I cried.

I didn't even pretend not to like I normally would. By the time I met up with Jace in the hall, there was enough mascara under my eyes that he helped me brush it away with his pocket square. It's a good thing I didn't have to give a toast at dinner, because I'd had just enough champagne that my ankles had finally given up on the stilettos Madison made me wear. I thought I'd fall over if I had to walk from the head table to the microphone set up at the front.

As soon as dinner ended and Mark McAdams took over the mic to open the dancefloor, I slipped out the back to go back to the bridal suite and put on my sneakers. It was the only compromise Madison would agree to, a pair of light-pink Converse with ribbons for laces. I pulled them free from where I'd stashed them at the bottom of the garment bag, turning around when I heard the door open and close again.

Jace smiled at me as he unbuttoned his blazer. "We don't have long, baby doll."

I dropped the Converse and my socks and started across the room, Jace tossing his blazer onto a table and shoving his sleeves to his elbows as he walked. We met in the middle. His lips came down onto mine, warmth blooming through my core as he pulled the hem of my dress to my hips and lifted me. I wrapped my legs around him, one hand at the back of his neck while the other worked to unbuckle his slacks.

My back met the glass of the window, the cold sensation sending a delicious tingle over my skin. Jace held me close, slipping himself between us so he could sink into me with enough force that I gasped. He moved fast, hard, like we could be caught at any moment and the idea of someone discovering us made this so much hotter. He slipped a hand between us and with three strokes of his fingers I was done, lost in a blur of sensations. He muffled my cry with his lips, letting out a final groan before he stilled against me.

As we caught our breath, he sat me on my feet. I smoothed down the hem of my dress, taking in the sight of him. His hair was still mostly styled, but a couple of pieces had come free and it suited him. The entire look was very Jace, the way his sleeves were pushed up so you could see the tattoos across his forearms, the slightly loosened of the tie around his neck, and the way his slacks hung low on his hips. He'd managed to tuck his shirt back into his pants before I took notice, but I stopped him before he could push his sleeves down.

I rolled them instead, making sure to really look at his tattoos as I did. There were words that I recognized from a book but couldn't remember which. A compass. Some roses. He lifted my attention to his with a finger under my chin before I could take them all in.

"You should show them off more," I told him before he could speak. "They suit you."

He smiled. "Whatever you say, baby doll."

He kissed me and we finished getting ready before rejoining the room of wedding guests dancing in the ballroom.

I DIDN'T REMEMBER the end of the night, just waking up the next morning in Jace's apartment with a bad a headache. I took the Tylenol sitting on the side table and went back to bed for a little longer. When I woke up, it was because the whole apartment smelled like bacon and coffee.

My head still ached, but the painkiller was otherwise doing its thing and making me feel a little more human. I wasn't even sure if I'd taken off my makeup from the night before. My face felt so dry and itchy. Despite my growling stomach, I took a detour to the bathroom. My face was clean, thank God. I bet I remembered to take off the makeup but not put on the moisturizer. I slathered it on, still blending it into my face when I walked into the kitchen to find Jace eating breakfast at the bar.

"I took your makeup off last night with one of those wipes you left on the counter," he said and slid a plate of eggs and bacon across to me.

I paused. My stomach flip-flopped. "The ones in the yellow package or the blue?"

"The makeup wipes," he laughed. "I wouldn't rub a Lysol wipe all over your face. I'm not an asshole."

I shot him a pointed look as I lifted the fork from my plate. "Really?"

"Not *that* much of an asshole," he corrected with a smirk. "You were kind of cute last night. You get snuggly and whiney when you're drunk."

"I don't get whiney!" I pointed at him with a piece of bacon before taking a bite. Shit, Jace was a good cook, better than anyone I grew up with anyway. Home-cooked meals were only for special occasions at my house and usually involved one side-dish or the main getting burned.

"Fine, not whiney, but you actually listened to me and did what you were told for once," he said, eyebrows raised like he was making some big point. "It made it a lot easier to get you in the car and take you home. I thought you'd fight me the whole way like you do most days."

"I don't fight you that much," I said and picked up another piece of bacon. "So, you brought me here, took off my makeup ... Did you undress me, too?"

"No. You did that part yourself," Jace said with a laugh, looking over me in a way that made my heart skip. "That's why your shirt's on backwards."

I looked down at myself, noticing the long list of participant names from a charity 5K Margot convinced us all to do a few years ago. The event logo should've been there over my heart, but I was sure it was across my left shoulder blade instead. Shit. What else had I done?

I let out a sigh and looked up at him, cheeks warm with embarrassment. "Did I do anything else?"

Jace leaned his elbows on the countertop. "You said you loved me."

Suddenly, it was hard to sit still despite the way every thought evacuated my mind. My first reaction was to minimize the comment, ride it off as just some drunken banter, but while most of the wedding was hazy, I vividly remembered the conversation with my mom, and she was right. I didn't want to settle for something that was just okay. I didn't want to chase after prestigious jobs that lacked the passion and creativity I desired. I didn't want to pretend that I wasn't dreaming about Jace Blackthorne and feeling giddy when I rolled over in the morning to see him in the bed beside me.

"I do love you," I said. I kept my eyes locked on his, my insides squirming as the smile spread on his face. "Anything else I should know?"

God, I hoped not.

"Yeah. I lied. You didn't tell me you loved me," he said as he straightened up and moved around the counter. He stopped in front of me, brushing a hand against my cheek. "But I dream about you saying those words, not to mention the other things I dream of you doing."

My insides were a jumbled knot, and I could hardly find my voice to respond. The way this man made me feel ... I couldn't hide my smile, because I did love him, even if he had tricked me into admitting it.

"You're such an asshole," I laughed and lightly slapped the side of his face. He caught my hand before I could lower it and moved it to his chest. He leaned in for a kiss and I tipped my head up to meet him, stretching to try to reach him when he stopped. He smiled at my frustration and brushed my hair away from my face. I stared back at him with the best pleading look I could, hoping he'd give in and just kiss me. He only smiled wider.

"I love you too, baby doll," he said and rested his forehead against mine. He took a deep breath in and finally gave in. He kissed me, a groan rumbling through his chest as he let it deepen. His tongue met mine and I tugged on the front of his shirt, hoping to get closer and feel his skin against mine again. He pulled away with that playful smile on his face.

"Get dressed. I want your help with something today," he said and let me go.

I groaned. "No better way to ruin the mood than to tell me to get dressed for work. I don't technically work here, you know?" I snagged the last piece of bacon from my plate and tucked it between my teeth.

"I could've asked if you need help getting dressed. I could lay out your clothes, so you know which way to put them on," he laughed.

"Asshole!" I stuck my tongue out at him before disappearing into the bedroom.

I COULD HEAR a second pair of shoes across the hardwood floors as I came down the stairs. I rounded the corner and saw two sets of legs, one wearing Jace's work boots and another wearing a pair of brown snow boots.

"What are you doing?" I asked, taking the final flight of stairs to the main room of the bookshop to see Jace standing feet away from Dottie. She lowered the book in her hands back to the stack on the floor to face me. Jace tucked the book in his hands onto the shelf before motioning to the room around them.

"Restocking and organizing," he said.

"I'm celebrating retirement!" Dottie laughed and stepped forward to pull me into a hug. It was something she only did on special occasions, like when I would appear in her bookshop on the first day of every Christmas Break and on the last day, when I'd see her before I headed back home for the spring semester. She smelled like vanilla and sugar cookies, reminding me that I still had to tell Jace about my family's plans for Christmas.

"You moved things around," I said when we parted, stepping back to take in the room. I knew Jace wanted to split the room for the brewery and the bookstore, but I wasn't sure how he'd do it. The bookshelves used to be in neat rows with an aisle stretching through the middle of the store all the way to the staircase in the back. Now, they were flush against the wall and the cash register and front desk area was completely gone. The lounge I frequented still sat in the front corner, a few small tables now just feet away.

"The bar will go here," Jace said and turned toward the middle of the room. He motioned toward the opposite wall that backed up to the storeroom where all his brewing equipment was. It made the most sense to put the bar there. He motioned with his hands to show how far it would stretch, taking up most of the wall. There was already plumbing on the wall for all the taps and there were hooks high on the wall where I imagined signs would go, like the display at Two Pines Brewery.

"It's nice," I said. "I think you can get a lot of people just on this floor."

Dottie waved a finger and me. "And there's room for all my current stock plus more."

"You always need more books," I said, letting her pull me to her side for another quick hug before she went back to her pile of books. Jace took her place, draping his arms around me and letting his lips linger at my temple a second longer than I'd expected.

"I wasn't kidding about needing help with the inventory, baby doll," he said in my ear. He backed away and joined Dottie along the wall to shelve books. I followed, letting out a deep breath and relaxing as I took in all the titles.

"I told him we had to keep my romance display," Dottie told me and pointed toward the table in the left window. It was labelled as a bestseller table but was compiled of her favorite romance books. Most of them weren't on bestseller lists, but I was sure the fact that they were her favorite made them bestsellers in the store. "I have to have my M. A. Jenson and my Callie J. Cody collection there even if it's not my bookstore anymore."

"Are they important authors or something?" Jace asked.

I felt like my heart was in my throat, making it difficult to breathe.

"Callie J. Cody is Dottie's favorite author," I quickly said. It wasn't a lie. Callie was her favorite. That's what I loved about Dottie. She never pretended to like something, but she would wholeheartedly support you and that's what she'd always done for me. She kept my book in stock, despite it not selling well at all, but she didn't pretend that it was her favorite just because she knew me. In the world of romance, Callie was a lot of people's favorite author and that was okay with me. She was my favorite, too.

"What kind of romance does she write?" Jace asked, not looking away from his work.

Dottie didn't hesitate. "Oh, it's pretty steamy stuff. She writes about rich people and their sexy problems. I can't wait for her next book. The woman is an actress, and she falls in love with her bodyguard."

Jace laughed and at first, I worried he found the plot to be stupid, but I could see as he turned to look at Dottie that he was surprised by her. Most people were. She was an older woman, retiring several years past the point where she could, and still spoke like someone much younger. She kept up with all the trends in books and what interested the masses. She was as easy-going as could be and it was refreshing coming from my world where all the adults were so stressed and unhappy all the time. Until I started reading more books and spending time with Dottie at the bookstore, I worried that being grown up was just depressing.

"What about the other one?" Jace asked.

"What other one?" Dottie asked. My heart sank. "You mean M. A. Jenson?"

"Yeah. What about him or her or whoever that is?"

"Pretty much the same stuff," I said, catching Dottie's attention for just a second. It dawned on her face and her mouth formed an O as she turned back to the shelf.

"They write the same kind of smutty books?" Jace said with a laugh.

"So they say," Dottie said with a shrug, casting a judgmental look my way before shoving a book onto the shelf. I shook my head, hoping she would help steer the conversation away from my secret life.

"Callie J. Cody is one of the bigger authors online right now, especially in self-publishing," I said, hoping this would pull Jace's attention away from the inventory at the table. Instead, it led to a conversation about the difference between traditional publishing and self-publishing and I had to pretend not to know as much as I did.

I was being stupid. If Dottie wasn't with us, I'd tell him the truth. I'd tell him about my pen name and my books and that podcast episode that had launched my career beyond my expectations, and I'd beg him to forgive me. But Dottie *was* with us. I had planned to talk with him yesterday after I talked with my mom, as soon as we were alone, but I got swept up in the wedding and the romance of it all and I forgot until now.

"Is there coffee somewhere?" I groaned, backing away from the shelves.

"Still hungover?" Jace asked with a laugh.

"I bet the wedding was wonderful," Dottie said as she shelved the last book from the stack at her feet. "Your sister has such a way with style and design. Make sure to tell her congrats from me when you see her for the holiday tomorrow."

"It's an obsession for sure," I told her, glancing toward the door for the back room and trying to remember if there was more than just brewery equipment behind the door.

"The only medicine you'll find behind that door is the hair of the dog," he said, rubbing my back before he leaned in to kiss my temple.

"What?" I asked.

"Hair of the dog. You know, get rid of a hangover by having another drink?" Jace said as he started for the stairs. No, I did not know and it must have shown on my face because he shook his head. "I'll bring down some coffee. Dottie, you want a cup?"

"I would love one," she answered, stopping next to me. I could sense the question before it came. She waited until the sound of Jace's footsteps on the stairs had mostly faded before she turned to face me with her arms crossed.

Dottie might not have any children, but she did a convincing cosplay as a disgruntled mother hen.

"I know what you're going to say," I said, hoping she would hold her rebuke even though I knew she wouldn't.

She let out a low hum, which only sent my stomach plummeting further into my shoes. "You haven't told him."

"I was going to yesterday until I got drunk and forgot," I told her and started toward the bookshelf again. It wasn't like there was anything to do there. I pretended to adjust the books, sliding one to the right a millimeter and running my finger along the shelf like there was dust to be removed.

"Marlee," Dottie started.

I whirled around to face her but I wasn't sure what I was going to say. There was no point to be made, no use in defending myself. There was nothing to defend anyway.

"Dottie, I fucked up," I blurted. I groaned and tipped my head back, stared at the ceiling tiles for a moment before I looked back at her. She didn't look back at me with the same judgement as before. There was a glint of understanding in her eyes and as nice as it was to know she was there to support me, I knew I was the asshole. "Shit. I have to tell him, but he's going to hate me."

"He won't hate you," she said, not missing a beat before the words came spilling from her lips. "Just tell him that you're M. A. Jenson. He seems supportive."

I stopped before I launched into all the reasons why I was a terrible person. Dottie didn't know about the podcast. I assumed she knew just because she knew me and she loved Callie's books so much, but maybe she didn't know about the podcast, or she hadn't listened to the episode with the sneak peek of my next book.

"I don't have any Styrofoam, so we will have to remember to take these upstairs later," Jace said as he returned with two mugs of coffee in tow. Dottie gave me a final serious look before pasting on a smile to take the mug from Jace.

"So, what's tomorrow?" Jace asked.

I wasn't sure what he meant. "Christmas Eve?"

"No," he said with a laugh. "Dottie said something about you seeing your sister for the holiday tomorrow."

"Oh," I said. I hadn't thought much about it, honestly. We did the same thing every year, but I guess things were different this year. Normally, it was a Sinclair pajama party for Christmas Eve, but Madison had Jared and Margot had Dax ... Still, Mom and Dad insisted on keeping the tradition, which was asinine to me. So, tomorrow would be all of us under one roof. Madison and Jared were bunking in her room at the cabin, Dax and Margot in hers, and I'd be in mine. I hadn't even thought about the event because I'd been so occupied by the wedding and the surprise trip Jace took me on.

"We're staying at the cabin tomorrow for Christmas Eve," I said.

He crossed his arms, holding me hostage with that stern look. Damn him.

"We are?" he asked with a scoff. "I didn't know we had holiday plans."

"Shut up, you love it," I said and slapped his arm, relaxing a little at his smirk. "My family does the same thing every year and my parents insist on keeping the tradition despite all the …"

"Change happens and you will all adjust," Dottie said and sat her mug of coffee on the shelf along the wall. "It's the first Christmas all three of you will bring boyfriends home for the holidays. Your mom and dad will adjust, too."

Boyfriends. Jace, my boyfriend, was coming to Christmas with me. Thank God for Dottie pointing it out, breaking the awkwardness and prompting Jace to look at me the way he was now. It was like he was proud of the idea, possessive almost.

My boyfriend.

"Well, Madison and Jared are married," I pointed out.

Jared scoffed. "Does it make a difference?" He moved closer to me, stealing my mug from my hand to take a sip of the hot coffee. "Will your parents make me sleep in a different room?"

Dottie laughed. "Little late for that."

"I think we should finish with inventory," I said, elbowing Dottie as I joined her at the shelves.

Chapter 26

JACE DIDN'T HAVE anything left in Madison's bedroom at the cabin, so it made the transition easy. He rolled a suitcase into my room while my sisters moved into their rooms across the hall. Our parents insisted on keeping the family Christmas tradition, which meant forcing all three of us and our significant others to spend Christmas Eve in the cabin. No one complained at the plans a month ago when we were discussing Christmas Break and Madison's wedding plans. But not even Dad could pretend like there wasn't tension now as Lori and Winnie Maxwell rolled their suitcases into the cabin.

"Where are Winnie and I staying?" Lori called from the first floor.

"Upstairs. The girls will show you," Dad yelled.

I turned to look at Jace, noticing that Madison was looking at me from her room across the hall. She shrugged my way before a bang down the hallway distracted me. A moment later, Winnie Maxwell dragged her suitcase past my room.

"Don't scratch the floors," Lori chided, following after her daughter on their way to the master bedroom.

"The wheel just broke at the top of the step," Winnie groaned.

"Then pick it up!"

"It's too heavy or I would."

"What did you pack that's so heavy for two nights?"

Jace shut the door to muffle the argument, leaning against the door and crossing his arms. "Fix your face. Your resting-bitch-face is showing and there will definitely be tension if you go down there looking like that," he said with a teasing smirk.

"There's going to be fighting anyway. There usually is, but especially this time with my dad insisting on bringing his new girl-friend to Christmas dinner before he's even divorced my mom." I had several reasons to bring my sour mood to the family movie night.

Jace straightened up and went to the closet, slipping his shoes off and kicking them inside. "Be nice," he warned.

"You going to put me in a timeout if I'm not?" I asked as I tugged open the drawer of my dresser to find a clean pair of sweat-pants. I wanted to wear the black joggers, but Jace had a point. I pulled out the flannel pajama pants that had reindeer on them. I didn't have to force a good mood, but I didn't need to actively rebel against the festive night either.

"Be nice or I'll send you straight to your room, baby doll," he said in my ear as he wrapped his arms around my waist from behind. "And don't make me come up after you." He nipped at my ear.

"Some threat," I scoffed and turned in his arms to face him. "Besides, I could take you."

I rose onto my toes to kiss him before he could respond. I could tell he wanted to argue, and that he knew exactly what I was doing by turning in his arms again and shoving my jeans down to my knees. I bent over as I removed them, bracing myself against the mattress as I let my ass brush the front of his pants. He took a step back at the contact and I glanced back at him to see him shaking his head as he lifted his suitcase onto the seat in the bay window.

I finished changing into my flannel pants and he put on a pair of gray sweatpants with a red shirt—it was the most festive thing in his limited wardrobe—and we left the room to head downstairs. Somehow, we were the first couple to arrive in the kitchen, and it made my stomach twist because I could tell from the way Mom's lips formed a tight line that she and Dad were arguing seconds before they noticed us coming across the living room.

"Jace, are you the reason there's all this craft beer in this fridge?" Dad asked, the humor in his face betraying his firm tone.

"Some of it is mine," Jace said, making my dad do a double take as he reached for a can in the fridge. "I mean, some of it I brewed. The rest came from breweries around the state."

"Brewed?" Mom asked, looking up from the gingerbread cookies she was dividing between paper plates. The pieces were different shapes and sizes, perfect for constructing gingerbread houses.

"He's opening a bookstore and brewery where the current bookstore is," I told them, opening a bag of gumdrops and pouring them into a plastic bowl. "It's why it took him so long to finish tiling the bathroom." I moved on to filling another bowl with pieces of peppermint bark.

"You're never going to let that go, are you?" Jace asked, taking a can of Sinclair Stout when Dad handed one to him.

"Sounds pretty permanent," Dad said. It was a judgement. He smiled and cracked the top of his can, but the tone was unmistakable. Business-like, the way he'd talk with someone in a boardroom and not my boyfriend across the kitchen at a family dinner.

Jace wasn't fazed. He'd grown up with this kind of tact, more of it even. "I moved out of the cabin a week ago, but I haven't forgotten about our deal. I promised I'd finish the renovations, and I will. I've been splitting my time between the business and here. I'm painting the den after Christmas and then I'm finished."

"I'm not criticizing," Dad said, pretending not to have seen my mom's pointed look telling him to back off. "I only meant that you made it clear that Crescent Peak was a brief stop on your way to Denver. You said you didn't know how long you'd be in the state because of the weather, and I just didn't think you'd be the kind of guy to settle for a small business."

"I know what you mean, and I know that the only reason I'm here is because you're close with my father and he asked you for a favor. I appreciate you opening your home to me, especially considering what you know about my past," Jace said, sitting his unopened beer down on the counter. "But I'm not my father and I don't want to live the way he does. I need the quiet life with a tightknit community, the kind of place that's different than that big seaside city where I grew up."

"The cold isn't stifling your powers?" Dad asked, staring in awe. "It takes an especially skilled warlock, usually a man well into his golden years—"

"Oh, it bothers me." Jace laughed, his eyes flicking to me for just a second before he looked back at my dad. "I think I've gotten stronger because it takes more focus and energy to do the simple things like light a candle, but it's so different here and for now that's enough. I needed to start over, be on the outside of the social circle for once instead of ushered in because of my last name and everything that comes with it."

The room was quiet for a beat and it looked like my dad was preparing the perfect speech, probably something about working hard and upholding the family name, but the moment was interrupted by a squeal and a giggle that lifted the mood and demanded attention. Always.

Madison scurried into the room, Jared following her with a red tinge of guilt to his cheeks. Madison averted her eyes once she'd caught our attention, pretending that they hadn't just been playing grab-ass or who the hell knows what in the other room moments before.

Newlyweds are gross.

"Cookie decorating?" Jared asked, plucking a piece of peppermint bark from the bowl I'd just filled.

"Gingerbread house construction contest," Dad called out, rounding the kitchen island to clap Jared on the back. The greeting in comparison to the one he'd given Jace was stark. "Hope you brought your construction hat."

Dax entered the kitchen with Margot just behind him. He pulled my mom into a brief side-hug and said, "I missed it last year, but I'm going to win this year."

He'd gained enough muscle after joining the Olympic team that he made Jared look small by comparison, which wasn't an easy feat. The two shook and hands slapped each other on the back in that hard way all athletes did for some reason. Dax eyed the candy separated in bowls across the kitchen island like he hadn't eaten in years. He probably hadn't had sugar in that long from the look of him.

"Beer, Dax?" Dad asked, opening the fridge and pulling out one of the Crescent Peak Books and Brews cans. I opened my mouth to point out how rude it was but got a kick to the back of my leg instead. I closed my mouth, not wanting to give Jace the satisfaction of a dirty look.

"None for me, thank you," Dax said and took a bottle of water from Margot. "It must have taken you all day to bake enough gingerbread for all of us, Jenn."

My mom shook her head, glancing briefly to the left as Lori and Winnie entered the kitchen. "It'll be a team competition."

"Glad I got a carpenter on my side," I chimed in, taking a step backward so I could purposely step on Jace's toes as payback for the kick earlier. He didn't even groan, the bastard.

"Carpenter?" Jared asked, intrigued now that the conversation had shifted. "I grew up working with my hands. I know my way around a table saw, but I haven't made anything since high school."

"I don't make things often," Jace said, scratching the back of his head and giving a shrug. "I mostly do renovations, a few household repairs, that sort of thing. I only started doing it to get credit for my high school internship class."

I laughed, the sound more uncharacteristic than I'd intended, but it did the trick. The room was looking at me now, but the attention wasn't for me. "He made the bar at the new brewery all himself and it's beautiful."

"New brewery here in Crescent Peak?" Lori asked, helping herself to the bottle of white wine sitting on the counter. She finished twisting the corkscrew into the top and popped the cork out with ease for as thin as she was.

"Crescent Peak Books and Brews," Jace said and picked up the can he'd sat aside earlier. He turned it so they could see the label.

Jace was asked enough questions between Jared and his interest in business and Dax's taste in beer that it kept the conversation going as we started the contest. We split by couples with Mom partnering with Winnie and acting mostly like it wasn't awkward to watch her almost-ex-husband dab frosting on Lori's nose halfway through the contest.

We paused to eat Dad's famous chili before voting on the winning house. Jace and I took the prize thanks to his vanilla wafer roof. We played a short game of charades while Mom and Dad dragged a plastic tote of gifts into the room and took turns passing them out. All of the girls got designer handbags except for Lori who also got a pair of diamond earrings from my dad.

As if it was bad enough that he couldn't wait for a private moment to give her her gift, the boys got signed sports memorabilia—Denver Bronchos' gear and signed footballs for Jared and Dax—except for Jace who was handed a little giftbox which contained a check for five-hundred dollars. Dad told Jared and Dax that he thought they could use the gear for the next Bronchos' season and promised to pay for them to attend a few games, looking away once Jace had pulled the check from the giftbox in his hands.

"I know I told your dad I'd let you live here as payment for doing the renovations, but I wanted to pay you for the work," Dad told him while Jared slipped into his new sweatshirt. "The invite for the games extends to you too. I'll let you know which games we get tickets for."

"Thank you, Mr. Sinclair," Jace said and extended his hand,

the men shaking like this was a business deal and not family Christmas.

Shit, it pissed me off. But Jace turned my face to his by my chin before I could utter a word, leaning in to press a kiss to my lips. It barely melted the tension I felt, but it was all the time the rest of the group needed to focus on making drinks and starting the movie on the TV above the fireplace.

I could hardly enjoy the Grinch's antics as I watched Lori fidget with her new earrings and my mom scroll on her phone from her armchair. Once the movie finished, Mom said she was too tired to stay up and went to the kitchen to pack away the leftovers. Lori volunteered to help and the two started their work in silence. You'd had thought they were in two different worlds the way they rotated around each other without speaking a word.

Dad brought a tray of beers to the living room, the last of Jace's cans from the brewery, and even Dax gave in an opened a can.

"I don't know if it's because I've been on a strict diet for training, but this is one of the best beers I've ever had," he said before taking another sip.

Jared nodded as he took a can from my dad. "It's good and this place needs more nightlife. Most people drive over to the next town for the bar if they want a night out."

Margot smirked and glanced at Dax. I'm sure it was some inside joke only they knew, probably something to do with that gym they spent so much time at in the next town, but it was the way they looked so relaxed that made me pause. They *all* looked so relaxed, like no one noticed how much of an outsider they were treating Jace.

"I never thought I'd like the small-town life, but it's a good change of pace. Everyone's been so nice here and I know I don't exactly look all that approachable," Jace said with a laugh.

"You're a summer warlock, right?" Dax asked, ignoring the way Jared leaned over to whisper to Madison, probably asking what it meant since he was the only non-magical person in the room. "I've met a few when I moved west. I go to school in California."

Jace nodded. "Yeah. I'm a summer warlock. I grew up near LA. Our coven has a club along the coast."

Dax sat forward a little like he was preparing to ask the real question he had. "You grew up in the rich club, right? Some of the warlocks I met at school told me about it."

I could tell from the twitch at the corner of Jace's lips when he smiled that he didn't care to explain. He nodded anyway. "Yeah. The Bougainvillea Club. My family's associated there, but I'm not anymore. It's been nice to experience something different, a quieter life."

Jared's beer hissed as he opened it, interrupting the conversation just long enough so I could lock eyes on Madison. It was an S.O.S and my shoulders relaxed when she straightened up and prepared to come to my aid for once. Maybe she wasn't all that bad after all.

"Marlee, your roommate is an autumn witch, isn't she?" she asked.

"Um, yeah. You know, weather control or whatever," I said. Now that I thought about it, Callie and I had never talked extensively about our powers. She'd seen me conjure ice cubes for drinks at our apartment and I watched her send a gust of wind across a courtyard that sent a guy toppling into a fountain on campus. He'd made fun of me at a party the weekend before.

"Where's Callie from? Kansas?" Margot asked and adjusted as Dax draped an arm around her shoulders.

"No, Oklahoma," I corrected, my voice catching in my throat as Jace pressed his knee against mine. "Um, she's from Oklahoma. Her family has a ranch there."

"Oh yeah! The Cody ranch," Margot said and crossed her legs in her seat. "The last time I saw her she told me about a storm that came through and broke a fence. She said they normally would divert bad weather around the ranch using their powers, but they were out of town or something."

"That makes sense," Jared said with his beer half-raised to his lips. "Tornados. The plains. They get some weird weather there. You think all the autumn witches and warlocks chase tornados like in Twister?"

Madison playfully slapped his knee, only making him smile wider at the joke.

"I bet it wasn't easy for you to leave your coven," Dax said, returning to the subject that had my stomach in knots. "I love the Cali sun, but I do get a little homesick sometimes. No, it's more like seasonal allergies or something. I feel a little under the weather, you know? Do you feel like that here?"

Jace's smile fell. He'd stopped pretending. I wasn't sure if the knot in my chest was panic, fear that he would say something to only push himself farther from the group, or if I was worried that he was the one rejecting them. Either way it made me realize how badly I wanted him to fit in with my family and have the close relationship with my dad that Jared and Dax had.

Jace let out a deep breath and sat forward, leaning his elbows on his knees. "I do feel like that here, but I'm glad for the change because things weren't good for me back there," he said, making eye contact with my dad for just a moment before looking back at Dax.

"I think we all want to escape from home and find ourselves. I've been there, man," Dax said.

"No," Jace said as soon as he'd finished. "I was sent away. The coven said it was me or my family and I decided to leave. It made the most sense for my situation."

"Jace—"

He ran a hand down my thigh to my knee, giving it a squeeze to silence me as he looked at the faces around the coffee table. "It would've caused more trouble if I had stayed. I paid off some people to leave me and my family alone and promised to get out. That's why I came out here and crashed at the cabin, but it's not why I stayed."

"Someone blackmailed your family?" Jared asked. He shook his head and ran a hand through his thick hair. "Is it because you came from money?"

"No, it's because I was in a gang," Jace said. The words were like a shockwave through the room. No one moved except for him as he pulled his right sleeve back to show off the large skull tattoo on his forearm. He pointed to one of the dark eyes. "I covered my gang tattoo here. I have a few others. It's not the whole reason I have so many tattoos, but it's the reason why some of them are so big."

"You were in a gang?" Madison asked, her voice soft.

Shit.

Somehow, I thought she'd known. I looked at Margot who looked even more stunned, her face a little paler than normal. Jared was the only person in the living room besides my dad who didn't look even a tiny bit terrified. Even Mom and Lori must have heard from the way they were watching us. Winnie's phone slipped from her lap onto the floor, the noise doing little to distract the group staring at Jace as he pushed his sleeve back to his wrist.

"I was. I had a bunch of guys working for me, running drugs. I never used, refused to touch the stuff after some of the things I saw," Jace said and looked up from his wrist. "Getting out once you're in is hard, especially as far in as I was. I paid my way out and I won't go back, not to the city at least. My dad is pretty pissed with me, obviously. I made some bad decisions, learned some hard lessons, and I think it's important that you know where I come from because I don't keep secrets from the people I care about."

Jace turned his attention to me, his eyes burning sincere holes right through my soul. I couldn't do it anymore. I had to tell him. No more distractions. I had to tell him the truth. I only hoped he would understand why I hadn't been honest, or this would turn into the worst Christmas ever.

Chapter 27

I TRIED to pull Jace away from the group once the attention was off him, but he insisted on staying to play a boardgame after Jared swore that he never lost a game. Put a bunch of business guys in a room with a Monopoly board and the entire night would slip away. Jace must've been invested in the game because he looked focused, almost angry when I tried a second time to end the night.

"Jace," I said, pulling his attention from his phone. He rubbed a hand over his face as he turned to look at me standing at the stairs.

"You can go to bed without me," he said with a small smile.

"He's stressing about the fact that I'm buying him out of the game," Jared teased and punched Jace's bicep. "He swore he'd beat me before calling it a night."

"I don't think I could make it another game, if that's the case," Dax groaned.

Jace didn't laugh with the rest of the group, sending me another weak smile before he looked down at his phone again.

I went upstairs to find a little red box sitting on the bed with a handwritten note.

I SAT the note on the edge of the bed and pulled the lid off the little red box. Sitting inside was a keychain with the Crescent Peak Books and Brews logo on it, a key attached to the end. My stomach sank and tears filled my eyes. I could feel the sob bubbling forth when I heard the door creak behind me. I whirled around before I could stop the tears.

Jace stood in the door for a moment, his eyes going from my face to the key in my hand. He let out a deep sigh and stepped into the room, shutting the door behind him.

"I'm sorry," I said. The worst part was that the apology was too late. I could see the truth in the tight lines of his face and the way his jaw was set. "How did you find out?"

He scoffed and pointed a hand toward the door. "After they mentioned your roommate. Dottie said she was her favorite author, so I looked her up and the last post she made online was some sneak peek only it wasn't just some fictional story."

"I didn't mean to … I tried to tell you."

"When?" he snapped and glanced toward the door like someone might come walking inside. He took another deep breath and lowered his voice. "All this time we've spent together, and you never once told me."

"I don't know. I would plan on telling you and things would go so well, and I wouldn't want to ruin it and that's just how it's been for—"

"Weeks?" Jace asked with a scoff. "I hadn't looked too deep into your author stuff. I assumed you'd let me in when you were ready. I'm such an idiot."

Jace shook his head and turned toward the door, taking a deep breath. He leaned over his suitcase, tossing in a few clothing items that sat beside it before zipping it. The sound of the zipper sent my heart into a frenzy.

"Jace, I need you to understand that I didn't mean for all this to happen. I didn't even mean to record us in my bedroom."

"But you sent it, didn't you? Then, you let that episode go live for all your readers to listen to all the dirty things that were meant for just us."

It stung. Fuck, it hurt like crazy.

"I didn't know that's what it was. I'd recorded something before that, and I thought that was what I sent to Callie to put in the episode. I didn't know until it went live, and I listened to it after writing. It was days later," I told him, following him to the bathroom. I heard the shower turn on and he stopped in the doorway a moment later, looking like I'd never seen him before. His jaw was tight, angry, but his eyes were soft and lost. It made my stomach plummet, and every argument turn to ash on my tongue. There was no argument. There was no fixing this and I hated it.

He shook his head and let out a long sigh. "Did you ever think to pull the episode or were your pre-orders just too high to consider it?"

"Jace," I started, tears slipping over my lips.

"I know everything between us started as a game of banter culminating into a hate-fuck that I still can't forget, but I didn't realize the game hadn't ended for you."

"I stopped playing the game a long time ago. You know that," I said, a final Hail Mary that I knew was as cheap as some of the shots we use to take at one another back when I couldn't stand the sight of him.

Jace shrugged like he wasn't sure what to believe. "When? Before that recording of us in your room?"

I opened my mouth in defense, but the truth was that the line was so blurred that I wasn't sure when I knew that I loved him. Part of me thought I'd fallen hard for him that day I met him.

Jace looked at me for a moment, his eyes screaming with frustration. I'd made a fool of him. At least, I'm sure he felt like that. He was questioning every moment we'd shared together; I could see it in the way he looked at me. Steam poured from the tiny bathroom behind him, a sad reminder of how we'd first met.

"I'm going to shower," he said, lingering in the doorway for just a moment before he closed the door and left me to cry alone in the bedroom.

I WAS STILL awake when Jace finally got out of the shower. He'd dressed in a pair of jeans and a sweatshirt, took the apartment key from my bedside table, and quietly left the room with his suitcase in tow. I never lifted my head from my pillow, just let the tears slide onto the fabric beneath me and try not to replay the fight in my mind until I finally fell asleep.

I woke up shortly after ten the next morning and double-checked the little red box on the side table just in case I'd imagined Jace taking his gift with him.

I hadn't imagined it.

I took a long shower and actually spent the time to dry and style my hair just to further procrastinate my trip downstairs. No one looked very well-rested. Winnie and Madison sat on the couch with bowls of cereal and Dax and Jared were across the living room and through the double doors to the den, watching football on the little TV mounted on the wall.

"Where's Jace?" Mom asked, pouring a cup of black coffee and setting in on the counter in front of me.

I pulled the mug closer by the handle, watching as she and Lori went back to transferring biscuits from a baking sheet to a more aesthetic Christmas tree tray. "He had to do something early at the brewery this morning."

I've never been happier that people saw me as a cynical, grouchy girl because neither woman batted an eye at my sour tone.

"My head hurts," I said and lifted the mug from the counter. "I'll be in my room."

No one said a word as I started for the stairs again, hardly keeping it together as I made my way to the second floor. I groaned when I finally reached my room and sat my mug on my desk. Coffee sloshed over the rim and onto the desk. I pushed my computer to the other side to avoid making this mess worse than it already was. Although, maybe frying my computer and losing my whole book would keep things from getting worse.

Shit. The stupid book.

I could pull the plug. I could delete the pre-order, losing all the money, but maybe it was the right thing to do. It didn't feel like it though. The book wasn't about Jace and me. It wasn't even inspired by our relationship. That moment we shared together led to me writing a single scene within the book and even then, I'd rewritten the circumstances so no one would ever guess at what had truly transpired between the narrators. The plot was nothing close to our real life. But being so honest with him, letting myself indulge in him, and God the sex …

I thought at first that I'd just never been so attracted to someone the way I was to Jace Blackthorne and that's why I was so struck by inspiration to write this book, but it wasn't that at all. I felt something deeper the more we talked and that's what led me to write this book that was yes, sexy as hell, but also contained some of the deepest and most vulnerable moments between two characters than I'd ever written. Jace gave me the confidence to write what I felt called to write and to show a side of myself that I'd never shown anyone and felt more real than anything.

And I fucked it all up because I couldn't tell him how I felt about him.

I wasn't the kind of person to dwell in my feelings. I'd allowed myself to do that before I fell asleep last night, so I did the only thing I knew how to do and got back to work on my draft. I'd finished it, so I started from page one and made changes as I went. The day slipped away as I relived the story, reading through the entire draft in nearly one sitting. I stopped just once for a snack and a bathroom break, resisting the urge to check my phone for a message from Jace.

The cabin was empty by the time I finished. It was dark, the gray clouds obscuring what little was left of the sunset. I went to the fridge to check what had been left over from Christmas dinner, finding a plate of ham and a couple spoonfuls of mashed potatoes. I made a meal of it, plopping it on a paper plate and sticking it in the microwave.

We'd finished all the beer over the holiday, and I wasn't normally much of a drinker, but I made myself a vodka Coke while the microwave hummed in the background. Once the plate stopped spinning behind the glass, I took the meal and the drink to the living room and sat on the couch. Monopoly was still sitting on the coffee table. They'd packed it all away in the box but hadn't bothered putting it back in the hall closet. I leaned back against the couch and lifted my feet onto the table, pushing the box onto the floor with my heels despite the ample room on the table.

I opened my phone to find dozens of notifications from my social media accounts. It had become more and more the norm the longer my book was on pre-order and Callie kept talking about it online. I ignored them and found my way to my sister's contact. I paused, my finger scrolling and hitting the call button before I couldn't calm my racing heart.

"I knew something happened. Tell me from the beginning," Madison said after answering on the third ring.

The sob burst from my lips before I could control it. I quickly put the phone on speaker and sat my mostly empty paper plate on the cushion beside me. I slumped in my seat and let my head rest against the cushion, so I was staring at the ceiling.

"He found out, didn't he?" Madison asked. I'd made the right decision in calling her over Callie. At least I didn't have to start all the way at the beginning.

"Yeah. He found the podcast episode," I told her. Part of me hoped I would never again have to explain this, but it felt like part of my punishment. Jace had been through so much in the last year and he trusted me after a stretch of choosing all the wrong people. I deserved to bear the shame like Hester Prynne. Maybe I was the

Arthur Dimmesdale of this story, and everything would only get worse after I'd confessed the truth.

Madison let out an audible breath and I could hear her adjust the phone through the receiver. "I'm sorry, Marlee."

"You can say *I told you so.*" I laughed because I wasn't sure what else to do. I would've said the words if the conversation were reversed. At least, I would've a month ago before I'd experienced what I had. I never understood romance novels as anything but fiction, but once I was dropped in the center of one it felt like floating in the ocean with the tide taking you farther from shore. And I'd welcomed the gentle waves and warm sun. What a way to go.

"No," she sighed into the phone. "But I did tell you that there's nothing like falling in love. I think you fell hard, too."

I resisted the urge to groan into the phone and held my breath, letting the tears slide down my temples as my vision of the ceiling blurred. "So hard."

"Do you want him back?"

"It doesn't matter," I said and straightened up, setting my hand straight into what was left of the mashed potatoes on my place beside me. "He hates me. He left last night and took my gift back. He doesn't want me."

"Sure, he does," Madison said with a laugh. "He was only so mad because of how deeply he cares about you. Have you tried calling him? You should let him know you're willing to work things out."

I carried my plate to the kitchen in one hand and my phone in the other. I'd been avoiding calling him because I felt so stupid, so unworthy of this relationship after lying as long as I had. Who could trust me after that? I wouldn't trust me.

I ran my hand under the cool water, feeling a little better just because the temperature made my witchy powers surge through my veins. I focused on that for a moment and let an ice cube form in my palm until I remembered how Jace had taken the last one I'd conjured from me.

"I'll call you later," I said and hung up before she could say goodbye. I left my plate on the counter and ran for the stairs. I didn't look put together in the slightest, fluffy pajama pants paired with a sweatshirt and my snow boots. I didn't care as long as I hadn't waited too long to talk to him.

I parked my orange Jeep along the street and got out, nearly falling on my ass when I hurried for the door. I tried the handle, but the door was locked. I knocked a few times, hoping he was just in the back brewing or checking stock. I'd just turned to start for the Jeep when the door opened behind me. I whirled around to face a dark-haired woman in the doorway. She eyed me suspiciously before she relaxed and placed a hand on her hip.

"He left a few hours ago," she said and nodded toward the street.

"Left? Where? I can wait until he gets back."

She shook her head, the apology there in her expression despite her annoyance at being disturbed. "Jace hired me as a manager a few days ago to help run things. I have a lot of brewing experience, so I can handle the business while he's away."

"What do you mean?" I asked. Shit. He hadn't just gone out for a break or to run an errand.

"His flight left at four. He waited to leave longer than I would've, but he texted that he made it in time to board. He'll be back in two weeks," she said, softening her tone.

I wondered if he'd waited so long because he was hoping I'd show up sooner. I wondered if he took me not coming as a sign. Maybe I should've just called him when I woke up this morning. I wasn't sure what was worse, how bad I had messed things up or the fact that I couldn't even do the classic "run to the airport" romance novel thing well. It didn't matter at this point. He wasn't coming back for two weeks and I was leaving for New York City in just a few days.

Chapter 28

"This is what you've been doing this whole time?" Margot asked as she flipped through the stack of paper on the table in front of her.

"Pretty much," I said and lifted my coffee to my lips. "When I wasn't with Jace, I was writing."

Margot sent a surprised look at Madison who simply nodded. I knew Margot was appalled by the whole thing. There was the fact that I confided in Madison—that alone was enough to shock anyone considering our past relationship. But Margot didn't know I was an author and this sexy book was what tipped things over the edge for her.

After the three of us met at the coffee shop, I filled her in on all the details of my budding career. At first, she was offended that I hadn't told her, but she understood after we started to talk about Mom and Dad. That's when I felt confident enough—or maybe I was just at such a loss at what to do next after everything with Jace—that I pulled out the draft of my book that I'd printed and placed in a three-ring binder.

Margot was picking through the binder one page at a time and it made my insides squirm to watch her scan each page. I exhaled before I realized it when she lifted her head to look at me. "And that's what happened with Jace? He's upset you wrote this book after you guys started dating?"

"No, it's not the book at all," Madison jumped in, talking loud enough that she drew the attention of a pair of elderly ladies from the next table. "It's because she recorded them having sex and it ended up in the podcast she cohosts with Callie."

"We weren't having sex!"

God, those little old ladies were mortified. They were pretending not to look at us before, but now they were both full-on scowling at me. Shit.

"So, what's the big deal then?" Margot asked as she turned another page in the binder. "I'm guessing it has something to do with whatever you might have said on the podcast. Did you talk about him?"

"No, Madison wasn't that far off except we didn't have sex," I said and sent her a pointed look. "We were just talking and some of the things we said were a little ..."

Margot nodded when I didn't finish, finally understanding. "And he's mad that what he said in private ended up becoming very public."

"And being used to promote a book he had no idea existed," Madison added.

Technically, he knew I was writing a book. I was remembering why I struggled to get along with her. Holy shit she was annoying. She might have grown out of her whole bitchy mean girl phase, but she was still great at poking her nose into everyone's business.

I groaned. "I didn't realize that's the recording I sent to Callie until days after the episode aired and then things just got away from me."

"Why didn't you just take the episode offline?" Margot asked.

That's what Jace had said. Why wasn't that the first thing I thought to do? I was so panicked in the moment that I wasn't thinking about anything. Callie didn't even know about Jace.

"I don't know. I just panicked and I didn't do anything. It's what I do when I'm stressed! I pretend it's not happening," I said.

The words felt unsettling. It was like the thought had been buried so deeply in my subconscious that I hadn't accessed the record until just now. It was true, though, no matter how uncomfortable. I did run away from conflict. I hid from problems. I pretended like everything was fine when it wasn't.

"What do you want to do?" Madison asked.

I wanted to run to the airport to keep Jace from getting on that plane like in all those sappy romcoms I used to make fun of her for watching. I wanted to call him, but he sent a text after I'd shown up at the brewery. His employee must have told him. Jace told me to give him space and not to contact him while he thinks about things. That's what I've always done, though, let the chips fall and anxiously wait and hope they landed in my favor.

Fuck, M. A. Jenson wouldn't wait on anyone before she made her move.

"I need to talk to Dad," I said and stood up from the table. "Hell, I want to talk with Mom and Dad. Can you guys come with me?"

"What?" Margot asked, a look of concern crossing her face as she stood up and tucked the binder under one arm. "You're going to tell them everything now?"

"Mom already knows. Well, she knows about me being an author, but not the podcast thing," I said and led the way across the coffee shop to the door.

"You told Mom and not me?" Margot asked.

I ignored her and stepped into the winter air, hurrying down the sidewalk toward my orange Jeep. Madison climbed into the passenger seat while I rounded the front for the driver's side. Margot was the last to get in, still grumbling about being the one person I didn't tell while I started the engine. I pulled into the street before I'd figured out where to go.

I could call them and tell them to meet at the house. I could go to the lodge where they both had rooms and hope to find them. I didn't have to figure out the details though, Madison reached across the dash to point at the next left.

"Go to the lodge." She had her phone pressed to her ear,

telling one of our parents to meet us there before she hung up without a goodbye and called the other.

"It might be better to meet with Mom first and then Dad," Margot said from the backseat.

"You're not her manager!"

"I can do this on my own!"

Madison and I exchanged looks. She smiled proudly before relaying her instructions into the phone. I glanced at Margot's reflection in the rearview mirror. She looked embarrassed. I knew she meant well, but damn. She really did insert herself into the middle of everything. I know I'd needed her in the past to mediate with our parents and Madison, but I couldn't let her carry things forever.

"Sorry," I told her, waiting until her eyes flicked to mine in the mirror before I took the left at the stop sign.

"No. You're right. You need to do this."

I steeled myself against the onslaught of shock, concern, and maybe even anger that would come my way once I'd said my part at the lodge. I pulled into the parking lot as Mom's SUV parked next to Dad's near the main entrance. They stepped out of their cars as I put the Jeep in park beside them.

"What's all this about?" Dad asked when I got out of the Jeep.

"Let's go to the suite where the bridal party met for the wedding," Madison called out from the opposite side of the Jeep. She said the words so firmly it was clear she was trying to steer the conversation away from becoming a fight in the parking lot.

No promises once we reached that room inside.

"I was finishing lunch when you called," Mom said and followed after Madison and I. "I would've appreciated a little heads-up first."

"We can't all eat brunch and a late lunch every day," I groaned, nearly getting squashed by the heavy door at the entrance before Dad surged forward to catch it by the handle. He shot me a warning look that I ignored to walk behind Madison. I could hear the furious tip-tap of Mom's heels on the hardwood floor of the hall as we walked, rounding the corner to the suite once she caught up with us.

"Most of my clients are in a different time zone, Marlee. Some of us have to adjust with a happy attitude."

I had barely gone a few steps into the room when I turned to face her. She stopped so abruptly that she nearly tripped over those ridiculous heels.

"Your family shouldn't have to adjust for your career all the time, especially not on vacation!"

"Marlee!" Dad snapped and slammed the door shut behind him.

I pointed at him. "You took a work call the day Madison got married!"

"Stop!" Margot rarely raised her voice, so it sucked the air from the room now that she had. She took a few steps closer so she could point a finger at my dad with one hand and me with the other. "We're going to talk calmly, or we won't talk at all. Everyone got it?"

Madison and Mom both agreed immediately, but my eyes went to Dad who looked ready to burst into a lecture judging by how puffed up his chest was and red in the face he'd gone.

"Yeah. Calm," I said, keeping my eyes on him.

He nodded and let out an annoyed breath that didn't ease the tension in the room a bit. "Okay. No yelling. But everyone needs to be respectful." His eyes pierced me with warning, but I didn't shrink the way I usually did. I wasn't going to let this argument just dissipate.

"Let's all sit," Margot said and motioned to the couches in the center of the room. Madison and Mom sat next to each other, scooting to make a space for Margot so Dad and I could take the empty couch that sat opposite them. Neither of us moved though. This was my meeting and just like he did in a boardroom, I wasn't going to sit down when I said my piece.

"This is about my career and what I want to do," I said, looking from my dad to my mom, who nodded.

"The writing," she said with a hum of understanding.

"The writing?" Dad asked, looking at her like she'd explain everything despite me being right in front of him.

"She told me at the wedding. She's published a book and has another on the way," Mom told him before looking up at me with a smile that I know was forced. It was like when an icicle would break from the gutters outside my cabin window, falling straight through the snowdrift outside where Madison and Margot would play to avoid listening to Mom and Dad's arguing inside. No one thought about me locked in my bedroom and how I could hear every word they said, hear about the affairs they'd both had on business trips, how much they'd argue about Madison and Margot, and how they rarely mentioned me during those fights.

Mom gave me an encouraging nod and said, "I found your pen name and took a look at your books."

"And the podcast?" I asked.

She shrugged. "Yes, I saw the podcast you cohost with Callie. I didn't realize you were so entrenched in publishing."

She didn't realize? I spent most my childhood with a book in my hand or tucked in my bag wherever we went.

"Did you listen to it?" I asked, not believing her when she nodded. "All of it, Mom? You heard the teaser? You heard me read that—"

"Yes! Marlee, yes, I heard the teaser from your book," she said, taking a moment to calm herself before she spoke again. "It's a little awkward to talk to your daughter about her book when she enacts a whole scene of it with her boyfriend and posts it to the internet."

"What?" Dad whirled around to face me again, his face bright red. "You did what?"

"I didn't mean to send that teaser!" I yelled over him, all rules of fair fighting going out the window and who gave a fuck anyway. They'd never been fair to me or my sisters. "I had something else recorded to send and then Jace came in and he must have hit the record button, or I did, whatever happened doesn't matter because I ended up sending the wrong file to Callie for the podcast and then it went live and everyone heard it and then my book ... Shit, it was just so easy to write that book after that."

"You made a ... *recording* of you and Jace Blackthorne?" Dad asked, voice shaking.

"They weren't having sex," Madison interjected as though it would make things easier to explain to him. He barely looked her way. He muttered something under his breath and pressed the heels of his palms for his forehead and walked toward the door.

"Jace didn't know," I said, lowering my voice as the guilt settled in my chest. "I didn't know until after the episode aired."

Dad slowly turned from the door, pausing a moment before he lowered his hands to look at me. "What did you record?"

"It's not bad, Peter," Mom said with a scoff. "It's just some sexy banter. It's pretty tame, really."

Dad groaned. "Is that why he left without finishing the job?"

"Is that all you care about, remodeling that stupid cabin so you can sell it and leave the last part of our family behind?" I asked.

"That's not fair and you know it's not true," Dad said, pointing at me.

"Well, you sure moved on fast. It's almost like you've done this before, like maybe when you were in Phoenix or Dallas," I said and crossed my arms. It didn't feel nearly as satisfying as I had always dreamed to say the words aloud. In reality, the words were bitter in my mouth and my eyes stung at the realization that they wouldn't make a difference anyway, not to the people I wanted to hurt with them. The last time my sisters looked like this was when our parents sat us on the living room couch to tell us Santa isn't real. Just like everything now, I already knew the truth then, too.

"Marlee, your dad's mistakes are not the reason we are getting divorced," Mom said gently.

"I know you made all the same mistakes he did, Mom. I've overheard years of arguments when everyone forgot about me. That's the real problem, I guess."

It was strange how quiet the room was, like we were in a vacuum. It looked like even the whole world outside stood still.

Mom cleared her throat and pretended to smooth her slacks over her knees.

"I'm sorry about what you heard," she said softly as she fussed over the fabric along her thighs. "Those conversations were private, and you should never have been included in them."

"That's the thing, I wasn't. Madison was always included in them. So was Margot. You guys always brought them up, but never me. Arguments about how Dad didn't understand the importance of Madison's social calendar and all her stress about her looks and fashion. Arguments about how Mom wasn't at enough of Margot's soccer games. Arguments about who worked more and didn't help with the kids enough, but that point seemed to shift all the time. One week it was Mom screaming the words and the next it was Dad," I said, trying to keep my voice from shaking.

Mom's mouth parted in surprise and once she recovered, she shot Dad a helpless look. There was nothing they could say to defend themselves. I'd heard it all throughout the years and she knew that. It didn't stop Dad from huffing and puffing like a steam engine as he tried to form a coherent sentence.

"Don't even start," I warned him.

He turned to fully face me. He sucked in a deep breath and let it out in a frustrated groan. "I thought I was doing a good thing. I thought it was mutually beneficial. I thought, of all my daughters, you'd be the least likely to be influenced by him."

"Influenced by him? Are you trying to say that all of this is because of Jace Blackthorne?" I asked, not caring about keeping calm and civil anymore. "This is why I wanted to meet and talk as a family, because my entire life has been about maintaining decorum and keeping up with the image of this damn family when it's hardly been a family unit to begin with. It's so fucked up the pressure you've put on all of us and I'm tired of it. I'm tired of pretending like I want to go to law school and prosecute high-profile cases or that I even care about my class ranking or GPA. I don't give a damn because it's killing me to keep up with things that feel soulless and—"

My voice cracked and I couldn't bring myself to finish. I wasn't even sure it mattered.

"You can be an author and still do all the things you want to do, Marlee Bear," said Dad.

"It's the *only* thing I want to do," I said past the thickness in my throat, staring straight at him until the tears blurred the hurt look on his face. "It's what I want to do most, and I've messed all of that up. I didn't write the stories I wanted to because I was worried they weren't important enough or were just stupid little romances when the truth is that love is the only thing that matters at all. I messed that up for myself, too."

I angrily swiped at my face, glad that I didn't bother putting on any makeup on this morning. Dad just watched as I worked to get a grip and calm the fuck down. I wasn't doing a great job of it from the way my heart continued to race in my chest each time I caught sight of him or Mom's sympathetic expression.

"And you wanted us here to tell us that we're the ones at fault," Dad finally said once I'd finally stopped crying. It's the calmest he'd sounded the entire time. That's all it took to summon the water works again. I held my breath for a moment until I felt in control just enough to sum things up as best as I could.

"You put pressure on Madison to build a fashion empire. You put pressure on Margot to go pro in soccer. You put pressure on me to be the smartest in my class and get into the best school I could. You never once asked me what I wanted to do once I got there. When I declared a major you just assumed what I'd do. I didn't want to disappoint anyone."

Ugh. I hated this. I hated crying like this. It made me feel stupid.

"Dad, do you know where Jace is?" Madison asked.

I was glad for the change in subject. Not only that, but I'd almost forgotten what Dad had said earlier about Jace skipping out on the last of the remodel at the cabin.

Dad shifted his weight to his right foot as he fished in his left pocket, withdrawing his phone a moment later. He shrugged as he unlocked the screen and began to scroll. "He hired a couple guys to do the painting and told me he'd already paid them. He said he'd left for business. I know his dad had been holding out on hope for him, betting he'd learn his lesson and come asking for a job with his company. I assumed that he left to meet with him."

Somehow, knowing that Jace was doing exactly what I had spent so long doing, made me feel worse. I finally felt like I was clearing the air with my family and stepping into the life I wanted for myself, and it felt like I'd forced Jace back into the box his own father had tried so hard to talk him into. He was giving up on his dream of small business and smalltown living for the Blackthorne name and legacy. It just didn't seem real. It couldn't be.

"He doesn't want that life," I said and shook my head. "He deserves so much better than that. Than this."

Dad gave a single laugh, like he couldn't believe I'd suggested that what Nolan Blackthorne had built was beneath Jace.

"Dad," Margot warned.

She didn't need to remind him of the boundary. He wasn't going to cross it because he was done. The conversation was over, and it was clear from the way he shook his head. He raised his eyes from his phone to me. I thought I saw them glisten for a moment, but he'd looked at Mom and my sisters before I could be sure.

"I'm not walking away from you or this conversation," Dad said and paused to clear his throat. "But I'm done talking about this right now."

He turned and pulled open the door. The room was quiet enough to hear every step he took down the hall until they faded into the distance and the suite door settled into the doorjamb after him.

Chapter 29

I HAD NOTHING TO DO. I didn't even have anything to write. I'd sent my book to my editor early just because I needed something to preoccupy my mind after I got back from the family meeting at the lodge yesterday. The cabin was painfully quiet, and I hated it. I'd even thought about trying to call Jace before I remembered how he wanted space. I left my phone on the charger when I woke up to avoid the temptation. If anyone wanted to talk that badly they'd know where to find me.

I wasn't that surprised when I heard the sliding door open behind me. I'd been sitting on the balcony through the master bedroom of the cabin for at least an hour, letting the chill of winter sooth my aching heart and recharge my powers. I'd been practicing conjuring ice into my palms, focusing on molding them into shapes rather than thinking about the real reason I was avoiding the rest of the cabin.

The clink of glass caught my attention, and I turned toward the sliding door. It felt like my heart slammed into my ribcage when I saw him. The ice in my palms hit the deck below and shattered. My dad held up the six-pack of beer bottles like it was a peace offering.

"I thought getting beer from the brewery might be a bad call," he said. I almost pointed out that telling me the fact was worse, but I stopped myself. I looked down at the shards of ice around my feet and kicked them toward the edge of the balcony, nudging them through the bars and over the edge one at a time.

"I thought I was too young for beer," I said as I toed the final shard over the edge.

"Not too young for Jace apparently," Dad murmured. He let out a sigh and sat the beer on the snow-covered table next me. "I'm sorry. I didn't mean—"

"Okay. Sure."

He sank into the chair to my right. "I only mean that Madison was always a little boy crazy, so I had to figure that out and then Margot had some interest in boys in high school, but not anything serious until Dax, and you ... Well, you never seemed focused on that, and I just didn't think—"

"It was a surprise to me, too."

Dad pulled two bottles of beer from the cardboard box and held one out to me. When I took it, he lifted a bottle opener to the neck and popped the cap off the top for me. He did the same to his bottle before clinking the lip of his bottle to mine and lifting it to take a sip.

"I didn't mean to insult Jace yesterday. I know his past and everything his family has been through. He's a little rough around the edges, hasn't always made good choices, and got really lucky things worked out the way they did for him," Dad said.

I scoffed into my beer, the glass making a deep whistling noise before I could lower it from my mouth. "I know. He told me about being in a gang, the case against him, his mom's murder. He told me all of it. At least one of us was honest, I guess."

I heard Dad let out a deep breath, prompting me to take a long drink from my bottle.

"Jace and I had a long talk when he first got here. Like I said, I know his past. I know his family. I know how his father responded and I ..." Dad groaned. I looked at him for the first time. His throat bobbed as he looked down at his beer. "I cried with him when he told me about his mom and how guilty he felt. He's made some bad choices in his life, but he's been a man when facing the consequences of his actions. And even though I told him I'd be his last stop to hell if he bothered you, I didn't think about you. You were right yesterday. I don't think enough about you and how you feel. I should've told you about Jace before you came home just like I should've asked you a long time ago about what your dreams are and ... I'm sorry, Marlee Bear."

I took a long drink before I lowered the bottle to my knees, watching the glass frost as I tried distracting myself with my powers. It wasn't working. My chest hurt. The knot rising in my throat and the burn behind my eyes was almost too much to hide and then Dad did something that he hadn't in years.

He placed a hand on my back and began tracing a figure-eight pattern like when I was a little girl. I used to get so pissed off as a kid, frustrated when I didn't feel like I was measuring up or like I wasn't being included with my sisters. My childhood nickname wasn't just some cutesy comparison to a fluffy bear with its head in a honey pot. It was because I acted like one. That's what Mom and Dad would say anyway. Only, Dad used the nickname like it was less of an insult and more of an asset the same way he'd call Margot Superstar.

The sob came straight from my chest, releasing the pressure that felt like it had been building all week. My chair scraped along the deck as he pulled me closer. I tossed my legs over his lap and buried my face into his chest as he traced that slow, soothing pattern across my shoulder blades. I didn't fight for control. I didn't want to. I was so damn tired of holding it all together. I let it all fall away and for once I felt better. I'd let loose on him and Mom both yesterday at the lodge, which felt cathartic in its own way. But I really needed my dad, too, just the way I did every time I would "unleash the bear" as a kid. Once I got all my frustrations out, I just wanted him to trace that figure-eight on my back and tell me things weren't so bad.

Only, I was pretty sure no amount of comforting would fix the lie I'd told.

"I really fucked up," I said once I'd calmed down enough to sink back into my own seat, pulling my knees to my chest.

Dad gave me a small smile and shook his head. "I don't know about that."

"He thinks this whole thing was just a winter fling that I used to sell more books. He probably thinks I used him the same way everyone around him growing up used him because his last name was Blackthorne," I said, nearly tipping my beer glass over when I bumped the table between us.

"I know how it all ended," Dad said with a deep sigh. "How did it all start?"

I felt the warmth creep into my face at the memory of Jace in that towel.

"I couldn't stop thinking about him after we met. I wanted to hate him, but I kept dreaming about him and every time I talked to him, he said something I needed to hear. He challenged me in a way no one else ever had, tough but honest like the way a close friend would. Only, he saw things that not even my best friend ever did. It felt like he knocked down all the walls around me when we were together or when I was even just thinking about him, and I think I needed that to tell the kind of story I've always been too afraid to put on paper. So, maybe he *did* inspire the book in some ways, but I don't see it like that. I think he made me come out of hiding for once and the book is just me expressing that. The story is sexy and maybe a little graphic at times, but it's not really about sex at all the same way my relationship with Jace wasn't just some fling. I just don't think he'll believe that though."

"Have you told him," Dad said, raising his brows in a question. I didn't have to answer for him to know that I hadn't tried. Not since our argument on Christmas anyway. "I'm sorry I made your dreams feel insignificant. I'm sorry I made you feel small, Marlee."

I wasn't sure what to say. I took another drink from my bottle, draining the last of the beer and setting the empty glass on the table.

"I wanted to talk to him in person. That's why I went to the brewery, but he'd already left. I can't just call him or text him. I need him to understand that this isn't just some stupid romance book and that he isn't just a fling. I need to tell him in person. If he could just see me ..."

Maybe I should've called. I could've at least told him how important it was that I see him in person.

Dad nodded and pulled his phone from his pocket. He tapped at the screen for a moment before he turned it so I could see the confirmation email. At the top was an airline logo and beneath was tomorrow's date.

"Your flight leaves at ten tomorrow morning. It's a few days earlier than you planned to leave, but you're right. I think you should see him in person," he said.

My stomach was churning. "Are you sure he's even in New York City? You just assumed—"

He nodded his head so confidently that it made my heart do an anxious skip in my chest. "He's in the city. There's a car scheduled to pick you up when you land. You'll go straight to him."

Fuck. Was this too crazy?

"I don't know ... How do I explain everything?" I asked, a knot forming in my throat again. Panic was starting to claw at my chest and I could feel the heat spread to my face.

Dad shook his head and gave a shrug. "Tell your truth, Marlee Bear. I know that even when it's hard, the truth always steers me exactly where I was meant to go."

My gut twisted as I realized what he meant. It was so like what Mom told me as we watched Madison and Jared take their wedding photos from the foyer of the lodge. In some ways, my parents' relationship was the best it had ever been. Once they'd finished working out the details on selling the cabin, it seemed like all the tension had vanished. Margot had buzzed around the welcome party with the expectations that our parents wouldn't behave themselves. I expected there to be fighting on Christmas Eve, especially when I found out that Lori Maxwell would be staying at the cabin with my family.

My dad had a point. It was the same one that Jace had taught me. If you live life by everyone else's expectations, the only person you will ever disappoint is yourself. Every time. And that's the worst kind of disappointment.

"Okay. The truth. It's the best I can do." I said. I sucked a deep breath through my teeth and let it out in a groan. "I need to pack. I need to figure out what to wear."

My dad laughed and reached for the pack of bottles behind us. He pulled a pair from the cardboard box and handed one to me. "There's plenty of time to enjoy another with your dad."

I tipped the neck of the bottle toward him so he could pop off the cap. I clinked my bottle against his before lifting it to my lips. I let the cool beer soothe my nerves, sending a familiar tingle of winter magic down my spine. It prompted me to sit a little taller. Regardless of what happened with Jace tomorrow, the truth brought me a step closer to living the author life I'd always dreamed. Because Dad was right. I was exactly where I was supposed to be.

Chapter 30

I BARELY SLEPT. I stayed up late packing for my trip back to New York. I was scheduled to fly home a few days later, but my dad's surprise meant I had to pack all of my things since I wasn't coming back for a few months. And all my things were spread throughout the cabin or left in Jace's apartment above the brewery. All my nicer things were in the apartment, which meant that I'd either be running to meet Jace wearing one of the many pairs of sweatpants I'd packed or my singular pair of jeans and ... I didn't even have a nice top to wear.

I stressed over the outfit long enough that I gave up on it and spent the night gathering my things and attempting to fit them all in my luggage. The Christmas gifts I'd gotten were enough to nearly pop the zipper on my suitcase, so I gave up on closing it and went back to choosing the outfit for the trip instead. That was, until I could hardly stand to look at my wardrobe anymore and I decided to distract myself by stress-cleaning the cabin.

Several hours later and I was seated in the back of Dad's SUV wearing my jeans, an orange sweater Madison gave me from the mercantile, and my leather jacket. I was running on two cups of coffee and the stress that I'd be late to get to my gate at the airport. My dad, however, seemed relaxed in the driver's seat, not noticing the way cars were passing us along the highway.

"It's going to be okay," Madison said quietly from my right.

I looked up from my closed copy of *Emma* by Jane Austen to meet her reassuring gaze. I looked past her where Margot was sitting with her phone propped on her knees, watching some soccer game. Mom was in an almost identical position in the passenger seat in front of her, only instead of her phone she was leaning over her laptop as she typed out an email.

I looked back at Madison and nodded despite the annoyance urging me to tell Dad to pick up the pace and get us to the airport before I lost my head. "I hope so."

The rest of the trip was quiet. My body relaxed once I saw Blucifer. The demonic-looking mustang felt more like an angel as we passed it to reach the Denver International Airport. Maybe I should've felt more anxious the closer we got, but I felt more settled than I had in the last twenty-four hours as Dad pulled to a stop beneath the covered carpark. Everyone climbed out of their seats and gathered at the trunk. Dad unloaded my suitcase while I said my goodbyes to my mom and my sisters.

"At least send a text when you get to there," Mom said as she pulled me tight to her chest. She pressed a kiss to my temple before she stepped back and sent me a serious look. "When you land *and* when you get to Jace's building. You know how I feel about you being alone with a driver."

"It's the same car service I always use when I'm in New York. Plus, she got an upgrade, and it's a nicer package than I've ever had with this company. She'll be fine," Dad said and closed the trunk. He joined us on the sidewalk, rolling my suitcase behind him. "Besides, you have that tracker you planted on her."

"What?" I asked and looked back at my mom who sent a glare at my dad.

"I'm kidding," Dad chuckled. "But we all share our locations, so just keep your phone with you. I swear that your mom and I won't be staring at the screen all afternoon."

"Send me a text," Mom repeated, a small smile tugging at her lips when she looked away from me to send Dad a warning look.

Margot wrapped an arm around my shoulders and pulled me to her side. "I'm sorry if all my anxiety has rubbed off on you. I hope you know that we all support your writing and we're just happy that you're happy."

"I know that, Margot," I said before she took a step aside, offering an encouraging smile.

"This is your big romcom moment, sis," Madison teased. She stepped in front of Margot so she could adjust the collar of my jacket. "I wish you had let me do your hair."

"Thank you," I said. It was the only thing that felt important enough to say and I could tell from the way she relaxed and chewed on her bottom lip that she understood what I meant.

"Anytime," she said and pulled me into a hug. "Just don't toss that sweater into the washing machine. It's cashmere."

I laughed into her ear before he took a step back, a twinkle in her eye telling me she was only half kidding. Madison followed Margot and Mom back to the SUV while Dad relayed the last of the information to me. I'd land at LaGuardia Airport by the afternoon. A man named Roger would be there from the car service to pick me up. Dad made me promise to verify the booking before I left with him. He told me to call him from the car as soon as I got inside, smiling a little when I pointed out how he'd scoffed at my mom for being overprotective.

"I like Jace. He's been through a lot, but he's a good guy and I know he cares a lot about you," he said.

"Let's hope so."

"I know he does," Dad repeated, firmly enough to hold my attention so I could see the seriousness in his eyes. He'd known Nolan Blackthorne for a long time, since Jace was a little kid. He'd known his mom, too. It meant something considering that when Nolan had no one left to turn to for help, didn't know what to do with Jace after the battle in court, and after burying his wife he had asked my dad to be Jace's fresh start.

"Thank you," I said, the words coming out in a whisper as I

reached for him. I held tight for a moment longer than usual, long enough to let him whisper an "I love you" into my ear before he pulled away and sent me a final wave before he climbed into the driver's seat again. I waited until the SUV had rejoined the flow of traffic before I went inside the airport with my luggage rolling behind me.

THE PLANE RIDE was smooth and gave me time to mull over what I was going to say once I reached Jace. I sent a text to Mom and Dad when I got off the plane. Dad sent me the details for the car service while I waited on my luggage to appear on the carousel. I didn't have to wait long before I spotted my giant suitcase, one of many black bags circling the conveyor belt.

I reached for it, but it was heavy enough that the weight plus the movement along the conveyor belt only sent it tipping on its side and my hands slipping from the handle. I nearly tripped over my feet. Before I could catch up with it, a man tugged it from the carousel and sat it on its wheels.

"Sorry. That one's mine," I told him as he straightened up.

He wore a black suit jacket and tie, a gold name tag pinned to his jacket. "Yes. Allow me, Miss Sinclair."

"Oh. Um, so, you're ..." I had just reviewed the information Dad sent me, so the name was fresh in my head. I checked his nametag anyway to be sure. "Roger."

Roger nodded as he raised the handle on my suitcase. "I was hired to drive you to Mr. Jace Blackthorne's apartment. The car is parked just outside. It's nice and warm. There's bottled water and I was told that you like coffee. There is a cup from a local roaster that I think you might enjoy."

Wow. Dad wasn't kidding about getting the upgraded package.

"Okay. Thank you. I appreciate it. Can we go now?" I asked as he extended his free hand to me. It took a moment to realize he was offering to take my purse. I slipped it from my shoulder and hung it from the crook of his elbow.

"Of course, Miss."

He kept close to me as we navigated the busy room, leading me out the doors. The black SUV was parked just outside like he said. He hurried forward to pull the back door open for me, handing me my purse when I asked him for it. I pulled my phone from the zippered pocket and texted my parents that I was in the car, raising my phone in an attempt to snap a photo of the back of Roger's head as he settled into the driver's seat.

I saw his eyes flick to mine in the rearview mirror and he turned in his seat to face me with a kind smile on his face just as I snapped the photo. He only smiled wider when I felt the blush heat my cheeks.

"No offense," I told him and lowered my phone. "It's just— My parents worry."

"I understand. I would have my daughter do the same," he told me and lifted the to-go cup from the cupholder in the front seat. "I was told you take your coffee black, and that you prefer a dark roast. The barista recommended several espresso drinks, an Americano, but I was insistent."

I took the cup from him, surprised that it was still so warm. By the look of the fine leather interior and the feeling of the heated seats beneath me, it wouldn't surprise me if the cupholder was even tricked-out to keep the cups insulated.

"Thank you, Roger," I said and took a careful sip. All the traveling had been exhausting, so the caffeine was welcomed. I was so relaxed as Roger merged into traffic that I almost forgot to send the photo to my parents. I thanked Dad for the upgrade. Maybe he felt bad considering everything I'd said at the lodge, or maybe he just wanted me to have the comfort on such a stressful day.

He started to respond, three little dots flickered on my phone screen before the message bubble disappeared. A few seconds later his message came through with a little red heart emoji. I dropped my phone into my purse and took out my book, going back to running my fingers over the textured letters on the cover rather than ever opening it. I was still so nervous.

My heart skipped when the car slowed to a stop under the portico. I took a few deep breaths to calm myself as Roger moved to the trunk to unload my suitcase. He opened my car door and stepped out. I immediately wished I'd found nicer clothes to wear. There were two doormen flanking the glass double doors and both were dressed nicer than I was. I should've known Jace would be at a place like this. He'd taken me to a hotel with a high-class restaurant on the top floor and we'd stayed in a suite that was larger than my apartment.

"Miss Marlee Sinclair is here for Mr. Jace Blackthorne," Roger told the doormen as we approached. They nodded and the older of the two opened the door for us so we could walk into the marble-laden lobby. A woman greeted me from behind a large mahogany desk to the left.

"This is Miss Marlee Sinclair," the doorman told her, hobbling toward the desk ahead of us. The woman's shoulders relaxed, and she reached for something in the top drawer of her desk.

"Would you like me to take your things to the apartment, Miss Sinclair?" Roger asked, pulling my attention from the desk.

"Um, no. Thank you for getting me here, Roger. I can take it from here," I told him, my stomach doing an uncomfortable flip when he inclined his head in understanding. This was a lot more formal than taking an Uber and the whole situation was starting to feel strange.

I looked back at the desk as Roger left, expected the woman to bring me a sign-in sheet for visitors. She rounded the desk to meet me, a hand outstretched. I took it and gave it a weak shake, glancing at the doorman who had taken hold of the handle on my suitcase and stood with it sitting in front of him like it was his duty to guard it or something.

"I'm happy to meet you, Miss Sinclair. We were told to expect you today. My name is Isabell Munn and I am the building manager," the woman said, her short hair bobbing around her face as she spoke. "Here is your key. Would you like Hector to help you to your apartment?"

I took the little gold key from her, glancing at the apartment number engraved in the gold bar attached to the keyring. *My* apartment? I was frozen and not in the comforting way a winter witch might be. I was in shock.

"No, um, I can get there myself," I told them, watching as Hector nodded and stepped away from my suitcase. He must've called the elevator because the screen at the top was counting down.

Six.

Five.

"There is a barcode on your keychain that you'll need to scan to get access to your floor," Isabell said as she led me toward the gold doors. "Scan that on the card reader just inside the elevator and then press the button for your apartment. Floor sixty-two."

Four.

Three.

"What's the apartment number?" I asked, flipping the key over in my hand. The only thing engraved along the gold bar was the floor number with the barcode on the opposite side.

Two.

One.

The golden elevator doors slid apart, and Isabell stretched her arm through the elevator. I didn't want to make her hold it forever, so I stepped inside of the mirrored compartment.

"Just scan that barcode and press the button. That gets you access to the floor. The key will work on your apartment door," she said and stepped back from the elevator. "Please call if you need anything, Miss Sinclair. Welcome to the building."

I wasn't sure to say. I was still working through the part where she'd said this was *my* apartment. The doors slid shut and the space went silent. The little scanner above all the buttons blinked red at me.

Chapter 31

I HELD the barcode to the scanner and watched as the red light turned to a solid green. I pressed the button once I found it and the elevator hummed to life. I could feel the pressure in my feet as it shot up, my ears popping along the way. It began to slow as the screen at the top continued to count, slowing as it reached the fifties and finally stopped on floor sixty-two. The doors slid apart, and I stepped into the marble hall, pulling my suitcase through the doors just before they closed with a ding.

I looked down the hall to see an emergency access door to the stairs at one end. The right end of the hallway went to a floor to ceiling window that overlooked the city. There was a small sitting area there, but no other doors. The only door was directly in front of me, the gilded number sixty-two hanging on the door.

What the fuck? My apartment?

I took a deep breath, the confusion turning to realization. My eyes burned and I tried to blink away the tears away as I shoved the key in the lock and turned, opening the door and walking into a little foyer. I left my suitcase there and set my purse on the floor beside it. I crossed the short hall in just a few steps, entering a large entertaining space.

Two modern leather couches sat in the corner facing a TV that was mounted on the wall. The tow wall to my left and directly in front of me were made up entirely of glass, windows that overlooked the city that I was sure added a lot of romance to evening dinners at the little kitchen bar on the opposite side of the room. That's where Jace sat at a barstool with a binder in front of him. My binder. The binder I gave Madison. The binder that contained that book.

Jace looked up from the binder, relief washing over his face and relaxing his shoulders.

"You did this, didn't you? You flew me out here. Set up the car service," I said.

"Your dad called my dad." He snorted and tapped the cover of the binder. "Your sister overnighted this to me. It got here practically hours after I did."

"How did she know where to send it?"

"I asked for her input on your Christmas gift. That key you found was just the first part of the gift. After what happened, I wasn't sure what to do. I left without giving you part two." He motioned to the room around us. The apartment. Part one was giving me a key to the apartment above the brewery, a place to stay during the holidays when I came to visit family. His new home. So, part two was giving me a whole floor in a luxury building in New York and Madison knew. I had to give it to her. She can rarely keep small secrets, let alone a whole apartment.

"I don't know what to say," I said, hoping he could hear me given how small my voice sounded. "I don't know. I'm just so sorry, Jace. We were never just a fling to me. You were never some experiment to try writing a better book. Being a dumbass, I announced that I was writing a spicy book because I got drunk before I came home for the holidays and I was fed up trying to write what I thought would make the world take me seriously as an author," I said as the first of the tears slipped onto my cheeks. "You unlocked a part of myself that I'd been trying to avoid my entire life, a part of me that worried the kind of books I wanted to write all along were just stupid or shallow romances and they aren't. You made me finally see that how I feel is worth expressing and I'll only be the best writer I can be if I'm honest and writing the stories that I want to tell. That book was never about you, not really. It's not our story, anyway. I hope you believe me, because I didn't want you to run off to New York to join your dad's business the way I went off to college for a degree that would appease my parents. I don't want you to be some businessman if you don't want to. You deserve to have everything you want just like you made me feel like my dreams are important."

The words poured from me, like the last drop from a pitcher. I was empty. There was nothing else I could say or do other than hope that he believed that I didn't want to hurt him and that I didn't use him to write this book.

"I saw red when I listened to that podcast episode. It hurt when I saw Callie's posts promoting your book as this sexy thing. It made me feel cheap and I reacted before I even knew what it was about," he said and flashed me a weak smile. "The truth is that I didn't look at any of your posts until after, on the plane. I looked at all your author things online, your first book, your website, your social media. I saw that post where you announced this book and noticed that it was weeks before you and I were together. You didn't even know I existed and you had already announced this steamy romance to the world between two people who weren't us, living this romance that wasn't ours, and a main character with a struggle to find herself. It wasn't *my* struggle, and I let my ego get in the way and I believed that this book was a reflection of me, when it never was."

"You're not mad that there's a recording of us in the podcast?" I asked. I was a little amazing at how calm he seemed.

He smiled. "It was pretty shitty, but I believe you when you say it was an accident."

"Why?"

"Because that scene isn't anywhere in this book," he said with a laugh, slapping his hand on the cover of the binder. "And I hope your readers aren't expecting it, because they're going to be disappointed."

"It was a major fuck-up and it all got away from me and then Callie kept pushing it out to promote my book and our followers ran with it. Even if she deleted the episode, other people posted clips that we can't delete and … I don't expect you to forgive me for that. I don't think I can forgive myself."

His smirk was the only reason I hadn't fallen apart again. That and the fact that he'd read my book. He read my book, and he knew it wasn't about him.

"I think I can forgive your little fuck-up if you can do one thing for me," he said, turning in his barstool to face me. He leaned his right elbow on the countertop. "Let me narrate the audiobook."

My whole body felt like Jell-O. God, this was better than I'd hoped. I pressed the back of my hand to my mouth to stifle the sob, calming myself enough to speak. "You actually read it? You read it and you don't think I should disappear from the internet?"

He nodded and rose from the barstool with the binder in one hand. He held it up for me to see with a small smile. "For the girl who finally stopped running and, baby doll, I'm tired of running too."

I close the distance between us, slamming against his chest. The binder slapped against the hardwood floor and Jace's arms wrapped around me. My legs slid around his hips as he lifted me into his arms, setting me on the kitchen counter.

"I'm going to need you to do that scene from chapter six," he said between kisses. He pulled back and sent me a challenging look as he pulled his white T-shirt over his head. "Now."

"I need you to whisper all those dirty book quotes in my ear," I teased as he took a step between my thighs. He gripped the front of my leather jacket and tugged it down my arms, pulling off my boots and socks while I slipped out of the orange sweater. Madison would die if she knew the way I tossed it behind me, her precious cashmere landing in the sink.

Jace kissed me hard, making me whimper when he bit my

bottom lip. He undid the button of his jeans as we kissed and I slipped from the counter and onto my feet so I could do the same, kicking my jeans to the side just seconds before he lifted me again. His jeans sagged low on his hips, revealing the top of a tattoo as he walked us toward one of the couches.

"Take these off," I said and reach for his jeans when he set me back on my feet. He sat instead, pulling me toward him by my hips so I was straddling him.

"Slow down, baby doll," he said with a laugh and placed a gentle kiss on my forehead and then my nose. I locked eyes with him for just a moment, taking in that challenging look I loved so much and that growing smirk as heat threatened to consume me. I let my powers flow freely, chilling my skin, and pressed a cool hand to his chest.

"Didn't you tell me once that fire and ice makes for a lot of steam?" I asked, loving how that smirk only spread wider on his face. I reached for the waistband of his jeans and he pulled my hand away, raising it to his lips to kiss my knuckles.

"You're a needy little thing," he said.

"I just know what I want," I said, sliding my free hand down his chest until he captured that one too. He smiled as he pinned both my hands in one of his.

"You will get what I give, baby doll," he said with raised brows. "When I'm ready to give it."

I hummed. "I know how to get what I want, so ..." I tipped my hips, feeling the pressure at the front of his jeans grow. He rotated so I was lying on the couch beneath him, hovering over me with my hands pressed above my head.

He laughed. "You really are a brat."

"I think you like that though," I teased, lifting my head to kiss him.

He pulled back, just far enough out of reach. It made my stomach squirm. Then there was that playful glint in his eyes, that look that always made my resolve crumble.

"I like every part of you, baby doll," he said, that onery look fading a little as he looked back at me. It was like he hadn't seen me in months and not just days, studying my face before kissing my forehead and brushing my cheek with his thumb. "I've missed this."

"Me too," I said.

The moment lasted just a second longer before he gave in when I lifted my head to kiss him again.

Chapter 32

CALLIE and I both squealed in surprise when the cork finally popped from the champagne bottle, sending a wave of foam over my hands and onto the hardwood floor of the apartment. I looked from Callie as she laughed to Jace who smiled behind my raised phone.

"Happy release day, baby doll," he said. Callie let out a girlish whoop and tossed her arms around me.

"To hitting number one in her category on day one!" She hugged me tighter and I felt like my cheeks would fall off from how much smiling I'd done since she'd come over.

Jace lowered my phone, passing it to me so I could view the recording. He'd snapped a few photos as well, to highlight the moment I popped the champagne. I uploaded the video to my social media accounts first, making sure to add a small screenshot of my "Number One Bestseller" tag to the corner of the video before I posted it.

"To finishing another semester of college," I said as I stowed my phone into my pocket.

Callie groaned as she handed me a full champagne flute. "No!

Today is all about you and your new book going viral and doing a thousand books in pre-order alone."

"It wasn't a thousand," I told her, letting her clink her glass against mine.

"Close enough," she said and took a drink.

Jace wrapped an arm around my waist and pulled me to his hip. "Worth celebrating." He kissed my temple and then left us to clean up the leftovers from dinner. Callie and I moved to the living room couches so we could watch the lights of the city. It had been a whole semester of living in this luxury apartment with Jace and I was still left in awe every night as we looked out at the skyscrapers. Living here made my commute to campus a bit longer, but it was worth it. Jace woke up with me each morning so he could drive me to campus before he started his day.

"Did you bring beer home?" I asked from my seat on the couch.

Jace looked up from the sink. The sleeves of his shirt were pushed to his elbows, and he'd sloshed enough water onto his front that it stuck to his stomach. I'd nearly forgotten what I'd asked when he noticed the way I was looking over him. He smirked and nodded. "I brought a variety from the brewery this morning. Extra Sinclair Stout, of course."

The look he sent me made me wish a little that Callie wasn't in the room.

"Oh!" Callie sat her glass on the coffee table and sat forward in her seat. "Speaking of CPBB—"

"No one calls it CPBB," I laughed. "It's Crescent Peak Books and Brews."

"Crescent Books and Brews," Jace corrected as he approached us with two cans of beer. "I'll bring you both glasses."

"Okay. CBB," Callie said and stuck her tongue out at me. I opened my mouth to correct her again, but decided it wasn't worth it. After opening the location here in New York City, Jace rebranded the business. He dropped the "Peak" from the name, though it was still there on the sign above my favorite little bookshop back in Colorado.

"Do we really want to talk shop right now? I thought we were celebrating," Jace said as he returned with two glasses and his own champagne flute. He settled onto the couch next to me, draping an arm over the back of the couch and giving my shoulder a gentle squeeze.

"It's part of the success story," Callie said with a tone of superiority, though I know she didn't mean it as such.

"I'm teasing." Jace laughed, getting a smile from her in response.

"I know that," she said and rolled her eyes before setting her gaze back on me. "So, Crescent Books and Brews NYC is all set to host our summer event. We just need a name."

"Sexy Summer of Books is out," Jace said with a laugh. "It sounds like a month-long event, like a discount on romance books in the shop and not a one-day event."

Callie groaned. "Well, you could run a summer discount on romance books. I'd gladly add to my TBR for a seventy-percent-off promotion."

"What if we just name it after the brewery so we can include everything. Crescent Books and Brews Romancefest," I said. I'd already run the name past Jace. He liked it and had already moved forward with the plans. He was stubborn enough that he said it didn't really matter what Callie wanted to call it since, as the business owner, he had the final say.

"Sounds great!" Callie said and lifted her champagne to her lips.

"I had another idea," I said, catching the way Jace stiffened next to me. This one, I hadn't run by him. "We're hosting a summer event here. What if we did a winter event in Crescent Peak?"

Jace let out a deep breath. "It's a small town. The brewery isn't big enough for a large event. What's the draw to get people there anyway?"

"It's Crescent Peak," I said and shifted in my seat to face him. "It's not a far drive from Denver."

"So, people could drive in. There aren't enough rooms at the hotel," he said.

"We book the hotel in advance for authors and vendors," I started, listing the items on my right hand. "We tie in local businesses. McAdams Mercantile is already on board with the idea. Madison said she'd even do merch for the event and run a booth for her business. The ski resort is a thirty-minute drive and my dad has taken enough of his business friends there to close deals that I bet he could ask the resort to do a promotion for the event."

"What about the venue?" Jace asked.

"The lodge would let me use the ballroom. We could do the book event and a book ball."

"I love this idea!" Callie chimed in before Jace could respond, a scowl growing on his face as Callie gushed about ideas for a theme. He waited, not patiently considering the way he tapped his foot against the floor, until she was finished to speak.

"If Crescent Books and Brews is hosting, there's still a problem with part of that," he said, sending me a challenging look. "The brewery can't brew enough beer for that big of an event."

He was right. I hadn't thought about that until now. He could tell, too, because his shoulders relaxed a little at the silence in the room. That challenging expression remained though, and I couldn't resist.

"You'll come up with something," I told him. He stared back at me with those raised brows, questioning, but the smile that tugged at his lips a moment later sent a thrill of victory through me.

"Whatever you say, baby doll."

Callie laughed and raised her glass to me in a toast. The conversation shifted to summer plans. After finals next week, Callie would be flying back home to Oklahoma. Jace had asked me a few weeks ago if he could plan our vacation. I agreed before I thought to ask him what he had in mind. I tried to go back on the agreement when I found out that it was a secret, but he was insistent on planning the trip.

"You promised to let me plan the trip and I'm planning the trip," Jace said when we returned to the discussion after Callie had left. Jace sat our empty glasses in the sink while I boxed up the last of the cake.

"And I'm letting you plan it, but you know I don't like secrets," I reminded him. "I just want to know where we're going." I moved the cake to the back of the kitchen counter. Jace turned from the sink to wrap his arms around my middle, kissing my neck.

"Can't a guy surprise his girlfriend just once?" he asked, nipping at my ear. I was not going to let him distract me. I turned in his arms and placed my hands against his chest, preventing him from leaning in to kiss me.

"You already have one suprise, so unless you'd like to like to go ahead and hand over that ring I know you have stashed around here somewhere—"

"I'm not spoiling our engagement. That one is a hard no," he said, tugging me closer by my hips.

"Then tell me about this summer vacation you've planned."

"And I thought you springing that winter book event idea on me was acting a brat," he said with a scoff, releasing me so he could go back to the sink.

I snagged the hand towel off the counter, but before I could snap him with it he plucked it away and draped it over his shoulder.

"We don't keep secrets in this relationship. I agreed that you get one, so pick: surprise me with a ring or a vacation," I teased.

"You can't sass it out of me," Jace said and pulled the dish soap from the cabinet beneath the sink.

"I bet I can figure out the code to the bedroom safe," I mused and moved the empty champagne bottle into the trash. "Bet you put the ring there. Or maybe your sock drawer."

I gasped when I heard the snap, feeling the sting at the back of my leggings a second after. Jace sent me a satisfied smile as he turned the towel in his hands.

"Ouch," I groaned and rubbed the spot on my left ass cheek where the towel had whipped me.

"Keep acting like a brat and see what it gets you, baby doll," he said, eyebrows raised as he twisted the towel in preparation for another swing. I turned to face him, shielding my ass.

"One secret," I reminded him, letting out a squeal when he rushed at me. He lifted me by my hips and sat me on the counter, pushing my knees apart to make space for him. He was close enough to kiss, just a few inches apart, and part of me wanted to sacrifice our little stand-off for that reason alone. He shook his head, letting out a deep breath.

"My coven agreed to let me back in. I wanted to take you home to my dad, the beach, and the Summer Solstice Ball," he said as he ran his thumbs back and forth on my thighs. "Maybe skinny dipping on the beach. I know a spot."

I slapped his chest but couldn't contain my laughter. "Sounds perfect."

"Perfect," he agreed and kissed me.

Epilogue

THE CHRISTMAS TREE glittered in the front window of the brewery, adorned with twinkling lights and bookmarks and a topper in the shape of a crescent moon. It was the first Christmas that Crescent Books and Brews was open for business and the bookstore and brewery had both done well, drawing more tourism from the surrounding areas that also boosted sales at McAdams Mercantile, according to Madison and Jared.

Madison's pink Jeep pulled to a stop just outside the front doors. Dax and Margot got here about thirty minutes before, Margot purposely timing their arrival with Mom and Dad's. She was still a little concerned about them arguing when they were in the same room together even though they were both way more tolerable and even kind of nice to be around now that they were divorced.

"Madison and Jared are here," I called from the front of the room.

"Peter!" Mom screamed from her seat at a table beside Lori. "Peter! Hurry up! They're here! You're going to miss them! Peter!"

"Mom, calm down," Margot said from a seat at the bar. Jared

laughed behind the taps, filling a glass for me. He sat the beer on the bar as I approached.

"I'm here," Dad said as he burst from the bathroom doors at the back of the room, still drying his hands on his jeans. "The one time I step away ..."

"You don't want to miss her outfit. It's so cute," Winnie said, leaning into the shoulder of the dark-haired man next to her. Winnie and Ben and had been dating for a few months now and he wasn't anything like what everyone assumed he'd be. She described him as a well-dressed, nerdy winter warlock, and she wasn't kidding. He loved all things computer science and ran his own company doing technology for businesses. He'd already refined the mercantile and the brewery's websites, even doing some basic graphic design to help with marketing. He was far from the normal gym bro Winnie usually went for, but they fit together like they were made for each other. It was almost sickeningly sweet the way they'd steal kisses when they didn't think anyone was watching.

"Where's my phone? Margot, where did my phone go?" Mom said with a huff, searching the table and then reaching for her purse on the floor.

Lori waved a hand, already poised with her phone raised toward the door. "I got it. I'll send it to you."

"You're getting a video or a photo?" Mom asked her, groaning when she finally found her phone in her purse.

"Video."

"I'll get a photo."

"Holy shit," I groaned, shaking my head at Jace who only smiled wider at the drama of it all. I took a sip from my beer and turned to face the door as it opened.

Madison came in first, wearing a red velvet dress with dark tights and a pair of red heels. Always the fashionista.

"Breakfast is ready in the back," Dax said, coming through a door and stopping next to Jace. "Make sure you try my waffles. I promise you'll love them. They aren't like other protein pastries. These are actually good."

"Where are they?" Dad called to Madison. She pointed toward the door as she walked toward us, her heels clicking along the floor.

"Jared's coming," she said, stopping next to me at the bar. "They say I'm the dramatic one." She pulled me into a hug. I opened my mouth to ask how she was, but the room exploded in gasps at the same moment.

Jared came through the front door with a backpack on his shoulder. He held a baby carrier by the handle, the top covered with a fluffy blanket.

"Oh! Get her out of there!" Mom cooed.

"Give me a minute. She fell asleep on the way here." Jared laughed and sat the car seat on a table. He flipped the blanket back and the tiny baby within gave a little whimper. He shushed her as he lifted her into his arms. "The perfect little witchy snowman. Who wants to hold her first?"

The baby was dressed in a white long-sleeved onesie that was decorated with buttons like the body of a snowman. She wore a white tutu and a little beanie with a fluffy ball on top.

"Jenn won the coin toss," Dad said with a smile and patted my mom's shoulder. Jared approached the table where mom sat, passing the tiny baby to her.

"Someone remind me the baby's name," Dax said, quiet enough for just Jace and me to hear. Madison left us to join Jared as he hovered around my mom, unloading baby items onto the table.

"Rosie. It's Joanne's middle name," I said, Dax nodding in understanding before he left us to join the crowd around the table. Jace lifted his half-full glass to mine and I met him halfway, the glasses clinking before he both drank.

"I don't think anyone is going to want breakfast for a while," he said and glanced at the table.

"You think Dax hid a ring in one of those waffles?" I asked.

Jace laughed and pushed the sleeves of his Crescent Books and Brews sweatshirt to his elbows so he could lean them on the counter. "No. He's waiting for the season."

"The start of the season?" I asked, keeping my voice low.

Margot and Dax had moved in together before the semester started. Margot was back on the soccer team and not only that, but back to her starting position and hopeful for a future in the pros. She was putting in extra time at the gym to make her final college season the best she could.

"The end," Jace said. "He got a ring a few weeks ago and told me he thought it would be best to surprise her with it after her last game."

"She'd like that," I said, glancing at the table where Margot sat next to our mom, baby Rosie now in her arms. I looked back at Jace. His gaze was still set on my family gathered around the table. He smiled when Lola gave a little whimper. Then, his eyes shifted to me.

"What?" he asked.

My body warmed. "It's just been a good year."

He smiled and reached across the bar to take my hand. It had been a good year, a really good year. We moved in together in New York City. Jace would go back and forth between New York and Colorado to check on both breweries a few times a year, but he spent most of his time wherever I was. My author career had grown and I was making enough money to be a full-time writer now once I graduated. We'd gone home to meet his dad and his coven and he was officially welcomed back. He and his dad had made up and we were set to fly out and spend Spring Break with him this year.

"Yeah. It's been good," he said and lifted my hand to his lips for a kiss.

"I love you," I said, watching his smile spread wider.

"I love you too, baby doll," he said. He rounded the bar to join me, pulling me to his side as we watched my family pass baby Rosie around the table.

Yeah. Things were good.

ACKNOWLEDGMENTS

This entire series came to me in November, just before the holidays, when I was between projects and needed a break from writing all the series, dark books. Like Marlee who felt like she needed to write something serious to be considered a "real" author, I never felt pulled to write anything light and fluffy. The idea for Winter Witches came to me slowly over the course of a workday and when I got home and finally got into bed after a long day, my mind just wouldn't shut up. I found myself plotting the entire book overnight on my phone while my husband slept beside me.

I was amazed. I'd never had a book come to me so quickly and never one like this. From there, it was easy to develop the world and subsequent books for Margot and Marlee. These books have felt like a cup of hot coffee on a snowy day before the fireplace and each year they have been what really kicks off the holiday season for me, and I will miss diving into the world of Crescent Peak. While all my books contain a romance plot, I never dreamed that I would write books like this, but I've discovered that there is a lot to be learned even in those "light and fluffy" romance novels that truly enrich our lives, even if it is just a moment of escape for some of us.

I have so many people to thank for bringing this book to life, starting with my wonderful husband. He inspired me to take that initial jump and stop waiting around for the perfect moment to start publishing. I have him to thank for giving me the push I needed to follow my dreams. I've had the best publishing team through this journey, and I have to thank Lucia Ferrara for all the great work she does editing this book and previous. I have worked with her on most of my books and it is always a smooth and enriching process. I have learned a lot that has made me a better writer, and I always enjoy her "just for fun" notes about differences between the U.S. and Canada. As someone who loves the little details, thank you for teaching me that those beanies with the pom poms on top are called a "toque."

As I've gone through this journey, I have brought some really great friends along with me. Thank you to Whitney for all of her support and always jumping in with a little bit of reality therapy when I need it. Someone told me a few years ago that "you are never really stuck" when things get hard and Whitney has really shown me what that means. Thank you, Whitney, for showing me that even when it feels like the universe is against you that your dreams are still on the horizon as long as you believe it and take small steps closer.

My progress wouldn't be nearly as streamlined if I didn't have personal assistant/ bestie Jill. She does the final proofread for my books and is ruthless in pointing out the tiniest details that pose an issue. I am so grateful for her scrutiny and support. Thank you for sitting me with through those long signing days and helping me refine my work. I always know when she hits me with a "Ma'am ..." that I've made a silly mistake or I'm overthinking things. I can always count on Jill to tell me what I need to hear and I'm a better writer for it.

I think Jill deserves a little extra recognition for Snow at Sunset specifically. Without her quick-witted idea during an afternoon of writing, we would not have the 'Simon Says' moments or the line *"Don't ever say another man's name while your hands are on me, baby doll."* I think she truly elevated that moment.

And finally, I want to thank the readers who have given my books a chance and those who have followed my journey for years. I appreciate all of your support, and I am happy to have you along through the publishing process. It means the world to have people read and enjoy my books, so thank you especially. I can't wait for everything I have in store for the future. Writing and publishing books is truly a dream come true for me, and I am so thankful that I am able to do it and share it with all of you. Thank you again for your support.

ABOUT THE AUTHOR

Amy Prokopis is a fiction author from Oklahoma who writes paranormal romance and romantasy books. She graduated from Oklahoma State University with a bachelor's degree in English and a minor in German before obtaining a master's degree in school counseling. Besides writing, Amy enjoys distance running and spending time with her husband, their son, and their Havanese, June.

ALSO BY AMY PROKOPIS

Visit my website to subscribe to my newsletter!

www.amyprokopis.com

Follow me on social media!

Check out more of my books here!